two are meant to be together and couldn't get enough of them. I have enjoyed reading this series and look forward to reading more books by this author." ~ Miss J

ANYONE WHO HAD A HEART

The Letter Club – Book 4

Elle Wright

PRAISE FOR THE LETTER CLUB

Nothing Else But You

"This was one of my favorites from an author period. It had everything I love in a novel. The characters and plot had me from beginning to end. Highly recommend." ~JuliaBookLandReviews

"I totally fell in love with this book, Gio is a dream and so is his girl. We get to know them through their letters and want them to get on in real life despite all the possible problems and obstacles. My new favourite author." ~JennyIndigo

"Wow! Loved it. I found the letters so great for a written style. The couple finding out about each other and falling in love without ever meeting. Awesome characters with so much emotion. A must read!" ~Laura Johnston

"This story was so touching. The plot is emotionally brilliant and the characters fit in perfectly. I love the emotional vulnerability and chemistry the protagonists have." ~PinkieIsShy

"Old fashioned letter writing has never been done better." ~Loni

If Ever I Fall

"The second book in "The Letter Club" series does not disappoint. I have to admit that I am a sucker for an old fashioned letter, so this story was right up my alley. If the idea of breaking out pen and paper seems archaic to you, then you may want to skip it.....but why on Earth would you want to do that? You would miss a phenomenal love story. Matteo is the love interest that everyone is looking for and Sophia is the girl that makes his heart melt."~RomanceReaderHB82

"If Ever I Fall is a great romantic read of a woman escaping harm's way, far away from her new love. The only way to stay in touch is through love letters. She learns more and loves more through the

love letters. Love From Afar Makes The Heart Grow Stronger. Great Read." ~Amanda Enriquez

"If Ever I Fall is about the romance between Sofia and Matteo by Elle Wright filled with danger, romance, and suspense. I became intrigued after reading the description to find out who Matteo was and what the truth about Sofia's family was. I was really surprised at the answers but you would have to read the book to find out." ~Nadia

"I enjoyed this new "Letter Club" story! It's an amazing read that is wonderfully developed and nicely written. I love the characters in this slow burn read. Matt and Sophia are so good together. What a match made for each other and a great love story with suspense, romance, danger and so much more." ~Mary

Never Without You

"These Letter Club books are fantastic! This is the third book I've read in the series and this one was just as good as the first two. It feels like you are part of trying to solve a mystery as you look for clues in the letters trying to figure out where each person lives. The love story is full of action, passion and steamy scenes! Highly recommend all of these books!" ~Midnight Maiden

"I gotta say, this book was everything and nothing like I expected. I could not put it down once I started it and did not want it to end when I got there! An utterly engaging story-line that grabs you right from the start, keeping you engrossed throughout." ~Sleep_Reader

"This is the third book in The Letter Club series. It is a great story. It is well written with wonderful characters that have depth. There is something to be said for the written word. Not only is this a sweet romantic getting to know you story but it also funny and contains enough drama, intrigue, and action that once I began reading, I couldn't put it down. I will definitely be reading the other books in this series." ~ L. Courter

"Theresa and Ethan bring us the next story from The Letter Club. They exchange letters and begin to connect more and more. These

www.BOROUGHSPUBLISHINGGROUP.com

PUBLISHER'S NOTE: This is a work of fiction. Names, characters, places and incidents either are the product of the author's imagination or are used fictitiously. Any resemblance to actual events, locales, business establishments or persons, living or dead, is coincidental. Boroughs Publishing Group does not have any control over and does not assume responsibility for author or third-party websites, blogs or critiques or their content.

ISBN 978-1-953810-03-8

For all the tough guys who love us fiercely

ACKNOWLEDGMENTS

The fires in California started while this book was in edits. While Redwood Falls is a fictional place, its setting is in one of the areas affected by the fires. My heart hurts from the lost lives, homes, wineries burnt to the ground, and large swaths of forestland that have been decimated. Thank you to all the first responders who work tirelessly to keep people, property, forests and wildlife safe. We appreciate you more than words can say.

Thanks to my beta reader who always catches the details, and to Boroughs Publishing Group for being there.

AUTHOR'S NOTE

Trigger Warning For People With Sensitivities To Certain Topics

While there are no explicit scenes depicting rape and suicide, both are referenced in this story. As well, there are instances of racism and antisemitism in the book.

ANYONE WHO HAD A HEART

Chapter One

How & Why
Max

Who falls asleep in the trunk of a car and is okay with it? I wondered about that as I moved my hand around until I found the trunk's emergency release. When dim light – thank god – hit my eyes, I checked to see where I was and learned nothing about the generic underground garage where the car was parked. As best I could without flashing the security cameras positioned in the corners of the half-empty structure, I climbed out of…oh shit, Ryan Trent's fancy schmancy car. I patted my hair, stuck my hand under my LBD to feel for my Spanx – yep, there – checked my ears, fingers, neck, and wrist to find all my jewelry in place, looked down and saw I was still wearing my favorite silver strappy sandals with the sensible four-inch heel, and then turned to search the trunk where I found my small evening bag. After grabbing it up, I felt around its bottom and found my keys, phone, ID, and credit card. Everything was where it was supposed to be in my bag and on my person, suggesting I'd passed out – I'll ponder that in a minute – and nothing untoward happened until I climbed out of the trunk at…crap, noon. On a Tuesday.

I leaned against the car and thought about where I was supposed to be today, and when. It took a moment, but I sighed with relief as I realized I hadn't booked anyone until one because on Thursdays I worked until nine. This boded well as long as I was still in Redwood Falls, which meant I'd have time to call a cab, go home, wash my face, change my clothes, get into my car, and head over to Shangri-la Spa, where I worked as a stylist.

In plain English, I cut hair, and was damn good at it. Bernadette La Pierre –not her real last name, but I agreed, Spreckle didn't have flair – who owned Shangri la, thought so too and gave me first chair.

After hoofing it to the elevator, I was delighted when it opened right away. I pushed L for lobby. The doors closed. Nothing happened. I pushed the "Open Door" button. That worked. I pushed L again. The doors closed. Nothing happened. Time was ticking, and I needed to get home. A silver button above the panel had "Call" inscribed in it, and I pushed that sucker a few times until a man's voice sounded in the elevator.

"Yes, ma'am?"

Ma'am meant there was a camera in the elevator and the guard? saw me. "Hi there. Listen, I keep pressing L and nothing happens. I mean, the elevator doesn't go up."

"You need a pass key to enter the building."

"Well, clearly I don't have a pass key, and I don't want to enter the building per se. I want to get to the lobby so I can call a cab and *vamos*."

"The lobby is in the building, ma'am."

Oh geeze Pete. This guy was a rule stickler. "Okay. Then how do I get out of the garage to the street if I can't take the elevator to the lobby?"

"You can't."

I knew that was a lie. Every garage had to have an emergency exit, and cars had to come in somehow.

My chin dropped to my chest and I counted to ten. "Listen, guard person or whoever you are, I have to get home. I don't care if I have to call the cops to come get me out of here. I'll be happy to tell them that I found myself in the trunk of a car, and then they'll question you about how you left me stranded down here without water, food, or a bathroom, when all I wanted to do was come up to the lobby to leave the building to get into a cab and go home after *I climbed out of the trunk of a car*."

The elevator lurched and began ascending. Twenty seconds later I exited the elevator, my heels clicking on marble tiles, as I made my way across an elegant lobby of what appeared to be a posh apartment building, and saw a security desk beside the front doors. This must be that new condo building they put up about a year ago on the far edge of the north end of town. The lobby had sloped-back leather chairs and a large square glass coffee table that separated a couple of poofy couches, over which were curved giraffe-necked lamps. The whole seating area sat on top of a red and white patterned area rug. Niiiice.

As I walked through the pair of heavy glass doors, I waved to a nondescript middle-aged man who looked like he'd spent his entire life as one of those guards who didn't talk or move outside of Buckingham Palace.

By the time I hit the sidewalk and touched my phone's screen to call a cab, I saw I'd lost eleven minutes of my life I'd never get back. Verna's Taxi Service was on speed dial, and the dispatcher told me I'd have to wait five minutes for the cab. Thrilled I was on my way home, but stuck waiting on the other side of a glass wall through which the palace guard was watching me as if I had pulled explosives out of my bag and was constructing a bomb, I started pacing up and down the block.

Now was as good a time as any to review the events of last evening as best I could remember them in the hopes of figuring out how and why I'd slept the night and morning away in the trunk of Ryan Trent's car. At the same moment I began contemplating that dilemma, Ryan's car pulled in front of the building and stopped. Then – shit – the passenger window slid down.

I should've kept walking, but sensing Ryan would slow roll next to me until I paid him the attention he believed he deserved, I bent at the waist and looked into the car to see him staring at me as if he was looking at a ghost.

"What the fuck, Max?"

"Good day to you too, Ryan."

"Get in the car."

"I'm waiting for a cab."

"Woman. Get. In. The. Car."

I drew in air through my nose and counted to ten. "I'm waiting for a cab," I repeated.

"Get in the fuckin' car, Max, or I'll come out and haul your ass in here. Your choice."

Somehow knowing he'd be good to his word, I waited until I heard the lock go, pulled the inset handle, and lowered myself into the plush sedan then touched my phone screen. "Hi, sorry. Truly sorry. This is Max Calapiano. I don't need you to pick me up." The dispatcher thanked me for letting them know and rung off. Then I turned to Ryan and said, "You have to take me straight home or else I'm going to be late for work, and I can't be late ever, but especially not today because Dana Hernandez is my first client, and she can be…difficult."

Ryan stared at me until I buckled up, shook his head, slid on retro Wayfarers, and drove out from under the building's extended wide portico. He then made an illegal u-turn and headed toward my apartment. I tilted my head, wondering how he knew where I lived. Before I had a chance to ask, he barked out, "What the fuck happened to you last night?"

"Ummm…" *Good question.* "I'm not sure what you mean."

"You really wanna play that game?"

"I'm not playing a game. I need you to be specific." *'Cause I can't remember shit about last night.*

"Specific, huh? Let's start with I walked into Henry's and saw Will Travers wrapped around you like a blanket. How's that for specificity?"

I remembered dancing with Will. We were having a good time. "We were dancing."

"He's married," Ryan shouted even though I was less than an arm's length away.

"I know," I snapped. "To Lola."

"And you're okay with that?" he snarled.

"With what?"

"That you were out with a married man?" His snarl was edging toward a growl.

Parts of last evening came back to me in a flash. "I was out with *my friend* Lola and her husband, Will. We were celebrating his promotion. Lola's preggers and was worried if she started dancing she'd hurl, and since she'd been able to keep dinner down without a problem, Will and I were dancing while she sat at the table toe-tapping *ten feet away from the dance floor*." I emphasized the last seven words by drawing them out.

Ryan had no response, and I glanced over to see his lips thin and his expression grim. "Since we're chatting, how is anything I do your business?" I felt his glare through his sunglasses laser across the console and thought, *Stupid. I should've kept my mouth shut.* We were less than ten minutes away from my apartment, and if I'd said nothing I could've made a clean getaway.

"Where were you the Saturday before last?"

Bizarre question. He knew where I was. I'd been out with *him* on our one and only date. "Ryan," I said his name like he knew better than to ask.

"Yeah. That's why what you do is my business."

"After one date? Are you insane?"

"You're a piece of work, you know that?"

That got my hackles up. "Excuse me?"

He didn't say anything for a few minutes, which I took as a good sign. We were done talking and I could jump out of the car, get upstairs and wash up, change and get to Shangri-la on time.

He swung his car into my apartment complex, followed the winding road around three buildings before he pulled into the spot next to my car across from my building. How did he know where I lived? We'd met at Bella Luna for dinner. I didn't give my address to guys I barely knew, and I always drove to meet my dates so I could get home on my own whenever I wanted.

After throwing the car in park, he turned off the ignition, yanked off his glasses and threw them on the dash, unbuckled his seatbelt and angled his body to face me. Evidently, he was not done talking. "Wasn't that your tongue down my throat in Bella Luna's parking lot?"

Well...

"Wasn't that your body I had laid out on the hood of my car while you squirmed beneath my hands while I was getting ready to put my mouth on your pussy?"

Apparently, I had a thing for his car. "Now you're being crude."

"You sure as fuck didn't think so at the time."

"I'd had too much to drink. You took advantage."

He laughed, but from the sound of it, he wasn't happy. "You don't get to lay that shit on me. You had two glasses of wine, and you didn't finish the second."

Ummm...

"Yeah." He stared at me. His sharp, amazing, preternatural green eyes scanned my face.

If I was being honest with myself – not him, never him – the only reason we'd stopped having sex on the hood of his swank sedan was because a couple of cars pulled into the lot and their headlights startled me back to sanity.

Ryan had helped me off his car, pushed me behind him while I straightened my clothes, and before he knew what I was doing, I'd made a mad dash to my vehicle and sped off. I'd checked. He hadn't followed me.

"Things got a little out of control."

"Can't argue with that." He ran his hand through his super thick, wavy dark brown hair. All night at dinner I hadn't been able to stop thinking about how I wanted to get my hands in that hair while I kept looking for the edges of contact lenses. Nope. Those amazing eyes were all his. "Why'd you run away?"

"The date was over." I shrugged. "I went home."

"Let's pretend that's not the lie it is. Then tell me, why didn't you answer my calls?"

Now I felt I was on solid footing. "I had nothing to say. We went out. I didn't want to see you again. I didn't return the calls."

He smirked. *Oh, shit.* That wasn't good. He knew something I didn't know, and I didn't like that one bit.

"Then why did you stick your tongue down my throat when you came straight to me at Henry's last night?"

Did I do that? I had no recollection of the evening after dancing with Will. "I don't know." He scowled. "Really. I don't remember much about last night."

"How drunk were you?"

I wasn't sure, but I thought I'd had three lavender martinis, which was odd. I never drank that much. What possessed me? I knew better than that. "Drunker that I thought, I'm guessing."

"You do that a lot?"

"Get drunk or kiss random guys?"

"Both," he growled.

Whoops. Wrong choice of words. "Excepting last night, I can't remember when I had more than a couple of glasses of wine. It's been a while." *For good reason.*

Now that I had enough pieces of last night puzzled together, I was pissed off at myself in a big way, but I'd deal with that later. I had to finish this and get to work. Unless I could wrap up this interrogation in two minutes, it looked like I was going in to Shangri-la wearing last night's clothes.

As much as I hated to ask, I had to know how I wound up in the trunk of his car. "After I, um, uh, kissed you, what happened?"

"No shit? You don't remember?" I shook my head, and he huffed. "You told me you wanted to get out of there, grabbed my hand, and started pulling me to the door. Will came over and asked what was going on and you told him we were leaving. He seemed to take it in stride, and we headed out. My phone rang, and I had to take the call. I gave you my keys and told you I'd meet you at the car, which was parked across the street from Henry's. I watched you until you got into my car. I couldn't've been on the phone more than five minutes. When I made it across the street, I found the keys in the ignition, and you were gone."

Ho-lee shit. I'd opened the trunk, put his keys in the ignition, climbed into the trunk, and shut myself in? That did it. I wasn't having another sip of alcohol again as long as I lived. Wine included. I'd waited years before I'd trusted myself enough to drink again. Now knowing what happened last night, I was never having another drop of anything alcoholic again. Ever.

"Then today," he continued, "when I was heading out to a meeting, I see you pacing in front of my building in the same clothes you had on last night." His hard glare skewered me. "Where'd you sleep, Max?"

All things being equal, if I told him I didn't remember, he'd think I was with some guy who lived in his building, which shouldn't matter, but he seemed to be a tad proprietary when it came to me, and I had to shut that down. The humiliation from telling him the truth would be horrendous, but it'd be better than him hounding me about who I was with last night. I didn't want or need him in my life, especially after this.

When I'd bolted from Bella Luna's parking lot a couple of weeks ago, I'd known down to my bones I could and would get lost in Ryan Trent, and that wasn't going to happen. After I explained about the trunk – god, this sucked – I'd cut him loose forever.

"In the trunk of your car."

His head jerked back so fast and far, it hit the headrest with a thump. "You're shitting me."

"Wish I could say I was. Ask the palace guard." His brows drew together. "The security guy at the front desk. I had to threaten him with the cops before he brought me up in the elevator from the garage to the lobby so I could get out of the building and call a cab."

I could tell he wanted to laugh, and he had the good sense not to, but his lips were twitching. "It's not funny. I put myself in danger, and that's not cool."

He sobered immediately. "You're right. It's not cool. I'm glad you're okay."

"Humiliated, but fine. I've got to go. I have to get to work."

"In last night's clothes?"

"No time to change. Thanks for the ride."

As I made to get out of the car, he put his big, warm hand on my arm. "Not so fast. We're not done, you and I. Nowhere near done."

"That's where you'd be wrong. Take alcohol out of the equation, and last night never happened."

"Got lots to say about that and our date, and I'm gonna say it when you aren't rushing to get to the salon. Pick up your phone when I call, Max, and if you can't, return the fuckin' call or the next person in your chair at Shangri-la is me."

He released my arm and I got out of his car fast.

How did he know where I worked? We'd first met at Beans & Roast, and we'd chatted over coffee. When he'd asked me out, I'd been too taken with him to say no. I mean, have you seen him? He's beautiful.

Over dinner, we didn't talk about our professions. Topics ranged from how many brothers and sisters we had, where we grew up, music and movies, mountains or beaches, big cities or small-town life. Then I'd near tackled him in the parking lot, and, well, I turned off the spigot before I drowned in him.

I didn't care if Ryan Trent threatened to show up at Shangri-la. If he did, I'd call the cops and report him as a stalker. Even if he was handsome as sin, had eyes anyone would get lost in, had a body like Aquaman, was a great conversationalist, and his kisses held the promise of unremitting hot, wild sex.

Chapter Two

Earth to Ryan
Ryan

The interminable meeting concluded and I got back to my office by late afternoon. I hated the political side of my job. Saw it as a necessary evil I had to endure. During the three-hour jaw-jacking session, my mind had wandered to Max Calapiano and stayed there. From the moment I'd seen her at Beans & Roast, I'd been gone for her. Short, spikey white-blonde hair with an inch of dark roots capped a heart-shaped face that held wide soulful brown eyes, a narrow pert nose, and pillow lips that fuckin' begged to be kissed and nibbled on.

She had a woman's body, all curves and soft places to hold on to and caress. But what had drawn my attention first was her laugh. She was joking with the barista, someone she clearly knew, and when he said something she found funny, her whole body was involved. Her shoulders shook, she threw her head back, and she bent a little at the waist, holding her stomach as the laughter moved through her.

Our first conversation sealed the deal. She was open, smart, warm, and loved to talk. I could listen to her smoky voice all day while waiting to hear her call my name when I was deep inside her at night.

She'd agreed to have dinner with me, and everything seemed to being going great on our first date. I hadn't been to Bella Luna yet, having been in Redwood Falls for only eight months, new to my job and the area. The Falls was a small community of about forty thousand, with surprising diversity and a mellow vibe that made it easy for me to say yes to the job offer. The food at Bella Luna was good, really good, and would make the cut in LA. Spending time with Max was better than being with anyone I'd ever spent time with, and up until recently, I hadn't been shy about how much I loved the company of women.

She hadn't been wrong when she said things got out of control. I'd forgotten where I was, my position in the community, hell, I'd barely remembered my name. The thought of putting my mouth on Max's pussy had made me stupid with lust, like the seventeen-year-old version of myself. I'd been thinking only with my little head. When we'd been interrupted, she'd run away so fast, I didn't process it until she was already gone.

I knew where she lived and worked, and I could've tracked her down, but given how skittish she seemed, I'd thought I'd allow her a little space before I made my full-court press. Last night, when I saw my newest lieutenant, Will Travers, wrapped around her on the dance floor, I nearly burst a blood vessel in my brain. I'd never been a jealous man, not with all the talent LA had to offer, but the thought of anyone but me touching Max made me see red. Once again, she'd enticed me and I thought we'd head to my place and get down to it. I'd make her mine and there wouldn't be any question in her mind as to my intentions.

One minute she was in my car, the next she'd disappeared. I'd gone to her apartment, saw her car there, but she wasn't. Then, around noon today, when I saw her pacing in front of my building in last night's clothes I near came out of my skin. Learning she'd spent the night in the trunk of my car was a funny drunk story until she'd said she put herself in danger. That was victim-speak. Which pained my heart in a way I'd never experienced. The thought that anyone had hurt her made me want to cry at the same time I wanted to track down and kill the SOB.

"Chief. Chief." Someone was squeezing my arm. "Earth to Ryan."

I turned my head to look at my Assistant Chief of Police, Camille Radcliffe. "Was I *elsewhere*?" I asked as if I didn't know I'd been miles away in Max Calapiano land.

"You were gone, Chief. Elsewhere would've been a short trip back compared to where you were at. Everything okay?"

"The usual. More shit than time in the day to deal with it, and we're stuck here listening to this crap. Why don't they send me the memo, tell me how it impacts the city and the department, and then I'll weigh in."

"You know better than that. Cut-and-dried is not the way government does things. Dilly, dally, and delay are the three Ds they live by."

I grunted. "Ain't that the truth."

After the meeting broke up Camille and I stayed long enough to glad-hand and say all the right things before heading back to the department's building, which was around the corner from city hall. The PD shared a three-story building with the fire department's and code compliance's administrative offices, which took up the top floor. Everything else was PD, including the basement with its weapons lockers, evidence room, and small jail with three cells. Central booking was located about twenty miles away at the county offices, where they had a large jail for prisoners awaiting arraignment or trial. The nearest penitentiary was well over a hundred miles away from Redwood Falls, and that suited me just fine.

After fifteen years with LAPD, I'd been more than ready for a change. I'd worked hard and had caught the notice of a well-regarded commander. True, having a rabbi helped grease my path, but I had to keep my nose clean, my head down, and get the stats to have risen through the ranks and make Commander about two years ago. That's when the recruiters really got serious. A few had approached when I hit Captain II and then Captain III, but I'd started to get the royal treatment after I'd been a commander for a year.

Redwood Falls appealed for a variety of reasons, not the least of which was location. Situated at the eastern edge of the Anderson Valley in Mendocino County, the small city was off the 128 about fifteen miles west of the 101 freeway. The air here was crisp and clean, and I'd felt my lungs clearing out after only a couple of weeks.

Close enough to Santa Rosa and stores I was familiar with, thirty-five miles to the ocean, I'd found enough of what I needed to feel comfortable in and around Redwood Falls.

The town had a quirkiness to it that made it unique and inviting. Before accepting the job, I'd made a few "clandestine" trips, checking out the city and its environs. A lot of old hippies, young hipsters, and the requisite number of mountain folk made for an eclectic blend of people and personalities. In my travels, I'd found head shops right next door to "antique" stores filled with taxidermy and antlers.

Since I was a kid, I'd loved the mountains, the trees, the wildlife, and the quiet. Everything Redwood Falls had in spades. As chief, I knew they had their fair share of crime in the city, but compared to LA, it felt as if I'd been airlifted out of a war zone and dropped into a sanctuary. I found it amusing and apropos that the spa where Max worked was called Shangri la.

Without even meaning to, my thoughts circled back to her. Knowing there was something ugly lurking in her past meant I had to go easier with her than I'd initially intended. One thing I'd learned in my thirty-seven years was that which was worth having was worth working and waiting for.

Trying to turn my mind back to the job, I refocused on the stats in front of me and was scrolling through reports when a knock sounded on my door. I yelled, "Come," and Will Travers stuck his head in.

"You have a minute, Chief?"

I almost laughed at how pissed-off I'd been at the thought of Max with Will. She'd shut that down with an emphatic *you idiot.* "Yeah, Will. Take a seat."

Will closed the door then let out a breath. Both actions told me my lieutenant found the upcoming topic uncomfortable and personal. "It's none of my business, and I don't mean to pry, but be careful with Max."

I was right. Uncomfortable and personal. "Careful?" I asked, not certain of the context of the caution.

"Lola and Max have been friends since the second grade. I've known Max for almost as long as I've known Lola. Max is good people, Chief. She leads with her heart, and she almost never says no."

I nodded, encouraging Will to go on, having learned these things about Max myself in the short time I'd known her.

"She had a rough patch about ten years ago when she was at Cal. Changed her. Made her more…wary. Again, none of my business, and you can tell me to get the hell out, but…she's not one-night-stand material."

Again, shit I'd sussed out already. But knowing whatever had happened went down when she was at college at Berkeley gave me a place to start digging. "'Preciate you taking the time to tell me. And while you're right, it's none of your business, gotta say, I'm not looking for one-night stands anymore."

Will chuckled and gave me a half grin. "Good to know, Chief."

Then my new lieutenant – and from that conversation alone, I knew I'd made the right decision promoting him – turned and left my office, shutting the door behind him.

Chapter Three

Ask Me No Questions, And I'll Tell You No Lies
Max

Everyone's eyebrows near hit the ceiling when I walked into work wearing an LBD and strappy sandals. "Don't ask," I warned my boss, co-workers, and the clients, nosy to the last one, some of whom were in various states of styling and coloring seated in chairs around the salon while others, who were waiting for their stylist, masseur, or esthetician, sat gabbing on the huge L-shaped sofa in the front of the spa along the far wall under the window opposite the reception desk.

Dana Hernandez walked in three minutes after I finished washing my face. She saw me tying one of the cotton wraps typically used by people getting facials around my LBD and said, "Wow. Walk of shame in the early afternoon. I'm dying to hear this."

Ignoring Dana's comment, and giving Bernadette, my boss, a look that said *Don't you dare pick up that thread*, I waved Dana over and told her, "I don't know what you're doing, but every time you come in here you look younger." The lie made Dana preen so fully, she forgot all about my walk of shame and spent the next forty-five minutes talking nonstop about her beauty regimen.

Bernadette wasn't so easy to derail. Three clients later, she cornered me in the back at the coloring station behind the sinks. "Do I know him? Is it someone local? Is it new? Is he good in bed?"

I almost never cursed at work, but after the hour I'd endured before I got to Shangri la, I didn't give a shit, and let it rip. "Jesus fuck, Bernadette. *If* I was seeing someone, I wouldn't talk about it here. This place puts the *National Enquirer* to shame. TMZ could ask almost any one of our clients for tips on how to dig for that last nugget of information without leaving too big a scar."

"Is that a yes? You're seeing someone?"

I shook my head as I blended two solutions to create Louise Gentry's soft honey blonde. "No. I'm not seeing anyone."

"You wouldn't lie to Bernadette, would you?"

"I would if I had to, but I'm not lying now." Bernadette frowned. "You're going to be disappointed. I won't bore you with the details, but I fell asleep with the dress on after partying with Will and Lola. You remember, Will got that promotion last week." Bernadette nodded. "I drank more than usual, overslept, and darted right over here so Dana wouldn't be kept waiting. Ta-da. The end." *And mostly the truth.*

Bernadette looked deflated. "That's as boring as all get-out. You're still in your twenties. You're supposed to be tearing it up, girl."

I had to hold back a laugh. Bernadette, who was on her third husband and they'd been together twenty years, talking about me tearing it up. "I'm twenty-nine nearly thirty, not twenty-one. I think I tore it completely and it's irreparable."

Bernadette put her hand over her heart at the same time she reared her auburn #6 poofed hair back and cried, "I hope to hell it's not torn, and I pray there's nothing to repair. That would be horrible for you."

I couldn't hold back, I cracked up. "I was speaking euphemistically."

"Thank god." Bernadette drew the back of her hand across her forehead. "You near gave me a heart attack thinking about such an awful thing happening."

"What happened?" David, one of the spa's masseurs, asked as he came out of one of the massage rooms wiping oil from his hands on white a Shangri la hand towel that had little green palm trees all over it.

"Nothing," Bernadette huffed. "Nothing good, anyway." She waved her hand up down the length of my body. "This is all going to waste."

David wiggled his brows. "I can help remedy that."

"He sure can," his latest client purred as she came out of the massage room.

David handed her a big glass of water and directed her to the door to the hallway as he said, "Now go sit up front and finish the whole glass, Adelaine. We don't want you to hold on to any free radicals."

"Heavens no," Adelaine panted. "My Harold would have a brain hemorrhage if I brought any radicals in the house, free or otherwise."

I took one look at Adelaine's St. John's Knits outfit and thought *I bet he would.*

"Now run along, sweetums." David made shooing motions. "I'll see you next week."

After the door shut and the click-click of Adelaine's heels couldn't be heard anymore, Bernadette said, "Well done you. She's coming every week now."

David puffed out his chest. "I can make anyone feel better. Even conservatives."

I dropped my head and shook it. "I've gotta get this goop on Louise's head. Behave. The both of you."

I was folding Louise's last foil when I heard the commotion up front. The receptionist, Gaia, gasped before she asked all raspy-voiced, "Can…can I help you?"

A three-quarter wall separated the reception area from the salon except for an arched cutout in which diaphanous rose-colored curtains hung. The overly dramatic entryway served as the official door to the spa, which was a little vee. To the left there was a curved hallway that ran along the salon's back wall, which led to the massage and estheticians' rooms. To the right was the entry to the salon. Unless a person was walking into the salon, none of the stylists could see who was up front, but we could hear what was being said.

Before whoever it was that made Gaia gasp and stutter could answer, a woman called out, "Chief? What're you doing here?"

Another woman said, "I'm sure he doesn't need a facial."

Yet another cooed breathily, "I bet he's here for a massage. All that crime fighting has to be hell on a body, even his."

These women. They had no shame. Apparently, the new chief of police was in the spa. I hoped there was nothing wrong.

"I'm here to see Max Calapiano."

I dropped the comb from my right hand into the bowl on my tray at the same time my left hand dug into the pocket in the cotton wrap, also covered with little green palm trees, and pulled out my phone. No calls. He hadn't called. Why was he here making good on a threat when he hadn't called? Clearly, warning him off by telling him I was going to file a police report alleging he was a stalker wasn't going to mean shit. Could this get any worse?

"Right this way," Gaia rasped, her voice all wobbly.

Yes, it could. It could get a fuckofalot worse.

Shoving the phone back in my pocket, I made sure my back was to the entryway. *Please, please, please. Let it be another person who sounds like Ryan.*

"She's right there," Gaia, the unwitting traitor, said.

"Thanks."

The heat from his big body hit me at the same time his musky scent did. Yep, I got a whiff of him even over all the salon smells. His maleness was undeniable.

"Max," he said softly. His warm breath hit the back of my neck, giving me tingles I did not want.

I turned and didn't look at him. I took in the now-silent salon – something that had never happened before – where every co-worker and client's mouth was hanging open, their eyes big and round. *Fuck.* I couldn't help but think about prey animals and how they stood perfectly still when they knew they were in danger, their instincts telling them if they didn't make a move the predator might pass them by and not notice them. Somehow, I didn't think that was going to work for me.

I focused on him and hated that he'd spent the past two weeks intentionally hiding he was the police chief. Not that it would've made a difference. Not at first. But knowing how he'd used his position to learn about me while I knew nothing about him, and, now that I thought about it, artfully steered our conversation at Bella Luna to anything and everything except our professions to continue his perfidy. And, oh-ho, how dare he get pissed about me dancing with Will Travers when Ryan was the person who'd promoted him. Given the size of that police department, Ryan had to've known Will was celebrating his promotion at Henry's.

Was that why Ryan had showed up there?

It took everything in me not to scream, "Get out."

"Chief," I snapped. His brows dropped, indicating he didn't miss the sarcasm laced through the honorific. "Someone break into my home?" I asked innocently, shooting the barb to make sure he knew how I felt about his unofficial snooping into my life.

"No."

"I forget to pay a parking ticket?" A couple of women chuckled.

"Don't think so."

"Huh. Then why do you want to talk to me?" *You deceptive, arrogant ass.*

He cleared his throat. "I think it'll be better if we speak outside."

"Ut-oh, Max," Bernadette muttered. "Do I need to call a lawyer?"

Pretty much everyone laughed as I narrowed my eyes at Bernadette. "I'll let you know." I turned to Louise. "I'll be right back, hon, to check on you. If you need anything, let Bernadette know, okay?"

Sweet, gentle Louise, the town's librarian, who had a front row seat to the Max and Ryan show, couldn't've missed how pissed off I was while *Chief* Trent stood there absolutely cool, calm, and collected, nodded rapidly and squeaked out, "Okay."

I held out my arm for Ryan to lead the way, and followed him through the folds of the curtains, across the reception area, and out the front door. I shielded my eyes from the bright sun beating on the west-facing storefront, then left him standing putting on his Wayfarers while I stomped down the block and around the corner, knowing everyone was leaning against the glass trying to hear what we were going to say.

I stopped on the far side of Henry's Bar & Grill where there were no windows, only bricking, and waited for Ryan to catch up. When he stopped a foot away, I leaned into his space. "What the hell is wrong with you?"

"You're standing there shooting fire and I'm here to ask you to a late lunch. Seems I should be asking you that."

I punched my fists on my hips. "Really, *Chief*?"

He sighed. "You got a problem with cops?"

"Nope. I got a problem with liars."

"Exactly how and when did I lie to you?"

"Thirty minutes over coffee, way more than two hours over dinner, and not one fucking word about who and what you are." He opened his mouth, but I cut him off. "Then knowing you looked into me, used your position to find out where I live and work…that's deceptive and an abuse of your office, *Chief*."

"Ryan," he growled. "I'm Ryan to you."

"You're no one to me." He grabbed my upper arm. He didn't hurt me, but his grip was firm. "Get your hand off me."

He released me and bent until his face was an inch from mine. "Last night you were climbing me like a tree."

I flung my arm back toward Henry's. "I was drunk."

"You weren't drunk outside Bella Luna."

I backed away from him. "We've gone over this already, and that's beside the point."

"Which is what exactly?"

"You have no business coming to where I work. We're nothing to each other, and it's going to stay that way. Now get gone, and stay gone." I made a wide pass around him and got as far as turning the corner before he was in front of me. Again.

In his deep manly-man voice, he gritted out, "When was the last time you got so hot for a man, Max?"

Damn, he was so fuckin' arrogant. "That's none of your business."

"I told you earlier, yeah, it is. We sparked, wildly, and you can stand there and try to deny it until the sun rises tomorrow, but we both know that'd be a goddamn lie. Now, you wanna tell me why the fuck you want to ignore something that good?"

No, I sure as fuck didn't. "We met over coffee. We had one date. I went home. Alone. I ignored your phone calls. Last night I was drunk and kissed you. That's the sum total of our interaction. Now," I lowered my voice, "I'm asking nicely. Please, don't contact me again. I don't want to see you anymore."

He sighed, dropped his head, held up his hands, and stepped back.

Even though it hurt to do it, actual pain-in-my-heart hurt, I knew walking away from him was the smart thing to do. I understood the concept of self-preservation better than most. Ryan Trent wanted to get close, and I couldn't allow that. Eventually, he would know the truth about me, and even if he didn't mean to hurt me, my heart and soul couldn't take one more lash of that whip.

Without another word or looking back, I walked to Shangri-la, opened the door, and went inside to work, deflecting everyone's questions with, "Police business. You understand. I can't talk about it." While they buzzed and speculated, they didn't bother me again. By nine pm, even Bernadette stopped probing.

I went home, took a much-needed shower, put on a pair of sweats and a t-shirt, then emptied the three bottles of wine I had in the house down the kitchen sink. I let the water run, then poured in vinegar to kill the odor. I didn't have the energy to turn on the TV, even though I was halfway through my latest binge show.

Lying under the covers in my big bed, I closed my eyes and waited until the emotions swirling through my bloodstream calmed. I knew I'd failed when the last thought I had was of Ryan's hands on my body, and his lips pressed against mine drinking me in while his tongue probed my mouth as if I held the nectar of life.

Chapter Four

Da Nile is not just a River in Egypt
Ryan

If any other woman had pulled that shit, I would've walked, no, run away, thrilled to be free of that drama. But this was Max, and her pull was undeniable. I'd had my fun for years, then I thought it was time to get serious and began dating. I'd had a couple of girlfriends a few months each, but no one had held my interest or had made me hungry with want the way Max did. Something frightened her so deeply she was willing to walk away from me even though I knew she felt this thing between us. There was something dark and deep haunting her, preventing her from being happy, and I was going to get to the heart of that beast and slay it.

But clearly not today.

I headed back to the office, planted my ass in my chair, and got to work. Somewhere around eight, Camille stuck her head in. "You pulling a late night?"

"Didn't intend to. Going to wrap this up in about fifteen minutes."

"Don't forget we got that meeting in Santa Rosa tomorrow at ten."

Santa Rosa was the largest city close to Redwood Falls, and sometimes their problems spilled over into my city. Mostly, every area department was dealing with the negative effects of tourism. Between the wineries, the forests, and the nearby lakes, many crimes were imported. But tourism was the lifeblood of most of the small towns and cities. Managing the problems was critical to keep revenue flowing. There were a few joint task forces with a number of area PDs working together to curb crime. Tomorrow was going to be an all-day deal.

"Yeah. I'll meet you here at eight."

"Got it, Chief." She flicked two fingers from her forehead then left.

After Camille went home, good to my word, I wrapped up what I was doing and headed out. Another of the perks of living in Redwood Falls, my standard of living went up exponentially. In LA, I'd lived in a small one-bedroom condo in Silver Lake I'd bought ten years ago. I sold it for double what I'd paid for it, and had all that equity. With that money I was able to buy, in a luxury building, a two-bedroom, two-bath condo five times the size of my last condo and my mortgage stayed the same. Yeah, I'd indulged and treated myself to a great car, but hell, I'd scrimped and saved for fifteen years. I'd earned my splurge.

Coming home every night was a pleasure. I had a long terrace off the open plan kitchen/dining room/living room that faced the mountains, and every night I sat out there enjoying the quiet. It'd taken months to get used to the relative silence. Sirens piercing the night were an unusual occurrence, and the handful of times it happened, I'd gotten a phone call about what was going on long before I'd heard the sirens.

There was a downside to the slow pace. Restaurants closed at nine during the week and eleven on the weekends. The coffee shops closed at eight, and while there were a number of bars, only Henry's and The Red Rail had live music.

I'd been used to the twenty-four-seven lifestyle LA offered, and I missed some of those conveniences and diversions. As it turned out, San Francisco was about a couple of hours away. Since I'd taken this job, I'd spent a few weekends there, and knowing what the city offered, and that it wasn't far, took the sting out of the few things I missed about LA.

Tonight, even after sitting on the terrace, I was still restless and couldn't settle. Watching Max walk away from me hurt in a way I'd never experienced. There was nothing rational about the way I felt, and understanding that didn't help.

Christ, I'd spent a total of maybe five hours with her. How could I be so attached, so certain about a person I barely knew? This wasn't lust. Well, okay, it was, but that wasn't what was making my heart feel empty like I was missing a piece of me. Something inside of me had staked a claim. Max was mine. I was as certain of that as I was my own name.

Insult to injury, she didn't trust me. Acknowledged, she didn't seem to be a trusting soul, but I better than most could help her with what had happened to her. No, I couldn't erase the memories, but I'd been trained to help victims and had helped hundreds of people regain power and control over their lives.

I wasn't going for the knight in shining armor award. I didn't want to save her, I wanted to… Okay. Now wait a damn minute. I haven't even taken this woman to my bed. Haven't spent a night with her in my arms. I needed to dial down the emotions and think of a strategy.

Somehow, I had to find a way in. There had to be a way to get Max to see she was mine, and I was hers.

***

The next day, after a fitful night of attempting sleep, I dragged myself into work at seven to get a little admin done before I had to head out to Santa Rosa with Camille. I didn't like being out of pocket all day, but this meeting was important. We needed to be an active part of the network of task forces working in our neighboring communities, and face time at these interjurisdictional gatherings with the top dogs was essential.

After catching up on my emails, I was cuing up last night's reports when Camille leaned into my office. "Ready, Chief?"

When I saw the time was 7:45, I nodded, figuring we might as well get on the road sooner than later. With no traffic, the trip should take a little more than an hour, but the 101 could get backed up, and I didn't want to be late.

Camille got behind the wheel of the Crown Vic, and that suited me fine. I didn't feel like driving. I needed to take this time to talk to her, ask questions. Get a feel for who'd be at this meeting and what to expect. She'd been with the Redwood Falls PD for nineteen years and knew the city and its neighboring communities better than almost anyone. Promoting her from commander to assistant chief was an easy process. No other applicant was better suited for the job.

She'd been raised in the Falls. Her parents owned and managed a small B&B in town, and the family had lived in a cottage on the back of the inn's property where Camille and her sister had grown up. Camille's husband was a history teacher at the high school, and her twin boys attended the local middle school. She didn't have the same depth and breadth of experience I did, but she was a cop's cop, and her roots in the community ran strong and deep.

"We got a call on a semi-regular last night," she said as we headed out of town. I nodded for her to continue. "Sigrid Giordano. Everyone calls her Ziggy." She shot a quick glance my way. "She's sort of a cousin of Max Calapiano."

Now I understood that glance. Small police department, and cops were the worst fuckin' gossips in the world. Though I didn't think Will would've said anything. More likely, a few of those women at the spa wagged their jaws. No doubt, Camille knew I was at Shangri la talking to Max. She also might know I left Henry's the other night with Max.

"How's she a 'sort of' cousin?"

"Ziggy's father is Max's father's brother's brother-in-law."

See, Camille knew everyone and their history, though the Calapianos were high profile. Big money from their vineyard and winery.

"Dominic Calapiano has a brother?"

"Yep. Lives in Connecticut. Some shit went down years ago after the brothers started the winery. No one knows what it was about, but Anthony Calapiano moved his family to the East Coast and he came back only when his folks died. His girls used to visit in the summer, but their lives are in Connecticut. I'm pretty sure Max's cousin, Anthony's oldest daughter, went to college at Stanford while Max was at Cal, but none of them returned to the Falls to live."

"So Ziggy?"

"Is a mess. Total wild child. Always has been. Her folks live in Santa Rosa, but she comes here to stir it up. Has two older brothers who manage to keep a lid on her most of the time, but she's walking trouble after she's gotten a couple of drinks in her, or if she's smoked a joint or two. She's model pretty, and men pant after her. Most of the trouble is man trouble, or men behaving badly because of Ziggy. Max is on Ziggy's official cleanup committee. Girl's a pain in the ass."

"What'd she do last night?"

"Last night was the culmination of a run she's been on for a few months now."

"Last night?" I sort of repeated.

"She had a rip-roaring with her boyfriend in The Red Rail. She threw a full beer bottle at him. Thankfully, he ducked, and the bottle broke against the dartboard. Glass and beer hit a few patrons. No one was hurt. Ziggy made tracks, but the bartender and a couple of the patrons know her and gave us an official ID. We'll catch up with her and bring her in for questioning. The Red Rail didn't file a complaint, and they won't. I don't see this going anywhere, but you have to know, she's on our radar."

Yet another piece to the Max puzzle, and a way to double back without being entirely obvious.

"Thanks for the update. Who's gonna be at this shindig we're going to?"

Camille ran it down, and my interest piqued when she said the operations captain from the Berkeley PD would be there. Before I left this meeting to return to the Falls, he and I would be talking about an incident from ten years ago.

***

Ten a.m. to one p.m. was packed full of worthwhile information including tactical briefings, sharing opportunities for available grants for equipment, hiring trends, gang updates, the lingering effects of the fires, and some discussion about recent terrorist hot sheets. I received a genuine welcome from the group of fifty men and women who'd been on the job for many years. A couple of folks had worked for departments in SoCal, but none in LA. I was asked a lot of tactical questions, and without a hitch, I was folded into the group like I'd been part of their team forever.

After we concluded our business, we had a catered lunch. All the departments chipped in for these quarterly meetings, and each department hosted the group in turn. Today, we were in a large room in the Finley Community Center, which had a huge sculpture of Linus and Lucy out front. Charles Schulz, the Peanuts cartoon creator, had lived in Santa Rosa for many years and was a hometown hero. I was told there are a lot of Peanuts things all over Santa Rosa, including a Schulz museum.

As if I'd orchestrated it, Captain Fredrico Alvarez from Berkeley PD sat next to me at lunch. He had a brother-in-law who worked for the LA County Sheriff's Department, and we traded stories. It was natural and easy when we segued into my Q and A.

"Hey. Were you in Berkeley PD about ten years ago?"

"Yeah. Beat cop for three years by then. Why?"

"You remember anything big happening at Cal ten years back?"

He squinted, then grinned. "Personal, huh?"

I drew in a deep breath and nodded. "Yeah. Someone who means something to me was caught up in I don't know what, but it was big and left a scar."

"GSW?"

I shook my head. "No." I tapped my chest. "In here."

"Sexual assault?"

"Maybe, but I don't think so. Doesn't feel like that. I'm not getting a free flow of information."

Alvarez chuckled. "Deep freeze, *ese*?"

Cops. Hard to hide anything from them. Especially the good ones. Fredrico Alvarez was particularly sharp and incisive. "Arctic."

Alvarez threw back his head and laughed. Then he tapped the gold band on his left ring finger. "Took me more than a minute to get here, man. Can't say I hated the war I waged to convince her."

My turn to grin. "I bet."

"Lemme think. The University of California Police Department shares concurrent jurisdiction with the Berkeley PD, so if it was big, we were there." He sat back. The thumb and forefinger of his right hand worked his 'stache as he thought. After a couple of minutes, he nodded. "Yeah. About ten years ago, give or take, there was a gang rape during a party at one of the frat houses. Fucked-up shit, *ese*. Brutal."

All the air left my lungs as my stomach dropped and bile filled the back of my throat. It took all my control to keep my lunch down.

"I took witness statements, but I remember the vic's name was something like Lali or Lisa. Maybe Laurie." He watched as I started to breathe again. "Mean anything to you?"

I shook my head.

"A relief, man."

"Fuck yeah." I took a beat to get my heartrate under control. "Any female witnesses?"

"Bunch of girls at the party. I know we talked to a lot of them. You want, I can look if you give me a name."

"Obliged, Fredrico."

"Rico. My friends call me Rico."

I gave him a chin lift. "Massima Calapiano. She goes by Max."

"The winery Calapiano?"

"Yeah."

"Aim high, *ese*, aim high."

***

By two-thirty Camille and I were back on the road, heading home.

"Saw you and Alvarez laughing it up," Camille said as she turned the car onto the entrance to the 101.

"Yeah. His brother-in-law is a deputy sheriff in LA. We were trading stories."

She nodded. "I heard there's no love lost between LAPD and the sheriff's department."

"More true when Baca was sheriff. He was an asshole and created a shit culture in the department. Things are better now. I've worked with a lot of solid cops in LASD."

"Cream rises, Chief. Like finds like."

I turned to Camille, whose gaze was fixed on the road. "You buttering me up, Assistant Chief Radcliffe?"

"Absolutely, sir."

I laughed. "Give it to me."

"The Santa Rosa PD has a drone program. Five officers and an evidence tech. I was thinking, we should get a couple of drones and liaison with them about their program."

"Find the money and how to sustain it in the upcoming budget year, and I'm in."

She flashed me a grin. "They must've been lying."

"What's that?"

"I heard you weren't easy."

"You got the part about the money, right?"

"Leave it to me, Chief."

Yeah. Great decision to promote Camille. As I was about to give her an *atta girl*, my phone rang. Will was calling.

I answered with, "What's up?"

"You know who Isak and Endre Giordano are?"

"Not really, but I'm going to guess they're part of Ziggy's family."

Camille turned her head when I said "Ziggy."

"Her brothers," Will said. "Her *older* brothers."

"I'm putting you on speaker." I upped the volume. "I heard they have a calming effect. The way you say it, I'm taking that as bad news."

"Well…" Will trailed off for a moment. "You're right. Usually, when Ziggy goes off the rails, they take her home and settle her down. Most of the time it's a good thing."

"This time?"

"Ziggy surfaced last night after having been MIA for a couple of days. Her brothers are tearing it up looking for her."

"Not going easy."

"Easy's three thousand miles in the rearview."

Camille made a noise in the back of her throat. "You think it'll do any good to bring 'em in?" she asked.

"Can't hurt to have a word," Will said.

"Make that informal," I told him.

"Right, Chief. You on your way back?

"We should be in around four, four-thirty."

"Copy that." He hung up.

"Told you that girl's a pain in the ass," Camille groused.

"Yeah, you did."

On the other hand, Ziggy's troubles provided me with an opportunity. Now I had a damn good reason to circle back to Max. Legit police business about her *sort of* cousin Ziggy Giordano.

I didn't think I'd thank Ziggy for being such a huge pain in the ass since she wasted department resources, but I was grateful for her family connections.

Chapter Five

Family Feud
Max

I was on the phone to Connecticut with my cousin Theresa recapping the newest Ziggy sitch when someone knocked on my door. I put my eye to the peephole and silently drew in a deep breath. Shit. Ryan Trent.

To make sure he wouldn't hear me, and to check myself in the mirror, I walked all the way to my bedroom before I said to Theresa, "Best not to say anything about Ziggy's latest predicament to Isak and Endre. Avoiding bloodshed and jail time is a righteous goal."

"For sure," Theresa agreed. "I almost can't believe she's at it again so soon."

"That makes two of us. When I know more, I'll call."

"Talk soon." She hung up.

More knocking, and I swear, I could tell he was losing his patience. I didn't look too bad. I had on my vintage Cal hoodie and yoga pants. Why I cared pissed me off. I walked back through the living room, turned the deadbolt, and swung the door open. "What?" I snapped. He looked so damn good it pissed me off even more. Like I needed to remember how fantastic he was.

"Nice to see you too, Max." I rolled my eyes. He chuckled. "May I come in?"

"Ah, no. Say what you gotta say and get gone."

"Police business, Max. I'm thinking you don't want me to talk about your cousin out here."

Fuckin' Ziggy. I shook my head. "C'mon." I stood back and let him in. As he passed by me – damn him, he came close on purpose – I could smell his unique musk and outdoorsy scent, which pissed me off. He had some nerve coming in here wearing a herringbone sports coat, a button-down open at the collar, and jeans that hugged his serious thighs. No man was supposed to look that good after a workday.

He walked into the living room and did a three-sixty. Total cop scoping out the place. Let him look. I was proud of my little condo. The living room/dining combo was adjacent to a decent-size kitchen with a small horseshoe counter. There was a slider at the end of the dining room that led to a little balcony that had a café table, two chairs, and a few plants, mostly succulents. The hall was perpendicular to the kitchen. On the left side of the hallway there was a little bedroom I used as my office/TV room/guest bedroom. The sage green wide wale corduroy sofa folded out into a double bed.

Across from the TV room was a three-quarter bathroom that had a man-size shower stall angled in the corner. At the end of the hall was my bedroom, which was big enough for my California king bed with its wood and iron headboard, plus a dark wood dresser and an end table with a scrolled iron lamp. A super-short hall held a walk-in closet on one side and a linen closet on the other. The hall dead-ended in a full bathroom.

Before I'd moved in, I had the floors redone in the whole place. Dark wood planks throughout, except the kitchen and bathrooms, which were Saltillo tiled. All the walls were painted pale sage green, and the large L-shaped sofa in the living room was russet corduroy with lots of funky throw pillows, some with tassels, some fringed, all in bright complementary colors. The sofa, the square distressed wooden coffee table, and the two ochre-colored wooden end tables that held scrolled iron lamps sat on a white shag area rug flecked with dark brown and tan.

Beneath the length of the front window was a long dark wood bookcase, on top of which sat a row of orchid plants. My cousin Theresa was a garden center nut and had a thing for orchids. She got me hooked. We traded orchid snaps all the time.

On the long wall in the dining room above the black bowfront commode were Ansel Adams prints, all taken at Yosemite. The dining room table was made of painted reclaimed wood, and the chairs were mismatched ladderbacks with large russet corduroy cushions.

The kitchen cabinets were crème white, a few had glass fronts, and the counters were white veined black granite. Three scrolled iron barstools sat in front of the horseshoe counter. It'd taken a while, and I'd gone to a ton of yard sales, antiques stores, shabby chic stores, junk yards, and reclamation yards until I found the pieces that had the vibe I wanted. Only the sofas and my bed came from a furniture store. There wasn't one thing in my home I hadn't chosen, including the frames for all the family photos lining the hallway, and the few small sculptures and knickknacks I'd picked up in my travels.

"Nice place, Max."

"What? You didn't break in and scope it out already?"

His jaw got tight and he looked like he was talking himself out of blowing a gasket. "Let's get this out of the way." He punched his hands on his hips, which pulled back the sides of his sports coat, revealing his gun in one of those belt holsters. I wondered if he'd had a gun with him every time we'd been together. If he had, I never saw it or felt it. "I didn't run your stats. You told me you worked at Shangri-la when we met at Beans and Roast, and you mentioned you lived in the Harmony condo complex over dinner at Bella Luna." He winged up a brow. "The first time I drove you home, I didn't know which unit you lived in, but I knew what your car looked like. When I saw it, I pulled in next to it."

Well shit. I might've told him about the spa over coffee. I didn't remember saying so, but it wasn't like where I worked was a state secret. I might've mentioned my condo complex over dinner since I thought the name Harmony was a bit much, but I didn't remember telling him that either. I'd been so caught up in his intense green eyes, dark wavy hair, and chiseled features I'd lost track of what my mouth was spewing.

I shrugged. "Okay. I'll give you that. But how did you know my unit number now?"

He looked at his boots for a moment. "Police business, remember?"

"About that. Why is the police chief taking care of 'police business'?"

He closed his eyes and I couldn't be certain, but I thought he muttered, "Fuckin' stubborn" under his breath. "Trying to be sensitive about your family situation, and sending Will when he'd rather be home with his pregnant wife, I thought I'd handle it."

Well. That pissed me off too. He was being considerate.

He sighed like he'd climbed thirty flights of stairs and was catching his breath. "Why don't we sit."

Sitting was not good. Sitting on my L-shaped wide-cushioned sofa was totally not good. Over the past couple of weeks, my brain had conjured indelible images of what Ryan and I could do with all that soft acreage, and I didn't need a reminder of my stupid fantasizing.

Yeah. All right. I'd get over myself and adult.

I sat at the end of the bend of the L, tucking one leg under my tush. He watched the move and his lips twitched when he spied my neon pink toenail polish. He sat on the edge of the cushion in the middle of the longer part of the couch with his hands clasped together between his long legs. His gaze leveled on mine and he asked in a gentle but professional tone he'd never used with me before, "Are you aware of an incident at The Red Rail a couple of nights ago involving Ziggy Giordano?"

Fuckin', fuckin' Ziggy. What new shit had she gotten herself into? "No."

"Allegedly, she threw a full bottle of beer at her boyfriend."

Before I could stop myself, I blurted, "Which one?"

Ryan's eyes narrowed and his jaw did that jumpy thing again. "How many does she have?"

"Well, it used to be two. Now, I can't say for sure." I twisted my fingers to keep from punching the sofa. Fuckin' Ziggy. "Did she hurt him?"

Ryan shook his head. "He ducked. The bottle hit the dart board and some beer and glass sprayed a couple of the customers, but no one was hurt."

"Well, there's that."

"Yeah." He sat back a smidge. "Do you know her boyfriends' names?"

"Nope. Ziggy isn't a big sharer."

Ryan looked like he wanted to say something about that but stopped himself. "Are you aware her brothers are looking for her?"

"Yep." I knew better than to tell a cop I was the one who sicced Isak and Endre on Ziggy. And I sure as hell knew better than to tell Ryan why I set her brothers on her trail. Only Theresa knew the story from a few months ago about Ziggy getting pregnant and not knowing which guy was the father. Ziggy's brothers would've beat the shit out of both the guys on GP, even though Ziggy had willingly participated in two relationships having unprotected sex. She'd had an abortion, and I thought after that debacle things would calm down. She was pissed as hell at me, but that didn't stop her from dropping in at two in the morning when she needed a place to crash. Who knew what new shit she'd gotten herself into. This time I didn't wait to call her brothers. I wanted her found and out of town ASAP. Christ, she was the walking definition of a hot mess.

"They're not playing nice, Max. Whatever's going on with their sister, these boys are terrorizing the town looking for her."

Damn it.

I modulated my tone to neutral, which took effort. I'd love nothing better than to be free of Ziggy's drama for a while. Like a year or two. I didn't think that was asking too much. "Is this you requesting I talk to them?" I was pissed at Ryan for being here. He could've sent any one of his seventy-five officers. He didn't need to talk to me about this shit, and neither did Will. I was double, triple pissed at Ziggy for putting my ass in this sling. And now I was pissed at Endre and Isak for being too damn heavy-handed, even though I knew that was what they did when Ziggy went missing.

"We'd like to talk to them. Informally," he rushed to say. "We're hoping to encourage them to take their sister back to Santa Rosa and keep her there."

I laughed sardonically. “Good luck with that.” I waved my hand before he said anything else. “I’ll ask them to give Will a call. They know him, and they won’t mind having an informal chat.”

“Obliged, Max.”

Great. Now was the time for Ryan to say, “Thanks for your help” and leave. Instead he sat there staring at me with a soft look in his eyes, his lids all hooded. Oh no he didn’t.

I unfolded my leg, and as I stood, I smacked my hands on my thighs. “Okieee dokieee. Unfortunate, but necessary chat. Thanks for stopping by. Have a good rest of your evening.”

He hadn’t moved more than his head as he watched me. “Max,” he said softly in what anyone with working ears would call a bedroom voice. I wanted to scream at him at the same time I felt like hanging my head in defeat.

I hated that I wanted him.

“No,” I snapped. “You don’t get to do this. I’ve made myself clear, and you have to honor that.”

He pulled in a long breath, but he didn’t move any of those fantastic muscles to stand. “I would if I believed you meant it.”

“What? You’re a mind reader now?” His lips parted and I didn’t let him say another word. “Out. It doesn’t matter what you believe. The only thing that matters is what I’m telling you even if I’m lying through my teeth. Which I’m not.”

He closed his eyes and dropped his head, then he put his hands on his knees as if he needed to push himself up. When he stood, my gaze followed the journey until it tilted back because, like a masochistic idiot, I had to watch him unfold that incredible tall, sculpted body at the same time I surreptitiously ogled his gorgeous face.

For giving myself away, I got a smug, knowing smirk.

Shitdamnfuck.

He held out his hand. “Let’s get something to eat. I’m starved.”

I crossed my arms over my chest. “I’m not.” Total lie. I’d meant to go Costco to do the big haul shop, and never made it. Since I had slim pickings, I’d planned to order in Chinese, and then he showed up.

“Get a drink and keep me company. C’mon. We’ll be in public. Take your own car.”

“Mandarin Paradise,” I shot out like a challenge.

He chuckled. He read me like a kindergarten primer. “I’ll meet you there.” Before I knew what he intended to do, his arm was around my waist and his lips were pressed against mine as he bent me back over his strong grip. I gasped and his tongue slid into my mouth, warm and gentle. He kissed me for only a few moments. Enough to remind me, as if I’d forget, the fire between us. The kiss was sweet despite its brevity, and in those few moments of connection I felt his promise that he’d take care of me, as well as full notice he wanted me in his bed. “I’ll order eggrolls,” he whispered against my lips. Then he righted me and strode out my front door without looking back.

***

Total cop. Ryan was sitting in the last booth on the right side of Mandarin Paradise, his back to the wall. He’d taken off his jacket and had rolled up the sleeves of his button-down. He looked good enough to eat, and if I added in hoisin sauce, we wouldn’t get out of bed for a week.

I shouldn’t be here. After he’d left, I threw the deadbolt and said *adios* in my brain at the same time I walked into my bedroom and put on a pair of jeans, my oldest, most broken-in pair of cowboy boots, and a black tank top, over which I pulled on a chunky moss green fisherman’s sweater that had a tendency to fall off my shoulder. I’d smushed some goop in my hair, pulled up a few spikes, swiped on fresh mascara, and ran cranberry lipstick over my lips.

As I was getting in my car, I asked myself why I wasn’t bailing. Aside from the absolute certainty that if I didn’t show, I knew he’d be banging on my door sometime tonight, ultimately, I decided it couldn’t be much worse eating with him when I spent almost all my free time, and a fair amount of headspace while at work, imagining what it would be like if I could have Ryan Trent.

His intense gaze didn’t leave my face as I walked down the narrow aisle to his booth. He stood when I got to the table, and I threw my beat-up slouchy bag on the seat and watched it slide across the red vinyl and stop at the wall. He shook his head and motioned for me to sit. At the same time as we were lowering our bodies onto the booth’s seats, Auntie Woo, which was what the owner, Mrs. Woo, insisted everyone call her, put egg rolls, dim sum, a pot of tea, and two small cups on the table. Two glasses of water were already there along with lemon wedges, a small condiment lazy susan, and a bowl of those wonderful thick, crunchy noodles I could eat by the truckload.

"Been a while, Max," Auntie Woo said as she smiled at me. "Glad you brought in the police chief."

How had I brought in Ryan when he got there before me? Never mind. I knew her question was meant to instigate an introduction.

"Auntie Woo, this is Ryan Trent. Ryan, this is Mandarin Paradise's owner, Mrs. Woo, who insists everyone call her Auntie Woo."

Ryan stood again, and Auntie Woo lit up. She was born in the Falls, but her parents were from China, and she was raised with and loved old-fashioned everything, especially the show of respect.

Ryan stuck out his hand, his focus on her completely. "Pleasure to meet you, Auntie Woo. I apologize for taking so long to get here, especially since everyone raves about your restaurant."

Damn. He was good. She was preening like a twelve-year-old after a ballet recital.

She shook his hand and clasped it with her other hand. "You've been busy settling in. I'm pleased you made the time to stop by." She released his hand and tilted her head, indicating he should sit, which he did. "Max knows our menu well. I'll rely on her to tell you about our specialties." She sent me a wink then left.

"I'm guessing she doesn't usually serve," he said as he put an egg roll and a dim sum on my plate using chopsticks, then repeated the action to his plate.

I did a quick head shake. "Sometimes when it's packed she does, but usually, no. Her kids help out after school, and she has a couple of cousins who work as servers full time. Everyone knows them. They've been with the restaurant since it opened in the early nineties."

He put hot sauce and soy sauce in one of the little cup-like dishes and mixed them with his chopsticks. "Mr. Woo?"

"Is an accountant. He does taxes for Shangri la and a lot of businesses in the Falls. He has nothing to do with the restaurant except when he eats here with extended family."

"Smart man." Ryan picked up a dim sum and dunked it in the sauce, then put the whole thing in his mouth. He bit down and closed his eyes as a loan moan bubbled in his chest. I watched a smile spread across his face as he chewed then swallowed. “Damn. That’s good.”

There was something really wrong with me. I was about to have an orgasm watching him eat a dim sum. Okay, you have to believe me when I say between the way he placed the food in his mouth, the way his jaw moved when he chewed, and that moan, I’d bet you’d feel like coming too.

“Aren’t you going to have one?” he asked innocently, but I swear, he knew I’d enjoyed the show, and he was baiting me.

Dangerous game. If I played, I knew where this would lead, if not tonight, soon. I was near combusting, and his green eyes sparkled like jewels on fire.

“You go ahead. Everyone should gorge on MP’s dim sum the first time they have them.” I reached for the eggroll he’d put on my plate. “How about I regale you with the house specialties and my favorites?”

His gaze held mine for a long moment, then he let it go. I knew he was regrouping for another assault, but it seemed, for the time being, we’d eat and make small talk.

While we waited for our orders, moo shu vegetables for me – hoisin sauce, remember? – and spicy shrimp and noodles for him, Ryan shared. I knew he meant for me to reciprocate, but for now I was happy to listen to him. Honestly, I was interested. At Bella Luna we’d talked about easy things, and he’d steered the conversation, but we never got really personal. Now, he jumped right in.

“I think I told you, I grew up in Torrance,” he said as if I’d asked. “You know it?”

“Not really,” I mumbled around my eggroll. “I haven’t spent a lot of time in SoCal.”

“East of Redondo Beach and north of Palos Verdes. Older houses. Mostly middle class, though some parts are rough. We lived about half a mile from the tiny stretch of the city’s beach.”

“We?”

He smiled. Such a little thing to ask about his family, but he liked that I did, and I couldn’t help it, I smiled back. “Me, my older brother, mom and dad.”

“How much older?’ He hadn’t said at Bella Luna, only that he had a brother.

“Six years. He was in college when I started high school. A bit too many years between us to be close when we were growing up.”

“Are you now? Close, that is?”

“Yeah,” he said softly. “He’s a dentist in Encino. That’s a neighborhood in the San Fernando Valley not far from LA.”

“Okay, National Geographic. I know where Encino is.” I leaned in a bit. “And I even know about LA. I hear it’s a really, really, really big city.” I batted my eyes a few times.

He laughed. “Smartass.”

“And proud of it.” I blew on my fingernails and rubbed them on the top of my chest. Stupid move. He watched my hand and his gaze traveled over my breasts, which weren’t really on display since the sweater was thick and loose, but still…I didn’t need his attention there. Diversion question. “He married?”

“He is.” He grinned, totally knowing I was trying to take his mind off my breasts. “He, Randall, and his husband Oscar have two little girls. Elizabeth is four, and Emory is seven.”

“Wow. Uncle Ryan.”

He gave me his sweet smile. The one that said he loved his family, was totally into being Uncle Ryan, and he had no trouble letting me know that.

“Yeah,” he rasped. God, why did he have to have such a sexy voice?

“Bet it’s tough living so far away from them.”

“It’s not ideal, but Oscar’s in show biz, and makes serious money. A couple of years ago they bought a house on a bluff in Mendocino, and since that’s not more than an hour away, we’ll see each other more than a few times a year.”

“Would I know him?”

“Oscar?”

I nodded.

He shrugged. “Do you like vampire TV shows?”

“Ohmygod,” I squeed and leaned halfway over the table, my chest hovering above the empty plates. “Is Oscar, Oscar Shelbourne who plays Lord Winston on *Dark Magic*?”

Ryan’s eyes got intense and hooded. His gaze held mine as he whispered, “I can’t wait.”

Ut-oh. I sat back and snugged my butt onto the vinyl bench. Somehow we weren’t talking about Oscar Shelbourne anymore. I didn't know exactly what happened to move us off safe ground, but that look in Ryan's eyes said *I'm going to fuck you for so long and give it to you so good you'll be screaming my name all night.*

I knew better. I shouldn't ask. I asked. "Wait for what?"

"To make you –"

Before he could finish his thought, which I didn't want to hear, though I knew pretty much what he was going to say, Mingmei came over with that stand thingie, kicked it open, and put the large round tray holding our food on the stand. "Here you go," she said in her soft, high voice. She put the platters with the food in the middle of the table, and she placed clean dishes in front of us. Then she put the moo shu pancakes wrapped in butcher paper next to my dish and asked, "Can I get you anything else?"

I wanted to say, *Yes. An emergency evacuation from the premises, please*, but I answered, "Not for me."

Ryan said, "I think we're good. Thank you."

Mingmei picked up the big tray and the stand, then said, "Enjoy your dinner" before taking off.

With my head down, I focused all my attention on unwrapping the pancakes, taking one out, putting it on my plate, re-wrapping the rest of the pancakes, then spreading hoisin sauce on the pancake. I heard Ryan chuckle, but I refused to lift my gaze, and concentrated on getting my moo shu vegetables onto the pancake without making a bigger mess of things than they were already.

Chapter Six

Viral
Ryan

Fuck. I'd pushed too hard and lost her. I'd been able to bring her around earlier, and when she agreed to meet me for dinner, I felt like I'd won the LA marathon. We'd been having a good time. Great food, easy conversation. She was the most relaxed I'd ever seen her, and I wanted *that* woman. Okay, I'd wanted her before, but the Max who'd been with me for half of the evening had eyes that sparkled with mischief and was full of sass, which she sharpened when she poked at me. When she asked about Oscar, she let it all hang out: happy, breathless, excited. I didn't check my reaction. How could I when she near came across the table with an eager expression, a bright wide smile, and holy shit, her full, luscious tits were nearly touching the dishes mere inches away from my hands. I was already lost in her before tonight. After…there was no turning back. My mistake: when her voice went higher than its usual husky and she let out a squeak, all I could think was I wanted to hear those noises when I was deep inside her making her come…and I about said so.

She'd retreated. I watched her shut down right in front of me. Eye contact became infrequent. Conversation was spare and awkward, and when the bill came, she insisted on paying for her half. Stupid shit that meant nothing. Staking her independence over fifteen dollars. I wasn't going to fight with her, especially since she'd gone back behind her military grade reinforced wall.

We'd said good night on the sidewalk like we were barely acquaintances. As much as I wanted to follow her home to make sure she got back okay, I didn't because I knew she'd take it the wrong way.

Now I was sitting on my terrace, staring at the trees, going over every moment we'd been together since she'd opened the door to her condo earlier this evening. I compared tonight to the other times we'd been together, and it dawned on me that when I talked about personal stuff, as long as everything was light and breezy, she loosened up. If I hinted at something deeper, a connection that meant emotions more than lust would be involved, she ran in the other direction faster than the speed of light.

What the fuck happened at Berkeley that put a permanent dark cloud over Max's heart?

As I stood up to go to bed, I saw the clock on the microwave said one thirty-seven. For a man who was supposed to be enjoying a less stressful life in Redwood Falls, I wasn't sleeping worth a damn.

The next morning, I was at my desk at seven-thirty reading Will's summation of an incident that occurred the night before involving a junior officer named Eric Foster who'd been on the job a little less than two years. Will had called me when I was on my way home from Mandarin Paradise and gave me a brief of what'd happened. I told him to write it up and I'd look at in the morning. The more I read, the angrier I got. This shit wasn't a minor rookie procedural mistake. It spoke to a deeper problem I would not tolerate in my department. I switched screens, and checked the personnel database set up for each department head, and looked up the officer's application. As I'd remembered, Foster had grown up in Willows, a small conservative farming community in Glenn County, about a hundred miles north of Sacramento. The officer had gone to Chico State, but commuted the half hour each way because there wasn't money to pay room and board. While in his last semester at Chico, he'd applied to the Santa Rosa Junior College Public Safety Training Center's police academy, and was hired by the Falls PD a week after he'd graduated the academy.

There was nothing in his record or background to account for his behavior. According to Will's report, Officer Foster was called to the small mosque at the south edge Redwood Falls to break up an altercation. When Foster arrived, he witnessed two young men arguing loudly near a motorcycle parked in front of the mosque. Seeing the level of agitation, Officer Foster called for backup, but he didn't wait – mistake number one – and walked up to the two guys in an attempt to end the fight without force. While trying to deescalate the situation, one of the participants threatened Officer Foster with bodily harm, which caused Foster to grab the guy's arm, twist it behind his back, and face-plant him into the mosque's exterior brick wall. Mistake number two. Of course, that's when all the cell phones came out, if they hadn't been out already, and recorded Officer Foster snarling at the guy, "I know all about you Black Muslims, and I'm not gonna stand for that shit in my town." Mistake number three, which qualified as a huge, hairy fuck-up.

By this time, a more senior officer had arrived, Officer Olmos, and he took the participant who threatened Officer Foster into custody, but he didn't arrest him. Thereafter, Officer Foster got the other participant's statement, and personal details, then told him to get on his way, which he did, on his motorcycle. All of this was recorded by Foster's and Olmos's body cams.

Officer Olmos called his sergeant, who called Will, who then directed dispatch to get Foster back to the station where Will met Olmos and Foster. Will took the threatening guy's statement and personal details, and released him. Then Will spent the next couple of hours talking with Officer Foster in front of his union delegate. Will wrapped up the night by putting Foster on administrative leave with pay pending an investigation.

Eric Foster's behavior was my first critical incident as police chief. Now I had to call the mayor, then I had to call the mosque's imam, and after that I had to call George Darnell, the head of the area NAACP. All that had to be taken care of in the next half hour before they were barraged by the local media.

Forty-five minutes later, after the mayor had blistered my ear, the imam thanked me for the call and said he looked forward to my lunch today with him and George. I'd actually called George first, and he had agreed to the lunch and told me he was anxious to hear what I had to say at our upcoming discussion.

By the time Will, Camille, and our community affairs officer, Miranda Cummins, were sitting at the oval conference table in my office, I was downing my second cup of coffee with a double Tylenol chaser.

"Miranda first," I said as I sat.

"The video is out there, and so far it has about seventy-five thousand hits on each platform. I've had calls from all the San Francisco TV stations, as well as all the newspapers in San

Francisco, Sonoma, and Mendocino counties. I've told them that at the present time this is a personnel matter that we can't discuss, but that you would be making a public statement this afternoon at three-thirty. I've spoken with the mayor's office, and we'll hold the press conference at the north end of the park outside city hall. The mayor will be in attendance as will the city council members who can be there."

The first thought that popped into my head was I wished Max hadn't shut me out last evening, and we'd gone back to her place where I would've spent the night showing her how much I wanted her. Then I would've slept wrapped around her, and I would've woken to her husky voice and incredible body, and I would've made sure our shower was memorable. If all that had happened, I would've been set up for today.

Instead, I was dealing with this clusterfuck on three hours of sleep. The only reason I didn't have blue balls was because I'd taken care of myself last night and again this morning in the shower.

"Not for public consumption," I directed my comment to Miranda, but I knew Camille and Will understood it was meant for them too. "At one, I'm having lunch with George Darnell and Imam Mansour. I'll ask them if they'll attend the press conference. As soon as I know, I'll give you a call."

"Copy that, Chief."

"You have anything else?"

Miranda shook her head. "No, sir."

"Keep me updated." She stood, nodded, and left my office, closing the door softly behind her.

"Talk," I told Camille and Will. "Say whatever you want to say. Don't censure yourselves. No judgments here, only solutions."

Camille began. "Let's start with Foster's nonverbal mistakes. He should have waited for back-up. He had the presence of mind to call for it, but I don't know where the disconnect happened and why he didn't wait. He put himself and the public in danger. For that alone I'd give him a formal written reprimand, take him off rotation for a week, and send him for training."

"Agreed," Will said.

"Then there was that whole strong-arming the idiot who threatened him, which he definitely did, the body cam caught the threat," Camille said. "There was no reason Foster couldn't've continued to try to deescalate. There was no indication the guy had a weapon. Only a big mouth. When Foster slammed the guy face first into a brick wall, procedure was violated, and Foster committed an excessive use of force violation. His lack of understanding that members of the community were watching, and that they'd record what he was doing, is incomprehensible. For that I would've recommended suspension, with a monthlong training follow-up."

"Yeah." Will sighed. "Agreed."

"There's no denying Foster said what he said." Camille shook her head. "Stupid ass. Not a lot of Black folk in Willows, but the town's heavily Hispanic. I wouldn't've expected this kind of thing from someone who grew up with a lot of brown brothers around him." She took a beat, as she often did when gathering her thoughts. "I know his mother raised him and his older sister. The father took off when Eric was about six. His background check came up super clean. Good guy. Responsible. Looked after his mom and sister. The only thing that touched his life that was a bit out of the ordinary was his sister's friend died when they were in high school. I don't know if you heard about this, it was about a dozen years ago. Three Willows high school students died within a couple of years of each other." I shook my head. I hadn't heard about that. "Small town, everyone knows everybody. But Eric was eleven when his sister's friend died, and there was nothing racial or sordid about it. Seemed illness related." She took a breath. "His behavior doesn't make sense. I can't credit what he said to anything in his background."

"How is he with," I motioned between Will and Camille, "both of you?"

Camille tilted her head. "Since we've always been higher ranked and senior to him, he's been deferential and polite. He didn't have a problem looking me in the eye. No tells I picked up on that said he has a problem with the color of my skin or with a woman in a command position."

"Same goes, Chief," Will said. "Always seemed like a nice guy keeping his head down while getting his footing on the job. I haven't heard any different from the sergeants or the senior officers."

This shit didn't come out of the blue. I asked, "Any indication he belongs to any hate groups?"

Will answered. "I looked. He doesn't have any social media accounts under his name or any variation of his name." I lifted my brows. "That's not uncommon for cops. If they're on social media at all, and a lot of them aren't, they go anonymous. That's especially true since those cops got popped for belonging to and chatting in hate groups. It was too easy to find them. Since then, the bad cops go deeper underground or to the dark web."

"Christ." I put my hands on the table palms down. "You on social media?"

"Nah. I let Lola overshare about our lives."

Camille laughed.

"You?" I asked her.

"I belong to a few sorority groups to keep up with my college sisters. Otherwise, I'm an emailer. You?"

I chuckled. "Outside of work, hardly. I'm the strong silent type."

Camille and Will grinned.

"Listen, to make sure the investigation isn't biased, and to ensure there's no appearance of impropriety, it's best not to have our IA look into the matter. Camille, I want you to put together a request for bids from former cops who have their own investigation firms. Tight window for a fast turnaround. I don't want to pay Foster to stay home on vacation. Make it clear the bid cap is twenty-four thousand dollars. This way, we don't have to go through the long internal city bid process. I'll okay your choice, and the outside investigator will report to you."

She nodded.

"Will. What was your impression when you spoke to Foster last night? I read your report, but I want to know your opinion."

"He's scared, Chief. He knows he's in deep trouble. I don't know if what he said is what he thinks and believes, and it slipped out, or if it was a complete brain fart because he was scared in the field. I'm with Camille. If you take the statement out of the equation, he's shown us he's not ready to handle tense situations on his own. He's going to get himself, his colleagues, and/or the public hurt. I don't know that he's cut out for this kind of work."

Fuckin' great. Before my time, but I wished his training officers found that out while Foster was still on probation. After this was done, Camille would be tasked with looking into who handled Foster's training. We needed to find out what went wrong.

"I'm guessing the investigator will come to the same conclusion." I stood. "Okay. Let's get on it."

***

Lunch at The Aegean went well. The imam and George agreed to stand with me at the press conference, for which I was grateful. I'd met the imam a couple of times before today at two Interfaith Council breakfasts. He was a soft-spoken man in his mid-fifties who radiated calm. George and I had lunch together not long after I became police chief, and we'd talked on the phone a few times since. George, an imposing man in his early forties, did not suffer fools gladly, but he was easy to work with.

I made it back to the office by three, and I called Miranda in for an update.

"Officially, the video has gone viral. We expect, and are prepared for, a thousand protesters whom we're keeping behind barricades across the street from city hall. We're blocking off traffic from Redwood north to Cedar and south to Oak. The mayor and two city council members will be attending, and the mayor knows the iman and George Darnell will be there and that they'll be in frame with you." She looked me up and down. "Are you going out there dressed like that?"

I chuckled. She was nervous. Redwood Falls didn't deal with this hoopla often. I was used to it. "You think wearing a dark blue blazer, a light blue Oxford button-down, and jeans is too caszh."

She realized I was yanking her chain, and shook her head. "I'll leave you to get changed."

"Good thinking." She left and I closed the blinds, locked the door, then changed into my uniform. When I walked out ten minutes later, Camille and Will were waiting for me in the hall. "Don't look dour," I told them. "Serious, but concerned."

Will pulled a comical face, and I shook my head. He might be from around here and hadn't had to deal with a media circus before in his career, but the man was cool down to his boots.

"This doesn't faze you at all." Camille didn't ask, she made an observation as she walked alongside me.

"You know I was assistant to the director in LA. I had four bureaus and twenty-one divisions reporting to me. That's a lot of cops in a city where there are a lot of problems, along with an active and unremitting media."

"Are you telling me we're small potatoes?"

I smiled at her. "I'm telling you shit happens, and we deal with it. Savvy?"

"Savvy, Chief."

We walked out the back door of our building and crossed the parking lot to the back entrance of city hall. When we got to the small rotunda up front, we found the mayor, the imam, George, the two city council members, Miranda, and the city's public relations manager, Bradon Fellows, waiting for us.

The mayor, Hiram Weatherstone, was an old-school politico who liked glad-handing, kissing babies, and telling the citizens of Redwood Falls that everything was wonderful. In other words, Hiram was not a fan of conflict, especially when it reflected badly on the city, which he took to mean it reflected badly on him.

"Mayor," I greeted him with my hand out, and he was forced to shake it. He was wary of me and my "big city cop" ways. I turned to the two city council members and shook their hands, then I greeted the imam and George. "Ready?"

The mayor looked like he'd swallowed a mouthful of bees. He nodded and followed me and my team out the double doors.

TV vans with satellite dishes lined Redwood Street, and were strategically placed in front of the protesters, blocking their view of the press conference. When they saw us walk out of City Hall, their chanting amped up, but otherwise they were peacefully assembled, and I hoped they stayed that way.

We rounded the side of city hall to the little park, and I moved to stand behind the podium packed full of mics. George stood behind me to my left, and the imam stood behind me to my right. The mayor, the city council members, and Bradon flanked George, and my staff flanked the imam.

The reporters quieted and I raised my gaze to look directly at them.

Chapter Seven

The Uniform
Max

"Dana. Sit your ass down. No one can see past that big head of yours."

Everyone was crowded around the small flat-screen Bernadette had wheeled out from her office and had set up on the reception counter up front. Clients were piled against each on the couch, and the staff was either leaning against the wall or sitting on the floor in front of the L-shaped sofa. I was standing by the front door watching everyone fidget while waiting for Ryan's press conference to begin.

We'd heard – salon, gossip, small city – something big had happened with one of the police officers last night, and I couldn't help but think that while Ryan and I were eating Auntie Woo's Chinese food, some idiot cop had created a situation big enough to have every area TV station carry the press conference live.

I tried not to think about my dinner with Ryan, but that ship sailed at about two this morning. After I'd left him standing on the sidewalk, I got in my car and didn't obey the speed limit as I made my way home. I changed into my most comfy nightshirt, grabbed my favorite afghan, laid on the sofa in the TV room, and watched *Back to the Future*, which I hadn't seen in years. Then I washed my face, brushed my teeth, gave myself the full moisturizing treatment, and went to bed, where I tossed and turned for way too long.

Frustrated, I got up, went to the living room, and read for a while. When my lids started drooping, I went back my bedroom and tried sleeping again. By two, I gave up trying and propped my pillows against the headboard, sat cross-legged against the pillows, folded my arms over my chest, and allowed myself to obsess about why Ryan Trent affected me.

God, he was gorgeous. Watching him across the table last night and seeing how unguarded he was, his expressions open and easy to read, he drew me in, and for a while, I was having a great time. I didn't think about what we were doing, where "this" was going, and what it might mean. I enjoyed him unreservedly, and it felt freeing. He was smart, funny, easy to talk to, and so fuckin' sexy I could eat him with a spoon. I'd had more fantasies about him in the past few weeks than I'd ever had about anyone, or in general, since I started having those type of fantasies.

Speaking of, a hush fell over Shangri-la and I understood why. Ryan walked up to a podium in uniform, and I swear – I know, I know, this sounds cheesy – he looked like a movie star. His white uniform shirt was crisp and bright and his jacket was so dark blue it was almost black. The gold stars on his collar flashed bright, his gold badge reflected the sun, and the gold braiding on the sleeves of his jacket were rich and thick. His hair with its wavy dip in front always looked like it was going to fall into his eyes, but never did. His stern square jaw was set in determination, and then he lifted his jewel green eyes, which lasered into the camera lens, and he began to speak in his serious tone, his voice deep and rumbling.

I heard what he said, but the meaning didn't penetrate because I was watching his mouth move. Geez, he had incredible lips. The bottom one was a bit thicker than the top and made me want to nip at it. I remembered every single moment when those lips were pressed to mine. He took kissing to an art form, and when I'd let him… No, that wasn't right…when I'd been lost in him, that talented mouth and his wicked tongue had transported me to a place where nothing but pleasure and bliss existed.

His statement finished, he began fielding questions from the media: calm, concise, and unflappable. He was in control of his message. No one pushed him to answer anything he didn't intend to answer, and he never wavered. When he told the press that his office would keep them apprised of developments he could share, he thanked them for coming, stepped away from the podium, and all the people who'd been standing behind him followed him back into City Hall as he walked away, straight and tall, in command of his body and the situation.

Holy shit. Knowing all that could be mine made my knees wobble.

Bernadette turned off the TV when the talking heads started to recap. "Well," she rubbed her palms against each other in a *that's that* move, "it looks like our chief is—"

"To die for."

"So commanding."

"Wears that uniform like a superhero."

"Is sex on a stick."

"Damn. I'd willingly have ten of his kids."

I had to literally bite the inside of my mouth to stop myself from saying, "I don't fuckin' think so, bitch."

In an internal *what the fuck* moment, I acknowledged that as the comments flew from those women's mouths, the more agitated I became. Then Dana, of all people, made the having his kids comment, and that tore it.

Ryan's children were mine to have, and the certainty of that feeling nearly laid me out. Spots floated in front of my eyes and I felt like I was on a tilt-a-whirl ride. I had difficulty getting enough breath into my lungs, and I pressed against the door and pushed my way onto the street hoping the fresh air would clear my head. After a few gulps of mouth breathing, I felt better, but I didn't think I could go back inside and tend to Dana while her flapping jaw continued its out-of-controlness. Instead of telling Bernadette I was taking a minute, I turned on my low-heeled boots and ran.

I took off like I sprinted in my spare time. Stores, people, conversations, cars, houses, and barking dogs were a blur of sight and sound as I sped my way to I had no idea where. My heart was pounding in my ears, but it wasn't from exertion. Fear, raw and real, was pumping through my veins. I couldn't stop running and without any intention or sense of where I'd propelled myself, I had to stop when I hit the dead end of a street.

I turned, half bent, and rested my hands on my thighs as I pulled in air through my nose. Shit. I'd run easily two miles and was at the top of a hill on Cottonwood Street. On this clear, perfect California late afternoon, I saw most of Redwood Falls laid out beneath me.

I backed up and leaned against the retaining wall – mudslides – and dropped my butt to the ground and wrapped my arms around my knees. Time seemed irrelevant as I tried to sort out what I was thinking and feeling.

An hour must've gone by. My ass was cold from sitting on the street, and I noticed I was shivering. I looked up and saw the city's lights twinkling below. Not an hour. Hours.

How had I not known night had fallen?

I had to stop my whirring brain from its incessant hum to take stock.

On the hottest days of the year, nights in the Falls were cool. Between the altitude and the thick forests surrounding the city, there were no steamy summer evenings here. Mid-June in the Falls meant the temperature could, and often did, drop into the low fifties. I had on a long-sleeve t-shirt, my jeans, and my ankle boots. During the day, working in air-conditioning, that was enough clothing. Now, not even close.

My phone was at my work station, my jacket and bag were at the spa, and my keys were in my bag. If the sun was down, the spa was closed. Bernadette didn't stay open late on Thursdays.

No use berating myself. I'd continue my psychotic break when I was toasty warm beneath my favorite afghan on my living room couch. Now I had to rouse myself to walk down the hill to find the first open store I came upon. I thought there might be a liquor store on the edge of the commercial district. They usually stayed open late. When I got to whatever was open, I'd call Lola, who had an extra set of all my keys. Then I'd have to wait for Will to bring them to me since she was pretty much on full bed rest. The pregnancy was kicking her ass.

As I was calibrating the effort it would take to unwrap my arms from my knees and then stand, headlights came up the block but didn't turn into a driveway. They came right at me and the car stopped a couple of yards in front of me. A police officer stepped out of the car – fuck, fuck, fuck – and spoke into the handset on his shoulder.

He gave some number and our location, then said, "Found her."

Squawking came out of the handset. I had no idea how the officer understood a word of it. At best the loud static sounded like computer-generated gibberish.

"Copy that. I'll wait."

He'll wait. Hell no. I knew for whom he was waiting and I had no intention of being here for the ensuing confrontation.

I couldn't seem to unhook my fingers from my arms, and my body started shaking something fierce. Before I could track the officer, he was squatting in front of me, wrapping one of those emergency mylar rescue blankets around my shoulders and inspecting me with his flashlight.

"Sorry," he said as he shined the light in one eye and then the other. "Are you hurt?" he asked gently.

I shook my head.

"Any bruising or head trauma?"

Again, I shook my head.

"Can you talk?"

I nodded. "Yeah," I whispered, and my voice cracked on the one word.

He gave me a small smile. "Can you stand?" he asked, his head tilting to the side. I forced my super-stiff fingers apart and released my arms, then I put my hands on the asphalt and tried to push myself up. When I listed to the left, the officer righted me and said, "Give me your hands. Let me help." I nodded and held my hands in front of me while concentrating on not falling over. "Ready?" He held my gaze. Geesh, he was sweet, and probably no more than twenty-two. I nodded again. "On three." He counted slowly and managed to get me standing at the same time another set of headlights came up the block at a crazy fast speed.

The lights blinded me for a moment and I fell into the officer's arms.

A sharp screech, the car door opened, I heard it thud closed, and like a flash, Ryan was standing next to the officer, looming over the both of us.

"Chief," the officer said with a frog in his throat.

"Rodriguez," Ryan's deep voice rumbled.

Before I was handed off like an unwieldy package, I squeezed Officer Rodriguez's hand. He squeezed back, gave me a chin lift, and went to his car.

"Can you walk?" Ryan asked softly as he wrapped one arm around my shoulders while pulling the mylar fully over me, his other hand securing the blanket, his fist lying against my chest.

I nodded, and slowly – my legs numb from having stayed in one position too long in the cold – I walked as Ryan guided me to the passenger side of his car. He took his arm off my shoulders, opened the door, and gently lowered me into the seat.

He'd left the car running with the heat on full blast. I closed my eyes, grateful for the warmth, and took a few deep breaths. Which made my nose run. I didn't have anything on me to wipe the dribble, and I sure as hell wasn't going into the glove box of the police chief's car, even if it was his personal vehicle. I dabbed my nose with the sleeve of my shirt. Of course, at that moment, Ryan got in the car.

He opened the lid to the console between us and handed me a bunch of napkins with the Beans & Roast logo on them. In my fucked-up emotional state, I took one look at the napkins and started crying. Shit. I wasn't a weepy, needy, clingy girl. I hated the way I felt, and yet I couldn't seem to get a handle on it.

Ryan growled. For real, a low growl sounded from in his chest, then his seatbelt clicked into place. I followed suit, and as soon as I was buckled in, he turned the car around and headed down the hill.

Busy blowing my nose and trying not to sound like a flock of honking geese, I didn't pay attention to where we were going. I figured he was taking me home, but I didn't have my keys and I needed to tell him that. When I looked up, I saw we were moving fast and I tried to orient myself. It took a couple of minutes to figure out where we were. Damn it. He was heading us in the opposite direction of my complex.

"Tell me the truth," he demanded in a stern tone. "Do you need to see a doctor?"

I shook my head and he stared at me for a moment, nodded, then turned onto Sycamore Street. A couple of minutes later, when I saw the new tall building a few blocks away, I knew he was taking me to his place.

A big part of me wanted to tell him to turn the car around, call Will to get my keys, and then take me home. I was in no condition to face whatever shit Ryan was going to dish out, and I sure as hell didn't want to have a scene at his place.

As strong as my resolve felt, in actuality I didn't have the energy to talk, no less fight to convince him of what I wanted.

He turned into a drive that went underground. A few yards in we stopped before a barrier arm and he picked up his keys and fingered a small disk on the ring and touched it to the silver metal column outside his window. The barrier went up and he drove down a level, made a left, and parked in a numbered spot about twenty feet away from two glassed-in elevators. At least this looked familiar. Hard to believe I'd climbed out of the trunk of his car two days ago. It seemed like weeks had passed since then. Even harder to believe...I'd known him for about a month.

Such a short time to have turned my life upside down, especially since half that time I'd been avoiding him.

He shut down the engine, got out, came around the hood, opened my door, and lightly touched my shoulder. "Give me your hand," he instructed softly. I lifted my arm from under the blanket and he placed one hand under my elbow and his other hand took mine. "Swing your legs out." I did as told, and he guided me up then leaned me against the side of the car. He bent in and picked up something from the well of the passenger seat. When I saw it was my bag, I nearly started crying again. He slung it over his shoulder, closed the door, and beeped the locks. Then he took one of my hands at the same time he angled his body alongside mine and circled my shoulders with his other arm. "Nice and slow," he rumbled.

Like an old lady, I shuffled to the elevators and when we got inside one, he used the same fob on a metal plate below the floor number buttons before he pressed "12," the highest floor in the building. The doors closed, and we whooshed up. The swift movement unbalanced me, and the arm around my shoulder pressed me tighter against his long, hard body.

Of all the thoughts to spring into my head, I said to myself, *Huh. He changed out of his uniform.*

***

The hot shower was a lifesaver and felt divine. I was long done with cleaning up – Ryan had fancy products, totally LA – and now I was standing under the rainfall showerhead hiding out. This big-enough-for-four shower had jet heads on the handheld and from two directional showerheads on the side wall. I'd made good use of them. My joints and muscles no longer felt mummified, and my skin was warm and supple again.

My brain and heart, however, were still a fucking mess.

We'd ridden up to his floor in silence, his arm around me keeping me steady. He'd left it across my shoulders as he walked slowly beside me as I did the old lady shuffle. We went down what seemed like a really long hall to the last door on the left. I'd noticed there weren't many units on the floor and expected to walk into something big and spectacular. From the little I saw, I wasn't disappointed. A huge space that looked like the living room, dining room, and kitchen, and huge glass doors lined the far wall, beyond which was a long wide terrace. He turned on a couple of lights and steered me down a hallway to the bathroom I was in. Now that I thought about it, this had to be the guest bathroom, because we hadn't gone into his bedroom to get to the master bathroom. If this was the "other" bathroom, I figured his must be amazing.

Light pale green glass subway tiles covered the bathroom floor including the walls of the Roman shower, which was behind a clear thick glass three-quarter wall. The subway tiles also covered the quarter wall that separated the toilet from the vanity, which was made of dark brown wood that looked like walnut. I was sure it wasn't a piece of furniture that had been an old chest of drawers rehabbed for the bathroom, but it had been designed to look exactly like that. The sink was a pale green glass bowl on top of the vanity, and all the bathroom hardware was brushed nickel. The mirror took up most of the wall above the vanity from ceiling to the white veined green marble countertop. The opposite wall was painted in a glossy sand color. Fluffy towels that hung on side by side on racks were the same color as the wall, and there were three large framed prints of beach scenes above the towel racks.

The lighting was directed spots from inset pots dotting the ceiling. Ryan had adjusted the intensity of the lights from bright to not quite dim. The room glowed, but the light didn't invade.

Even though neither of us had said a word, he'd been solicitous and gentle. He'd guided me to the closed toilet and lowered me onto the seat, then he placed my bag at my feet. He took the mylar blanket off my shoulders, folded it and walked out, but he didn't close the door. A couple of minutes later he came back with a dark blue hoodie and a pair of blue sweatpants. Both said LAPD, and the hoodie had a badge and the word "Officer" beneath it. He laid the clothes on the countertop, walked out again, but this time he shut the door.

The good news, it seemed I wasn't going to be interrogated. The bad news, I had to deal with *me*. I turned off the water, stepped onto the super-fluffy sand-colored bath mat, grabbed a towel that was warm from an apparently heated towel rack, and wrapped it around me with room to spare. I loved bath sheets and was so glad Ryan didn't have stingy towels. I used an oversize – yes, warmed – hand towel to wrap around my head, and I reached down to the floor to grab my bag and plopped it on the countertop. I felt for my phone and sighed with relief when I found it, but I didn't want to deal with what had to be ten million texts and voice mails. Instead, I rooted around until I found my wide-tooth comb, which I washed.

After I'd toweled my hair nearly dry, I ran the comb through it, then mussed it with my fingers. The heat, still swirling in the bathroom, had put color in my cheeks, but my eyes told a different story. I hadn't had a full-blown panic attack in probably eight years. The last time was when I was in therapy and "had a breakthrough," which was code for I lost my shit in the therapist's office. I wasn't a sharer, and I hated that I had to go to therapy, but my cousin Theresa, who had been getting her PhD in Shrinkdom at Stanford, told me I wouldn't get past my trauma unless I worked it out with a professional. I loved Theresa like no one else, and I trusted her with my life. She'd helped me find someone I could work with, and after a couple of years in therapy, I "had the tools" to keep myself from going under.

Until today.

In a classic textbook move, after graduating UC Berkeley with a BS in anthropology, I'd returned to the Falls to stay within the circle of my family. After therapy, I understood myself well enough to know I wasn't ready to go on digs to get field experience before starting a PhD program. Pressure and unmet expectations were not my friends. After graduating magna cum laude from one of the best schools in the world, I went to beauty school and became a hair stylist. Decent money, an honest living, no pressure, and most of the time it was fun. More importantly, I was home, only miles away from my immediate family. Someday, I might go back for my PhD, but clearly, I wasn't ready yet.

Here's the thing: Wanting Ryan was a unique kind of pressure. To the world, I was a happy, somewhat snarky woman who liked uncomplicated relationships with men. Adult playdates were my stock in trade. I kept my playmates far from the Falls, and I made sure they were the type of men who were happy living on the periphery of my life. After what I'd been through, I knew that was all I could handle. About four weeks ago, sitting over coffee at Beans & Roast, my subconscious had decided otherwise. My conscious mind hadn't gotten the memo, and when the two started the war inside my head, my behavior became…shall we say, erratic.

Today, the war had escalated, and now I had to decide which détente I was going to find acceptable.

Chapter Eight

The Heart of the Matter
Ryan

Keeping a lid on my emotions and acting rationally was one of the reasons I'd risen in the ranks in a highly politicized big city police department. I didn't lash out. I didn't blow up. I didn't let a person or situation get the best of me. I didn't yell, and I'd followed protocol even when I was setting out to change it.

Until 5:20 pm today, nothing had happened that had gotten under my skin. True, I wasn't happy one of my officers had fucked up colossally and was filmed doing it. I wasn't thrilled I had to play the political two-step most of the day. And I damn sure wasn't tickled to be fielding questions from ravenous reporters salivating to make the officer's fuck-up their next Pulitzer Prize-winning story. Scrutiny was part of being in a command position. I couldn't say I enjoyed that aspect of my job, but I knew how to tolerate it.

Had I still been working for the LAPD, I wouldn't've known about the call that came into dispatch at 4:05 this afternoon. In a big city police department even with friends in all the right places, routine calls didn't get passed along to command staff unless the calls involved family, and even then, there were delays. Will had shared that Annette, one of the dispatchers in the Falls PD, was a friend of Lola's, which, by extension, meant she was friendly with Max. Moments after Annette put out the call to our officers on patrol, she contacted Will. At 5:20 Will was in my office playing a recording of the call. I had gotten back to my office only minutes before Will came in, having spent well over an hour enduring the mayor's play-by-play debrief of the press conference. I was still in my starchy uniform.

Nine-one-one. What's your emergency?

Okay. All right. I don't know if you're who I should be talking to, but, but, something's happened to Max.

My stomach dropped to my knees.

Please take a breath, ma'am, and tell me who you are, where you are, and what happened.

I'm Bernadette La Pierre and...oh god, oh god...and I own Shangri-la Spa on Piedmont.

Okay, ma'am. Tell me what happened.

We had just finished watching the press conference and everyone was returning to their work stations with their clients. Dana Hernandez told our receptionist Gaia that Max, who's Dana's stylist, wasn't there and no one knew where she was.

Who's Max, Bernadette?

I knew Annette knew who Max was and what she looked like, but Annette played it by the book, which was the right thing to do.

Massisma Calapiano. She's my best stylist. She was with us when we were watching the press conference, and poof... I'm sorry, I'm sorry. (sobbing) She disappeared. A few of us went outside looking for her, but we couldn't find her anywhere. Her car is in the lot behind the spa, her bag is in the back room, and her phone is at her workstation. No one...saw her leave. She's...she's vanished. (more sobbing)

That lid I'd mentioned…fucking gone.

Okay, Bernadette. You have to do one more thing for me. You need to describe Max.

Can I send you a picture? I have a photo.

Yes, ma'am. But I need a physical description to give to the officers right now.

Okay. Okay. She's about five-eight. She has short spikey platinum hair with dark roots. She's really pretty. She's...she's so pretty, and funny. (sob hiccup) Big brown eyes and she's really curvy. Oh, oh...she was wearing jeans and a maroon long-sleeve t-shirt.

That's great, Bernadette, stay on the line, I'll be right back with an email address where you can send the photo.

Will stopped the recording and put his phone back in his pocket. "Every available car has been out looking for her, Chief, and Officer Olmos has been at the spa for about an hour taking everyone's statements. I'd told him to get Max's phone and bag and have another officer bring it back here. Forensics got the phone about a half hour ago and they're looking to see if she received a call or text that took her away from work." I nodded. "I recommend holding off from alerting her family until we're sure what we're dealing with."

"No more than four hours, Will. They'll need to know by then."

"Yes, sir." He opened his mouth then closed it. I waited for him to say what he had to say. "I went to her apartment, Chief. It's undisturbed. Bed's made, clean dishes in the dishwasher, nothing looked out of place."

"You did the right thing. No stone unturned."

"Yeah. My thinking too."

Max and Will had been friends for a long time. Ryan guessed Will was feeling this as much as Ryan was, but for different reasons. "I want updates every fifteen minutes."

Will closed his eyes for a moment, pain written all over his face. "Will do, Chief."

After he left, I closed the blinds and locked the door. I nearly tripped returning to my desk. I felt nauseous, my hands were shaking, and my heart was racing so fast I thought I was having a heart attack. I yanked off my jacket, tie, and shirt, and nearly fell to the floor. A few years ago, Oscar had taught me yoga breathing. Now, I sat with my legs crossed and forced myself to control my breath. I must've been sitting in that position working on the in and out air exchange for a good ten minutes before I felt some semblance of control return to my body. I stood and shucked off the rest of my uniform and put on my street clothes, then I opened the blinds and unlocked my door.

When Will came in a few minutes later, any calm I had achieved flew out the window, and all my years of containing my shit was history.

"Officer Rodriguez has been canvassing the businesses around Shangri-la. Two people told him they saw a woman fitting Max's description running through town. They didn't see anyone chasing her, but they said she was moving fast." He grimaced. "That's all I got so far."

My fists were balled on my thighs as I nodded. After he left, I closed my eyes and saw red.

If Max was hurt in any way, I was going to kill someone tonight, and I didn't give a shit what that meant for my tomorrow.

***

Five updates later, and Will still didn't have any news. "Here's her bag, Chief." He laid it on the corner of my desk. "The phone's inside. Forensics went back three weeks. All the calls were to and from friends and family in her contacts list. She deleted a few robo calls, and blocked those numbers, but nothing else. Same for the texts. All people she knows. Innocuous chatter. Jokes. A couple of silly vids. More than a few to Lola." Will shook his head slowly. "Max is good at cheering her up."

I'd bet my car Will hadn't told Lola yet. "Did Forensics search the bag?"

"They did, and everything in there is what you'd expect, which suggests no one's touched it since she went to work this morning. Her wallet seems to have all her credit cards, but there's no way of knowing unless you want us to search her apartment for her bank records."

I had to grit my teeth to keep my voice calm and level. "Not yet." Foolish perhaps, but I was holding out hope this wasn't a horror story, but a misunderstanding. If we didn't find her by nine, I'd order the search. "I'm guessing there were tons of unidentified prints on the bag."

"Fifteen sets outside Max's. Hers are on file from when she got arrested during a protest when she was at Cal."

I wanted to chuckle. So like her. I knew she had fire, and she cared deeply about many things. "Occupy Wall Street?"

Will nodded. "Yeah. She was all worked up about that."

I bet.

***

Dispatch notified me a moment after the call came in. Officer Rodriguez had found Max. I got the address and jogged down the stairs next to my office. I put the portable bar lights on the roof of my car and did eighty on residential streets. When I turned up

Cottonwood, I killed the bar lights and put the heat up to maximum. If she was outside all this time, she had to be freezing.

As I crested the top of the hill, I saw Rodriguez with *my* woman in his arms. Yeah, I wasn't rational and didn't even try to rein it in. I jumped out of the car and had to restrain myself from ripping her out of Rodriguez's hold. When I was close enough to see her face, my heart skittered. She looked whole, but like someone had put her through the wringer. Her makeup – she never wore much – looked cracked. Black dots and smudges trailed beneath her eyes, and her lips, a faded red, were puckered.

"Chief." My officer gulped.

"Rodriguez." I reached out for Max and saw her squeeze Officer Rodriguez's hand. He squeezed back, gave her a chin lift, and went to stand by his car while I tended to her.

"Can you walk?" I asked as I placed an arm around her shoulders and felt her body shaking.

Max wasn't a small woman. She was taller than average, and, thank god, had meat on her body in all the best places. But right now, she seemed like a waif in the wind shuffling beside me, her body clearly struggling to stay up. I wanted to scoop her into my arms and hold her against my chest, but didn't because when she remembered this moment, she'd be pissed off that I had. While fighting with Max was entertaining most of the time, whatever it was that caused this *thing* to happen had shaken her deeply, and from this moment on I wanted her to remember I'd treated her with care.

Slippery mylar fucker was sliding off her shoulder and I had to use my other hand to keep it from dropping. When we got to my car, I lowered her into the passenger seat, closed the door, and went over to Rodriguez.

Turning so I could watch her through the window, I waited for Rodriguez to report. He tilted his head to the side to indicate the top of the street and said, "She was sitting in front of the retaining wall with her arms wrapped around her knees. I did a scan and saw no bruising or blood on her body or in the surrounding area. There's no evidence anyone else has been here. Her eyes were clear and her pupils reactive. She was able to answer all my questions and talk. Given how slowly she moved, I'm guessing she was sitting there for a while. She's cold and a little shocky, but I didn't think a bus was warranted."

I nodded for him to go on.

“We didn’t have time for more than a medical Q and A. You arrived a few moments after I helped get her upright.” Damn straight I did.

A few lookie-loos were on their front porches or peering out their windows. “Canvas the residents.”

“Will do, Chief.”

As I walked to my car, I saw Max wiping her nose on her sleeve. After I got in, I handed her a wad of napkins from the coffee shop. She looked down at them and burst into tears. I wanted to beat the shit out of someone, but, as I’d suspected since we began this touch-and-let-go dance, the dragon that needed slaying lived inside of Max.

***

Finally, the shower stopped. She’d been in there for over twenty minutes, and fifteen minutes ago I started telling myself my ass had to stay attached to the couch even though I wanted to go into the bathroom to make sure she was all right. After she’d stopped crying, the ride home had been heavy with silence. It killed me to stay quiet and keep my hands to myself, but I knew she needed space to settle. She’d allowed me to help her upstairs, and I’d put her in the hall bathroom with my sweats, which I knew were too big, but it was the best I could do, for now. Tomorrow, I’d see where she was at. My guess, she’d want to go home, and I was fine with that since I’d be going with her.

The bathroom door latch snicked open and a shaft of light hit the hallway. A little steam floated in the air. Max stepped out, dwarfed by my sweats, and turned her head toward the living room. I stood but didn’t make my way over to her, even though I was dying to wrap her in my arms and hold her close. She’d been skittish and seemed overwhelmed by everything. I wasn’t going to crowd her. Tonight went at her pace.

“You want something to drink?” Unless she slurped water while she showered, she had to be a little dehydrated. She nodded and headed over to me, walking a little better. Her muscles were looser after the hot shower and her limbs behaved as they should. “Coffee? Or I have tea.”

"Cham…" she cleared her throat, "chamomile?" Damn she sounded rough. Like she hadn't talked in weeks.

"I might." Moving my hand back and forth, I indicated the sofa, the dining room, or the stools at the kitchen counter. "Sit while I check."

She eased onto the sofa, which made sense. If she'd been hunched over on asphalt for hours, she'd want soft under her sweet ass. Wow. She was fresh faced. No makeup. This was the first time I'd seen her this way, and the effect was remarkable. She had a few tiny freckles over the bridge of her nose, her dark chocolate eyes looked brighter without the black she used around them, and her lips were light pink. A far cry from the blood-red lipstick she wore.

My Max was a natural beauty.

After I was sure she was comfortable, I went into the kitchen, flipped on the lights, and opened one of the wide drawers. Everything in here slid on silent casters or opened on silent hidden hinges, and then they closed on their own, requiring a slight touch to get them going. I gotta say, I wasn't the kind of guy who looked for luxury, but it was damn easy to get used to.

My mom was an earth mother, flower child, hippie-dippie kind of person, and for a housewarming gift she'd sent a fancy carved wooden box with about thirty different kinds of organic tea. She knew I mainlined coffee, but she was big on providing options and alternatives, if not for me, for potential guests. Right now, I was glad for her never-ending attempts to broaden my horizons.

Were I making the tea for me, I would've taken down a big Dodgers mug, filled it with water, and put it in the microwave. For Max, I put on the kettle. When I'd moved in, I had a filter installed under the sink – another of Mom's suggestions, this one to help reduce my plastic usage – so the kettle was filled with filtered water.

"You hungry?" I called as I took down a cup and saucer from a cabinet above the coffeemaker. When I didn't get an answer, I leaned on the counter and saw Max watching me like I was performing a magic trick. Her expression held a little awe, and her mouth was slightly open. Apparently, she thought my caveman tendencies extended to being useless in the kitchen.

"Um…ah…yeah. I could eat…some." Her voice was huskier than usual, but it didn't sound like she was talking through gravel this time.

"Fruit and yogurt some, or grilled cheese some?"

She tilted her head and one side of her mouth went up as if it wanted to smile but couldn't quite get there. "You have fruit and yogurt?"

I pointed to the bowl on the counter filled with apples, bananas, and oranges, and grinned. "I have blueberries and strawberries in the fridge."

"Huh," she sort of grunted, "I'm impressed."

I wanted to tell her had I known my food choices would've done it, I'd've taken her grocery shopping on our first date. Instead, I said, "My mom's a vegetarian. We grew up eating healthy."

That got me a genuine smile. I'd pay good money every day for the rest of my life if she smiled at me that way. "Tea and grilled cheese with a side of strawberries." Her gaze held mine, then she added, "Please."

"You got it." She could have anything she wanted. I was hers. I wished she knew that. There was nothing I wouldn't do to make her mine and keep her happy and safe until we were older than dirt.

While I worked in the kitchen, she leaned back on the sofa and watched me as if I were a subject she was observing. I didn't mind. I liked her eyes on me, especially when I was doing something to take care of her. The kettle started to sing and I poured the hot water into her cup and wedged the tea packet on the side of the saucer. I put the honey, the sugar bowl, nonfat milk, a teaspoon, a linen napkin, and the cup and saucer on a tray and brought it into the living room, placing it on the coffee table in front of her.

She watched me with an intensity I'd never seen, her expression fierce at the same time it was cautious, like she didn't know why I was doing this. If she'd given me a chance weeks ago, she would've understood: for her, I'd do anything in my power to make her happy.

I never questioned why I fell hard and fast. I'd accepted she was my "one" the moment my heart started tripping in my chest at Beans & Roast. I hadn't been looking for my forever, but when I found her, I knew Max was it down to my marrow.

"Thank you," she whispered.

"Let me know if you need anything else," I whispered back.

She nodded, and I took that as my cue to return to the kitchen. While I was cooking, I glanced over to make sure she was doing all right. She didn't add anything to her tea, which I'd noticed at the

Chinese restaurant, but better to give her options than make a supposition. I'd been treated to her opinion of my suppositions and didn't want to give her any reason to backslide. Every time I checked on her, she was leaning back against the arm of the sofa, sipping and staring at me.

I made three sandwiches—I was famished—washed strawberries, cut off the leafy bits, and put them in a bowl. I brought over everything on another tray. After I laid it on the coffee table, I sat on the sofa in the middle. Close enough, but I wasn't crowding her. I grabbed up her plate and handed it to her, then I got my napkin and plate, and sat back.

"Mmmm," she half moaned as she bit into the grilled cheese. "God, this is fantastic. It tastes like you made it on a real grill."

Even now, after whatever had happened that made her flee Shangri-la, she was open, expressive, and sweet. "I did. There's a small grill on the stovetop."

She picked up the sandwich and examined the bread. "Geez Pete. There are grill marks and everything."

I couldn't help it, I chuckled.

She gave her head a small shake. "A leftover from childhood. My father curses like he gets paid for it by the word. My mother was none too pleased his children followed his example. Instead of punishing us for swearing, she rewarded us with quarters for every substitute word or phrase we used instead of cursing."

I knew she had a younger sister and a brother. She'd shared that over dinner at Bella Luna. "Lemme guess. You earned the most money."

She grinned. "Yeah, but it was really a contest between me and Luca. Donna's always been the good girl. Whatever substitute word I used, she copied. Luca had a hard time complying. Though, to be fair, he didn't really try. Dad laughed every time Luca said fuck. Not exactly supportive parenting."

"I imagine your mother had plenty to say to your father after you guys went to bed."

She was chewing and slapped her hand over her mouth as she leaned over her plate and laughed. I waited as she swallowed, coughed, gulped down the rest of her tea, and swiped her fingers over her eyes. "We're Italian. My mother had plenty to say to my father right in front of us. They had no trouble going at it: arguing, kissing, yelling, whispering while in each other's arms, whatever they felt the minute they felt it, all while us kids were a rapt audience. They still do."

Given Max's mercurial temperament, and her ability to let whatever she had to say fly, I didn't doubt what she told me was true. Considering she'd grown up with all that openness, the mystery that was buried deep inside her must be a horror show for her to keep it hidden and let it impair her ability to express what I knew she felt. Every time she kissed me, she was all in, and it wasn't only sex. She pushed powerful emotions into me with every swipe of her tongue, tug on my hair, press of her body against mine…every moan, whimper, and groan. We ignited like we'd been doused with lighter fluid, and I wanted to burn with her until we were ashes.

"I'm guessing by that amused look on your face," she waved her half sandwich at me, "your parents waited until you and your brother went to bed."

"Hmm…sometimes. They're the poster couple for opposites attract. My dad's a rocket scientist type who works in the aviation industry, and my mom's an artist who does huge pieces in paper. Think massive decoupage." Max's eyebrows rose. "She's a let-it-all-hang-out type, and he's reserved and circumspect."

"Well, that explains a lot," she said, finishing the last of her sandwich. I was thrilled she'd eaten. Color had come back to her face and she seemed more herself.

"Please, elucidate." I passed the bowl of strawberries to her and watched as she bit into one and a line of red juice ran down her chin, which she caught with the back of her hand before it dripped onto her lap. My dick was so hard it hurt to move.

She dabbed her chin with the napkin and then cleaned her hand. "Great strawberries. You get them at Adam's Market?" I nodded. "Figures. They have the best produce anywhere. It's worth it to pay a little more. Plus, I like supporting Adam. He's the mellowest dude I've ever met. You know, he opened that market when I was a kid, and now he supplies fruits and cheeses to the winery when they have their pairing evenings."

"Fascinating. You were going to explain…"

"No. You want me to explain. Elucidate to be exact. Are you an Ivy Leaguer?" I shook my head. "Stanford?"

"UCLA."

"Wow. A real homey. I'm surprised you came way up here."

"You're stalling."

"I'm evading."

"You're Italian." I threw my hand out. "Let it rip." Her expression froze, and in that moment I realized whatever happened today at Shangri-la had something to do with me. Bernadette said they'd been watching the press conference and then Max disappeared. What did I say or do that upset her so much that she ran? She had to tell me so I could fix it. I wasn't going to let her retreat behind her internal fifty-foot wall again. She needed to start trusting me. I leaned forward. "Hey, hey. Come back, Max. I'm right here. Talk to me. No judgment. Promise."

She shook her head over and over. I reached out and rested my hand on her knee. The touch startled her and brought her back into the room. She tucked her lips into her mouth then pursed those fuckin' luscious lips, and I could see the wheels turning in her brain as her eyes sparked.

I squeezed her knee. "Tell me. I'd never hurt you. You can tell me anything." I didn't care I was begging. I needed her to believe her heart was safe with me. I moved closer and moved my hand to her thigh. She looked down at it but didn't ask me to remove it or brush it away. "You're safe. With me, you'll always be safe."

She huffed a small laugh filled with incredulity. "You're the most dangerous person in my life," she rasped.

I gave her a small smile. "Elucidate."

That got me a smile back. "You must be hell on wheels in interrogations."

"I've had my moments." I leaned in closer. Our faces were inches apart. "I'm not interrogating you, Max," I whispered. "I'm trying to give you somewhere safe to land. Talk to me."

She took a deep breath, looked at her lap, and let the air out of her lungs. "I like you." She said it with death sentence implications. I turned it around.

"Great news. I like you too."

"Yeah. I got that." That came out like an accusation.

"I didn't think I was hiding it."

"You don't do subtle." Definitely an accusation.

"I can do subtle, but I didn't see the point since I wanted you to know I like you." We were talking in code. She was mine and I was hers. She seemed to know it, but if she needed to dance around the truth 'til we got there, I had all the time in the world as long as she stayed no farther than she was from me right now.

"See…well…see, that kinda overwhelms me." I knew that, but I didn't know why. When she let her body do the talking, she was broadcasting on all channels she was into me in a big way. I didn't think there was a disconnect between her mind and her heart, but there was a roadblock she'd put there. The damn thing was so solid the Army Corps of Engineers couldn't've done a better job.

"Massima, look at me." Her head snapped up at the use of her proper name. "I swear, I promise, I vow, I won't hurt you. I'd eat a bullet before I hurt you. You. Are. Safe. With me."

"God," her shoulders sagged and her body seemed to fold in on itself, "I wish I could believe you."

As much as I wanted to knock down at least that first line of fortification, she'd had a shit day and was exhausted. This conversation wasn't helping. "C'mon. Let's get you to bed." I stood and held out my hand. "The guest bedroom is down the hall right next to the bathroom."

"What about all this?" she asked as she looked at the trays with our empty plates, and the bowl half filled with strawberries.

"It's not going anywhere. I'll get to it in the morning."

"Such a guy," she muttered. She took my hand and let me help her up.

I put my arm around her waist, and even under the bulky oversize sweats, she felt terrific. She leaned her head on my shoulder as we made our way to the hallway. When we approached the door to the guest room, she looked up and murmured, "Your room. I don't want to sleep alone."

Torture and elation. Max, finally in my bed, where she belonged. Yet I knew I wouldn't sleep a lick. Not when I could smell her, feel the warmth of her delicious body only inches away, and the most I'd be able to do was kiss her forehead and say good night.

Chapter Nine

Come Clean
Max

No, I wasn't stupid. Well, not intellectually, and usually not emotionally. At best I was confused. At worst, I was about to jump off a cliff and become splatter. I didn't want to be alone. I knew I wouldn't sleep a wink in a strange bed. It always took me a couple of days to acclimate when I travelled. With Ryan down the hall, not only wouldn't I sleep, I'd spend the entire night wishing I was by his side. So why bother with the charade? I knew he knew how I felt about him. It terrified me that he knew, and in equal measure it paralyzed and thrilled me that he felt the same way.

Someone who wasn't carrying around steamer trunks filled with remorse and regret would be jumping for joy that a man like Ryan wanted her. Me? I wanted to hide in the battlements and hoped he went away at the same time I wanted to cleave to him and never let him go.

Tonight, I'd try going with the latter.

We stopped at the end of the hall and he reached into the room and turned on the lights. Both lamps on the beside nightstands glowed warmly in a big room painted a light smoky gray. The ceiling was trimmed in wide white crown molding with detailed corner blocks. A beautiful walnut sleigh bed – California king, of course – had a white and gray patterned comforter and two plain dark gray shams leaning against the headboard. Above the bed was a large abstract work of art made of torn thick paper in white, gray, and hot pink. The piece was floating in a huge plexiglass box.

All of a sudden, I wasn't tired anymore.

"Wow." That came out in a rush of reverence. "That's some piece. Your mother is wicked talented." I moved out of his grasp and climbed up on the bed – the mattress was at least four feet from the floor. I shoved aside the shams, and the pillows beneath them, and stood as close to the work as I could, taking in the detail and intention of every overlapping piece of paper. On the bottom left corner of the piece written in calligraphy in oxblood ink was "Shaula Trent."

I turned and told him what he already knew. "She's a Scorpio." Shaula was the second brightest star in the constellation.

He was smiling. "Indeed. November second."

"Who's the astronomer?"

"My grandfather. When my mother was born, he told my grandmother that his little girl was his second brightest star, my grandmother being his first."

"You inherited that."

"What?"

"Gooeyness."

He laughed and came to the bed. He toed off his boots and, still laughing, he grabbed a sham, got on the bed – he didn't have to climb up – put the pillow against the footboard, laid down, and looked up at me. "I'm hard-pressed to think of anyone in my life who thinks I'm gooey. The opposite, in fact." He patted the bed. "Grab a pillow. The view from here is great."

I took the other sham and laid beside him, staring up at the amazing work of art. "Does it have a title?"

"*Daybreak*."

"Ahh. I see that. So cool."

"I'll tell her you said so."

I flipped to my side and smushed the sham to prop up my head. "She knows who I am?"

He turned on his side and put his elbow on the bed and held his head in his hand. "She does."

"That freaks me out."

"Why?"

"It's intimate when you talk to your parents about someone new in your life. The implications are weighty. Unless you tell your mother about every woman you date."

Those brilliant jewel eyes were dancing. "I've never mentioned anyone to my mother before you."

"Gooey and freaking me out even more."

"Apparently, I can't help being *gooey* around you." He grinned when I narrowed my eyes. "Anything I can do to help with the freak-out?"

You know, I didn't want to do this. I knew what the pain of losing him would feel like. All that bullshit about forgetting pain so you could recover, move on with your life, love and be loved, was just that, bullshit. I remembered in white-hot detail how it felt when my heart squeezed so hard inside my chest I couldn't breathe, eat, sleep, think. I remembered how long it took to get myself back to where I needed to be to move forward. How I had to lay my guts out on the floor of a shrink's office every week for two years before level became a way of life. I didn't want to do that ever again. Especially not because of him. Letting myself have him and losing him would break me.

I shook my head. Then I lied. "I'm really wiped."

He closed his eyes and I could feel his frustration coming off him in waves. He wouldn't push. He'd been so incredibly patient and caring all night. But he wanted to move me past this. He wanted an us. Hell, as far as he was concerned we were already an us. He'd told his mother about me for crissakes.

I couldn't do this.

Call me a coward, I didn't care. I had to protect myself or I'd implode.

I sat up and asked, "Do you have an extra toothbrush?"

He opened his eyes and the blank expression he wore hurt to see. "Yeah. You need a t-shirt to sleep in?"

"That would be great," I said as I slid off the bed, waiting until my toes touched the floor.

Now that I turned around to take in the rest of the room, I saw a long walnut dresser opposite the bed with a large rectangular mirror above it. There were a few framed photos on the right side of the dresser and a long narrow ceramic dish in the center that held change and a couple pairs of cufflinks. On the far side of the room was an alcove with a plush gray easy chair and ottoman, and a matching loveseat. The furniture faced the wall that held a large flat-screen TV. There was a small round wood and glass coffee table in front of the grouping that sat on a white and gray area rug, which looked great against the dark wood floors.

Ryan opened a dresser drawer and pulled out a Red Hot Chili Peppers 2002 tour t-shirt. Damn, even his vintage tees were cool. He handed me the shirt and then walked down a little hallway to his bathroom. He came back with a toothbrush and toothpaste.

"Thanks."

He smiled and nodded.

I went to the other bathroom to do my business and get ready for bed. The tee hit my legs not quite mid-thigh. A little shorter than I'd hoped, but he'd seen me in my LBD so it wasn't like my legs were a mystery.

When I came back into his bedroom, only the light on left side of the bed was glowing and he was in bed on the right side with the sheet and comforter bunched down around his waist. Ho-lee shit. I tried not to react, but his wide fantastic chest was on full display. I swear, my mouth went so dry I couldn't swallow. Yeah, Aquaman had nothing on Ryan. Even the light smattering of chest hair was perfect. Enough to run my fingers through, and rasp over my breasts when… I had to knock this off. My gaze went up and hit his and I saw the smug all over his face. Damn. I had to work on being not so obvious.

I went around to my side of the bed, which was really my side of the bed when I was home. Let's try not to read too much into that. I climbed in and scooched under the covers.

"To turn out the light, hit the switch next to the headboard."

I raised up on my elbow and reached around and found the switch. I flicked it down and the room fell into darkness. He had light gray Roman shades on the room's three windows, and all of them were down.

Talk about intimate. I could hear him breathing and his scent surrounded me. No way was I going to fall asleep.

"Good night," I whispered. *Thank you for taking such good care of me,* I thought. *Thank you for not making me feel like a basket case. Thank you for being such a good guy.*

"'Night, Max. Sleep well."

Yeah, like that was going to happen.

I heard the sheets rustle, and even from way over here, I felt the mattress depress when he lay down. He was a big dude. I turned on my side, my back to him, and put my hand under my cheek. I tried to regulate my breathing and I did that mental exercise of putting each part of my body asleep, starting with my toes.

I didn't get past my knees and I was out.

***

Someone was yelling. Totally in distress screaming. Me. I was shouting, "Don't, please don't," and then I felt strong arms around my waist yanking me toward the middle of the bed.

Ryan's big, long body surrounded me, his legs tangled with mine, his mouth was at my ear, and he was saying softly, "Shhh. You're safe. It's all right. I've got you," over and over.

How mortifying. It wasn't bad enough I'd lost my shit yesterday and the whole damn police department had been out looking for me, now I was that idiot who had nightmares while sleeping in the same bed as the man who'd made sure I'd been found.

Fuck it. I was too exhausted and past humiliated to care.

I untangled my legs from between his and turned in his arms, burying my face in his magnificent chest. "Sorry I woke you," I mumbled.

"Shhh," he hushed me again and began making soothing circles on my back with one hand while the other stroked my head. Geez, that felt nice. With steady, calming motions he made me feel safe and protected – talk about gooey – and in his hold the world seemed to melt away.

Like this, he didn't seem dangerous at all. He was someone I could turn to and he wouldn't judge. Ach. Everything about him was sucking me in deeper. I shifted slightly in his hold and realized I'd been lying against his serious erection. I'd felt him before when we'd kissed and groped in Bella Luna's parking lot. I guessed the same was true when I climbed him at Henry's, but only Ryan remembered me in his arms. A shame, really. He was larger than life in so many ways, and I'd known from the get-go he would be untamable in bed. But in this moment, he was as docile as a lamb. Well, a worked-up lamb, but he didn't communicate that with more than his body's biological response to having a woman in his bed.

No, I wasn't going to sell myself short. I knew all his responses were about me. Anyone else would be doing handstands while squeeing at the top of her lungs. Part of me was that silly person who derived unbridled glee at being the woman who caught this imposing man's attention. The other part was a fucked-up mole who freaked out at the sight of light.

But yum. It seemed he was wearing nothing but boxer briefs, and I was wearing a thong that was little more than dental floss. Actually, I didn't like thongs, they hurt, but I hated panty lines more, and the jeans I wore yesterday hugged my ass. I was vain enough to not want to ruin a good ass lift, and usually I went commando under jeans, but for some reason yesterday morning I put on a thong. I knew why I was dwelling on this. With every sweep of his hand, Ryan came closer and closer to the lowest part of my lower back. Two more passes and he'd be in tush territory. I didn't think he was making a play, but I wouldn't mind if he did.

Right. Not a sane thought. It would take less than a minute of kissing him before I lost all rational cognition and things went from *this is nice* to *countdown to detonation.* We didn't seem to have a middle ground. You know, that place when things started heating up and you thought, *yeah, this is going somewhere I like, let's keep at it.* It seemed we began at *I need to fuck you now*, and went straight to the hood of his car from there.

A random inexplicable thought: What if we fucked right now? We'd get that supersonic lust out of our system and then we could examine the reality of what was really between us. Yeah, bad idea. There was no way one schtup would be enough. Fifty maybe. Probably a hundred and fifty to be sure.

I liked sex. For the most part, my bedmates had been adequate to good lovers. Some were more playful than others, some more enlightened, but over the years – and really, there hadn't been *that* many – I found myself making the effort more because I needed some sort of male contact since I didn't do relationships. A couple of guys would've been happy for more regular liaisons, but I didn't let those wishes gain traction. In fact, it'd been over seven months since I'd been with anyone, and didn't that say it all about me that I hadn't noticed until now.

Sex with Ryan wasn't something I liked, it was a craving, and I knew if we got started, I'd be insatiable.

Sighing, I found I'd melted into his body. Somewhere in my mental musings he'd stopped shushing, and I'd become boneless and completely enveloped in his scent, his body, his protection, and his care. God, I loved the musky man-ness of him. Sort of outdoorsy mixed with a cocktail of pheromones that I found irresistible. I bet his skin tasted great. His lips, tongue, and mouth were a gourmet meal. I had no reason to believe his body would be any less scrumptious.

I snuggled even closer, if that was possible, and without thinking about what I was doing, my tongue poked out of my mouth and the tip touched the dip between his pecs. Dayumm. A smorgasbord of man, and I was ravenous. I flattened my tongue and slid it across his defined pec to his hardened nipple. Before I could really get into it, he pulled me up and pressed his lips against mine. Okay, we could do that for a while before I got back to that delectable body.

He pulled back a fraction of an inch and whispered against my lips, "*Glikia mou*, not now."

I spoke English, Italian, and passable Spanish. I had no idea what he said, but it sounded heartfelt. "Huh?"

"*Glikia mou*," he whispered again, then pressed his lips to mine again briefly. "Greek for sweet one or sweetheart."

Whoa. Gooey, but in a good way. I didn't mean to sound breathy, but I did when I asked, "You speak Greek?"

I felt his smile against my lips as I gazed into his amazing eyes. "A few words. Mostly endearments. My mother's Greek. Well, her parents are. She was born in Long Beach."

"Wow." More breathy. I was turning into a Valley Girl. "I'm guessing Trent isn't Greek."

He chuckled, his warm breath tickled my lips and chin. "English. Very. Way back before the Romans English."

Well, that explained the reserved father and fiery mother. Her people had a lot in common with my people. With that thought bouncing around my head, I muttered, "It's all that Mediterranean."

Geez. His eyes actually sparkled. "What's all that Mediterranean?"

Stupid mouth spoke without my permission. "The way we go from zero to fuck me."

He bust out laughing, and I wanted to crawl under the bed and stay there for a week. Through his waning laughter he said, "Certainly a contributing factor."

“Then why not now?” Yeah, my mouth was running away from my brain at maximum velocity.

His hand came up from where it was resting on my waist and cupped my cheek. “Because I want you when you’re with me one hundred percent.”

Damn. He was being considerate again. “It’s annoying you’re such an adult.”

“Right about now, *glikia mou*,” he kissed the tip of my nose, “I’m annoyed at myself too.”

The bulge between us lay testament to his statement. “What now then?”

He smiled and I saw it in the crinkles around his eyes, and I felt it against my lips. Then he untangled us, rolled off the bed, leaned across the mattress and held out his hand. Without overthinking what we were doing and why, I allowed his fingers to twine with mine and crawled across the mattress toward him.

Chapter Ten

Moonlight
Ryan

From before we were sitting on the couch eating – if I had to time it, I'd say it was when Max had leaned back and starting watching my every move – I'd been nearly coming in my briefs. When she walked into the bedroom in my t-shirt, I almost lost it, and when she climbed into bed, I wanted to curl myself around her and never let her go. As expected, I didn't sleep, but I was damn glad she was next to me for a lot of reasons, not the least of which was, she was safe. I still got heart palpitations thinking about how crazy I felt when I didn't know where she was and what had happened to her for *over three fuckin' hours*. Knowing I was the reason she was safe, warm, fed, and now sleeping appealed to my chest thumper. I was man enough to admit I regressed to Cro-Magnon from time to time.

She'd fallen asleep quickly, which was a bit of a surprise, but not. She *was* wiped, even though she'd used that as an excuse to avoid the heavy she didn't want to discuss. I wanted the shit bogging her down out on the table so we could deal with it and move on, but I understood she wasn't up to it. Not after panicking the way she had after my press conference. I lay as still as I could, listening to her breathe as I tried to figure out what had set her off. I had a feeling it had something to do with what was going on at the spa during or after the press conference and less or nothing to do with the event itself. I'd had a taste of the viperous nature of some of those women. I could only guess what they were saying when they saw me on TV.

Just as I was about to drift off, Max started travelling in her sleep. Agitated, jerky movements at first, and then she was nearly thrashing when she started screaming. I was on her before she barely got out the words, “Don’t, please don’t,” which made my skin crawl imagining what plagued her. It took a while to get her to settle down, and then we were cuddling. Wrapped around each other in a way I’d been fantasizing about since the moment I saw her at Beans & Roast.

There was no controlling my dick. She was right up against me from her soft hair to her painted toes, and she felt and smelled divine. A Rubens painting come to life in my arms was too much for me to forbear. I hadn’t been so out of control of my cock since I was fourteen years old.

Fucking hell, when she ran her tongue over my chest, I couldn’t control the short but powerful ejaculation that shot up from my balls. I wanted her like I had never wanted another woman. The urge to spread her across my bed and pound my body into hers was so overwhelming I nearly cracked a molar.

The self-control came from a place of love I didn’t know I had in me. The nature of my job had me being selfless for a living, but this was different. Nothing I wanted, desired, or yearned for mattered as much as what she needed.

In the middle of this tumultuous night what she needed was gentle, tender care.

Gooey.

Only Max could turn romance into an indictment.

But, for all the backpedaling, I saw what she hadn’t admitted yet to herself. She was beginning to trust me. I wanted to break out the Lagavulin and throw back three fingers – a few times. Instead, I led her into the living room, opened the glass doors to the terrace, placed my phone into the dock, and put on Luther Vandross.

Then I took her into my arms, and with the cool mountain air curling into the living room, we danced to the gooiest music on earth.

***

The moon had dropped beneath the treetops. We were heading into early morning. “Don’t you have to go to work in a few hours?” Max muttered into my chest, the words muffled but understandable.

“Am I stepping on your toes?”

She looked up, her dark brown eyes fathomless. “You’re trolling for compliments.”

No lie, this woman made me laugh more than anyone I knew. Sharp tongued, but sweet as sugar. “Am I?”

She narrowed her eyes. “Puh-leaze. You know you’re a good dancer.”

I enjoyed slow dancing. Any guy who didn’t was a moron. I got to hold a woman against my body and move with her to music. There was not one thing wrong with that. In my pre-Max days, slow dancing was a way to gauge whether the woman had rhythm and if we’d be good in bed. It wasn’t foolproof, but aside from being with an all-out klutz, and that’d never happened to me, any woman in my arms was a win.

Max in my arms was transcendent. We weren’t dancing as much as gliding, our bodies in sync in a way that said we were made for each other. “I have a good partner.”

“Now you’re buttering me up, which is pointless. I’m here, aren’t I?”

“I noticed, *glikia mou.*” She smiled at that. She liked me saying endearments to her in Greek. I was grateful I’d paid attention to my grandparents when they spoke in Greek so Randall and I wouldn’t understand what they were saying. From them, I’d learned enough of the language to get by. “To answer your question, I texted Camille when you were in the bathroom. I told her I’m taking tomorrow off.”

“It’s good to be king, huh?”

I chuckled. Would that were true. “I answer to too many people to be king. But I enjoy a certain amount of autonomy.”

“Ha.” She laughed against my chest. “You should watch your own press conference.”

See, I knew it wasn’t the press conference that set her off. It had to be those petty, nasty spa clients. Max came off hard and tough, but under that veneer was a soft, caring woman with a good heart and a lot of sweet. She’d be susceptible to caustic barbs, and those women were well practiced at slinging napalm. “I was king-like?”

“Trolling again.” She looked up and fluttered her eyelids. “You need reassuring, Chief?” She dropped her voice low to huskier than usual, trying to seduce me with her taunts. “You need me to tell you how big and strong you are?”

I twirled her away from me, then yanked her back against my body. “I need you to behave yourself.”

She gave me a three-year-old’s pout. “You’re no fun.”

"*Agápi mou,* I'm the best time you're ever going to have."

"Arrogant and gooey at the same time. How do you," she yawned, "manage it?"

"Bedtime." I took her hand and walked over to the dock and grabbed my phone, then I walked us to the sliding glass doors and locked up. "I'll answer all your questions later today."

"Even what you said in Greek?"

My love. "Especially what I said in Greek."

***

Max detoured into the hall bathroom, and I got another pair of briefs out of the top drawer before I went into my bathroom. I needed to clean up and change. I laughed when I wadded up the soiled briefs and threw them in the hamper. Starting at about ten years old, I couldn't count how many times I'd wrapped my underwear in my shirts and then buried the ball in the hamper so my mother wouldn't see the evidence of my wet dreams. Somehow, in my kid's brain, it didn't dawn on me she'd unroll the ball when she put my clothes in the wash.

I was half lying against my propped-up pillow, my hands locked behind my head, when Max came into the bedroom, her bag dangling from her right hand.

She stopped in the doorway, punched her hands on her hips, drawing up my t-shirt a little, which was a fine fucking view of her delicious thighs, and blew out a noisy breath, her bag bouncing against her leg. "You call that behaving?"

"What?" I asked innocently. "I'm just sitting here waiting for you."

"Riiiight," she said sardonically. "Shoe on the other foot, what would you say if I effected the same pose and you walked in?"

"Thank you, Jesus."

She gave me a bright smile. "Nice compliment." She pulled up her bag and dug out her cell. "I noticed you and I have the same phone." She tilted up her chin at my cell connected to the slim white cord that led to its charger. "You have an extra? My phone's nearly dead."

I reached into the top drawer of my nightstand and pulled out the extra cord and charger. "Give it here. The plug's on this side." She handed over her cell and I twisted my body half out of the bed to plug the charger into the surge protector strip under the nightstand. As I sat up and placed her phone next to mine, I caught her admiring the view. "Like what you see, *glikia mou*?"

"Well, you certainly won the genetic lottery at the factory."

I grinned. As compliments went, that was a ringing endorsement from Max. "Get your sweet ass into bed. We need to get some shut-eye." I lay down and watched as she stomped around the foot of the bed as if what I'd said pissed her off, but she couldn't hide her lips hiking up into a smirk.

She dropped her bag next to the bed, climbed in, and didn't even try to pretend she was going to sleep on that side. She got under the covers, scooched over and put her head on my left pec, slung her arm over my abs, and threw her leg over my thigh. I hit the light switch, then placed my arm over hers.

Yeah, she knew she was mine and I was hers.

I leaned down and kissed the top of her head, her soft hair tickling my lips. "*Kalinikta, agápi mou.*"

"*Buonanotte, bello.*"

Chapter Eleven

Crash
Max

Ryan was still asleep. I had no idea what time it was since I couldn't reach my phone, and those Roman shades worked unbelievably well. No gaps on the sides or anything. It wasn't pitch black as it had been at night, but it could be nine or noon. Sometime in the night – more like early morning – we'd turned in our sleep and now I was more than spooned, I was surrounded. My head was on one of Ryan's heavy arms, and the other lay over my waist. His face was angled between my shoulder and my neck, and one seriously thick thigh was wedged between my legs and the other was on top of my outer leg. Not complaining. I was warm, snug, protected, and claimed. I pondered the whole claimed woman thing for a moment and decided I was okay with it as long as it stayed in the house. Geez. What was I thinking? All this should scare the hell out of me, but it didn't.

Not after last night.

All night, from the moment he took me out of Officer Rodriguez's arms until we passed out like we'd been sleeping together for years, Ryan had been sweet, kind, gentle, funny, considerate, and loving. I was completely freaked out by the whole strong, quiet man thing for a while, but after he'd held me and soothed me through the aftershocks of that horrible nightmare episode, something in me shifted, and I decided maybe I *could* do this.

We could take it slow. Stop laughing. No, we couldn't go slow. We'd broken the emotional speed barrier already. We were in deep, and we both knew it. But I could go slow with letting him inside the dark dungeon of my trauma.

I wanted to believe him when he said he wouldn't hurt me and he wouldn't judge me. I needed him to mean what he said. I was skating on the thinnest ice I'd been on in ten years, and I sure as fuck didn't want to fall into the water and get frozen out.

That cheerful thought reminded me, I had to pee. Three times while we were dancing – he'd danced with me for nearly two hours: the two most romantic hours I've ever had in my life – he stopped and got me a glass of water. Yes, I made him bring the trays into the kitchen and I put the strawberries in the fridge. He'd been worried I was dehydrated, and I didn't have it in me to argue with him.

Aside from his gooey choice of Luther Vandross – who I loved and adored, but damn, talk about playing on my heartstrings – Ryan knew when to murmur in my ear, move me silently around the room, and when to make me laugh. He seemed to enjoy our banter. He was good at it. Quick-witted with a dry humor I appreciated, he never got mean or caustic. As tough as he was – and let me tell you, after that press conference, I knew he had a backbone made of steel – he didn't have a mean bone in his body. Arrogant? Absolutely. Pushy, bossy, and high-handed? Without a doubt. A handful? Oh yeah, and then some. But I was no walk in the park. I needed someone who knew how to diffuse a bomb because I was combative and combustible.

I tried to move and his arm around my waist tightened, which really didn't help the bladder situation. I was going to have to rouse him, and I felt bad about that. I'd kept him up most of the night. Before I had a chance to get him awake enough for me to move out of his hold, my phone rang. He turned over and picked it up, which was high-handed and presumptuous in the extreme. Except when he answered, "Trent," whoever was on the other end talked to him and he responded with, "Tell him I'll be there in forty minutes."

Huh. We had the same ring tone. Let's try not to read too much into that.

He put his phone down, turned over, and hauled me to him with one arm. "G'morning," he whispered in my ear, then ran his tongue around its outer edge.

Damn. One sweet little move and I was ready to fuck his brains out.

"Hey," I said into his chest. Did I mention I loved his chest?

"You slept," he stated.

"Yep." I raised my head to look into his jewel eyes. "You too."

"Best sleep I've had in a long time."

I smiled. Another nice compliment. "Who was that?"

"Camille. The mayor wants to meet, so now I've gotta go to work on my day off. As I said, not a king."

"Well that sucks."

"It does. But I should be back in a couple of hours. Do you want me to drop you at your place, or do you wanna stay here?"

"My place. I need clean clothes, and I have to go food shopping. I texted Bernadette last night and told her I was fine, but needed to take a few days off. She fussed, but I smoothed it out. Anyway, it's no biggie to go to the spa to get my car. I'll hop a cab over after I get dressed."

"No need. The officer who brought your bag to me drove your car back to your place first. You're all set."

Geez. He'd been helping me even when I didn't know it. Such a good guy.

"Thank you."

"Whatever you need, just ask. I've got you."

So it seemed.

"You gonna spoil me?"

He smiled. "Like a queen." He placed both of his large hands on my face and kissed my forehead, then each eyelid, each cheek, the tip of my nose, the hinge of my jaw on each side, then my mouth. No tongue. Only soft lips pressed against mine for a few lingering moments. "I have to get ready," he said against my lips.

"Go. You want coffee?"

"I'd love a cup of coffee."

I kissed his mouth quickly before I stuck my tongue down his throat, as I was wont to do. "You got it."

He slid out of bed and I watched his fantastic back, ass, and legs as he walked down the short hall to his bathroom. Damn. He must work out every day. Disciplined. My idea of a workout was when I spent an entire day at Santa Rosa Plaza and Coddington Mall.

I used the hallway bathroom, brushed my teeth, freshened up and put on my clothes, which felt icky, but I'd change the minute I got home. I left his t-shirt and sweats folded on the edge of the vanity, then put on my socks and boots.

I went to the kitchen to make him coffee and saw it was 9:15. Huh. I probably didn't get more than five hours sleep, and I felt really rested. The magic of sleeping with Ryan.

He had one of those easy-peasy Italian single-pod machines. I wasn't much of a coffee drinker, and didn't feel like tea, so I had a glass a water while his coffee dripped into his LAPD mug. I knew he took it black and liked it hot. I considered bringing it to him in the bathroom, then figured he'd have a glass wall as his shower divider and I sure as hell didn't need to see more of him than I already had. Not that I didn't want to, I mean, who wouldn't, but I didn't trust myself with what I'd do if I did.

I'd folded a piece of paper towel into a square and I put the mug on the paper towel I placed on top of the glass circle inset into the little coffee table in his bedroom alcove. I picked up my bag, unplugged my phone, and went back to living room so he could get dressed without me ogling him.

I barely sat my tush on the sofa when my phone went off in my hand. The caller ID said "Unknown." Typically I wouldn't pick up, but Ziggy was known to switch phones every time she dumped a boyfriend. From what Ryan had shared, I'd say Ziggy and the guy she threw the full beer bottle at were no longer an item.

"Hello."

"Oh, hi. Sorry. I'm trying to reach Chief Ryan Trent." Oh shit. I grabbed the wrong phone. Fuckfuckfuck. I had to think fast. Okay, okay. I got it. I'd pretend the call was forwarded.

"You've reached his line. He's in a meeting right now. Can I take a message?" There. That sounded professional. I'd pass along the number and no harm done.

"Sure. Tell him Captain Fredrico Alvarez from Berkeley PD called with the information he wanted on that ten-year-old case. He has my number."

My heart stopped at "Berkeley PD" and my stomach hit my ankles at "ten-year-old case." I tried to swallow, but my throat had closed up.

I swear, I promise, I vow, I won't hurt you. I'd eat a bullet before I hurt you. You. Are. Safe. With me.

That fuckin' liar.

"I'll let him know," I managed to say.

“Thanks.” Captain Fredrico Alvarez from the Berkeley PD hung up.

I grabbed my bag, ran into the bedroom, switched phones, and to make certain Chief Trent knew why I fuckin’ left, I got the paper towel from under the coffee mug, pulled a pen from my bag, and scrawled on the paper towel “Captain Fredrico Alvarez from the Berkeley PD called.”

Then I ran down the hallway, through the living room, and out of his condo, making sure I closed the front door quietly. Ten feet from his door was an emergency exit, and I took the stairs, figuring I needed that damn key fob to get to the lobby. I didn’t want to go through the same dance with the palace guard yet again.

As I jogged down the steps, I called Verna’s taxi and the dispatcher said they’d have someone there in three minutes. Hallelujah. I bolted out of the stairwell, ran through the lobby, ignored the palace guard, and hit the sidewalk at the same time the cab pulled up.

I was in my apartment for ten minutes. I threw whatever I could get my hands on into my large suitcase, put my laptop, iPad, and phone into my “fancy” knapsack, and ran to my car. My jacket was lying on the passenger seat. Perfect. I’d stuff it in my bag. I made it out of the condo complex and hung a right to head to the 101. At the first red light I hit, I called my mom and told her I was going out of a town for a quick getaway. She took it in stride since I did that sort of thing from time to time. Everyone in my family loved to travel, and I was particularly fond of impromptu jaunts.

I made sure I modulated the tone of my voice so I sounded happy and normal, and Mom bought it lock, stock, and barrel.

Three hours and fifteen minutes later I was sitting on a plane headed for Boston.

Chapter Twelve

One Call
Ryan

Usually I didn't dress in the bathroom, but the torture of seeing Max want me and not being able to do anything about it was cruel to both of us. Plus, I didn't want to fight a hard-on the whole way to the mayor's office.

What a pain in the ass going to this meeting was. I wanted to spend the entire day with Max. Make sure she was back on her feet. Take her out. Have lunch and dinner away from the Falls. Give us time to enjoy each other as we'd started doing when we were dancing.

Damn. Those couple of hours were the best of my life. She was sweet, funny, sassy, and she was *with* me. I knew, after we made sure she was free once and for all from whatever tormented her, I'd have even more of the woman I'd glimpsed last night. The smart, loving woman who gave me some of her heart when she was in my arms dancing, and was snugged up against me in my bed. If those few hours were a preview of what a lifetime with her would be, I'd be one hell of a lucky, happy man.

I got pissed off all over again thinking about having to wait to be with her because Hiram was having a hell of a time wrapping his mind around the reality he had to live with. I'd told him a few times that I couldn't share personnel information with him unless we were in a closed-session meeting with our attorneys regarding a lawsuit or a legal settlement. Even then, the information I was permitted to share was limited to the suit or the settlement. After I'd told him those absolute facts, he'd called the city attorney in to explain "the truth," with me present, certain there'd be a different answer.

Disappointed and angry he didn't hear what he wanted to hear meant I was his whipping boy until the investigation was over and we made a decision about Eric Foster's future with RFPD. I think I'd mentioned I hated this part of my job.

I came out of the bathroom in my button-down tucked into my jeans. I ducked into the walk-in closet – as in walk-in, turn around, sit on the chair in the corner, look in the three-way mirror walk-in closet – and went to the safe. I took out my gun, my holster, and my badge, put them on, grabbed up my boots, pulled them on, then selected a blazer and shrugged into it.

I came into the bedroom and smelled coffee. I looked over to the alcove and saw my LAPD mug sitting on the little table. I walked over to it and smiled. She knew how I liked my coffee. I took a sip and noted it had cooled a little. She must've made it right after I went into the bathroom.

Figuring she must be in the living room, I stopped at the nightstand to pick up my cell so we could leave straight away. This way I'd have enough time to walk her into her apartment and make sure she was okay before I left. There was a paper towel with writing lying on top of my phone. I leaned down to see what it said and choked on my coffee. I put down the mug knowing what I'd find before I looked. I ran into the living room, checked the terrace, ducked in the hallway bathroom, saw my folded clothes, and even went into the guest bedroom.

Max was gone.

Goddamn it. One fuckin' phone call and the bottom had fallen out. The hell of it was, usually I took my cell into the bathroom in case of an emergency – mine or the PD's. The phone didn't cross my mind when I walked away from the bed. I was being an idiot thinking of how Max was probably eagle-eying my ass, and I was preening hoping she was enjoying the show.

Fuck.

By the time I got to her condo, she was gone. She'd kill me if she knew I had the keys to her place, but after she went missing Will gave me a set and swore me to secrecy. She'd probably kill him too.

Her bedroom looked like she'd torn through it. Open drawers with clothes hanging out, hangers akimbo or lying on the floor of her closet, some with clothes on them. There was a big empty space along the back wall behind her shoe racks where a large suitcase must've been. The medium and small pieces of luggage were still there, listing to the side. She must've taken another shoulder bag. The one she'd had with her at my place was lying on her bed.

More evidence of her mad dash was on display in the bathroom. Drawers were half open, and there were all sorts of things strewn over the counter haphazardly.

I wrapped my hand around my forehead and leaned on her vanity. I told myself she'd come back to me. I was hers and she was mine. She knew that. She'd *felt* it. She'd come back to me. She had to.

Max ran away when she needed to process deep emotions, and knowing I was digging around in her darkest secrets were the deepest fucking emotions I could've stirred up. I understood she felt betrayed, but I wasn't betraying her. I was trying to figure out what was wrong so we could get past it. She had to know I meant for us to spend our lives together. She had to know I'd do anything to make her happy. Getting information from Rico was me trying to help her. Fuckin' hell, I wished she'd stayed and threw things at me, screamed at the top of her lungs, anything so I could've explained why I was digging where she thought I didn't belong.

In the middle of her vanity was a round mirror on top of which was an assortment of tiny perfume bottles. I picked up the smallest one with a brushed glass stopper that looked like a flower. I pulled out the stopper and caught a whiff of the scent she'd worn the night we went to Bella Luna. I put the stopper back in the bottle and stuffed it into my jacket pocket.

I went into her little kitchen, turned on the light above the stove, then walked out of her home, and locked the door.

Perfect that I was numb and felt dead inside. I could sit and listen to the mayor and not give one shit what he said about any topic he chose to cover.

***

Four hours later, I was sitting in my car at the edge of Crissy Field staring at the Golden Gate Bridge. Her perfume bottle was standing in the well, the little door hiding the compartment was up. I'd put the tiny, delicate thing in there before I went into the mayor's office. No one got to have any part of Max but me.

What would happen now was an exercise in waiting. I'd built my reputation on being patient and seeing the long game. When it came to Max, I knew the long game already. She and I would spend the rest of our lives together. We would have a home, children, a couple of dogs, barbeques in the backyard, holidays with family, vacations alone where we stayed naked and in bed most of the time, birthday parties, graduations, and everything two people in love for a lifetime were supposed to have. She was my future, and I sure as fuck wasn't giving up my future.

If I was a different kind of cop, I would've put out a BOLO the minute I knew she was gone. She wouldn't have gotten far before someone stopped her and brought her back. But she'd never forgive me for doing that. It was bad enough she was nursing a heavy dose of pissed off and betrayed. I sure as fuck didn't need to add a serving of cornered and apprehended.

I watched a plane in the distance turning over the Pacific, and knew in my heart she'd gone to SFO and had gotten on a plane. Most likely, she went to her family in Connecticut, probably figuring if she put a whole country between us, I wouldn't find her. Even if I didn't have cops who'd lived their whole lives in the Falls and had known Max since childhood, I would find her.

She'd packed my heart in that suitcase, and I intended to get it back.

I pulled out my phone and called Rico.

Chapter Thirteen

Circling
Max

A preface: Running away wasn't really going to hit my wallet. When I was twenty-six, the trust fund my grandparents set up for me vested. The same age requirement applied to all their grandchildren's trust funds. I wasn't rolling in it, but I didn't have to worry about a retirement plan, and I got to take great vacations whenever I wanted. Yeah, I also splurged on bags and shoes, but only sometimes. I had a job because people needed to be gainfully employed and have a sense of purpose. I didn't want to work for my family's winery or vineyard. We would've fought every day if we worked together, and I loved them too much to have a repeat performance of the split between my father and his brother, my uncle Tony, who moved his family to Connecticut and never returned to California. As previously mentioned, my aspirations after getting my degree at Cal weren't happening, and I'd wanted something of my own that kept me close to family. For the most part, I liked working at Shangri la, and unless and until that changed, or I got my shit together and went back for my PhD, I was where I wanted to be.

I had a few minutes on the plane before we had to stow our electronics. I texted Lola to tell her I was off on one of my last-minute vacays, and I sent substantially the same text to Bernadette, who I knew would be none too pleased. When the flight attendant closed the cabin door, I knew I'd lucked out. I had a seat in first class with no one next to me.

After we took off, I got a blanket, lifted the arm between the seats, and sort of stretched out. I was leaning next to the window – I'd pulled down the shade – and I had one of those little pillows behind my head. I had to bend my legs or else my feet dangled into the aisle, but I was semi-comfortable. I was going to force myself to go to sleep even though I didn't know if I could calm my brain. One thing for absolute certain, I refused to spend the next five and half hours crying.

It took a while to drift off. First there was the safety lecture and demonstration, then the pilot chatted for a few minutes about climbing to forty thousand feet to try to avoid turbulence over the Rockies. Really, I didn't need to know that. Then, because it was first class, they were dropping food the moment the seatbelt sign dinged off. I'd gotten a bottle of water, and told the flight attendant to skip the food. Even if I couldn't sleep, there was no way was I eating. There was a slim chance I might work up an appetite if they brought out Dunkin' Donuts, but I didn't think so.

My stomach was in knots, my heart hurt, and my head was pounding. Something vile had lodged in my esophagus, and that rock lay heavy in my chest.

The whole time Ryan had been broadcasting caring and gentle – okay, I'll give him that, he'd taken good care of me – he knew he was betraying my trust by digging into something that wasn't his to learn. IF I'd gotten to a place where I could've told him about that horrible, life-altering disaster, that was mine to share. I couldn't even begin to wrap my mind around one cop telling another the "facts" without knowing what I knew, the hidden shit that still gave me nightmares ten years later.

The thing about drifting, as opposed to sleeping, was every now and then I was more present than out of it. The couple behind me were flying back home from their honeymoon, and I was treated to snippets of their recap. Their drive up the PCH in Malibu and into which canyons they'd gone to fuck. The cottage in Carmel that had a hot tub with well-placed jets. The hotel in San Francisco with a sofa that was the perfect height for anal, and they giggled about fucking in a vineyard in Yountville. Thank god they didn't fuck in my family's vineyard. I didn't want to see them. Putting faces to their activities was plain wrong, but when the new wife had to go the bathroom, my seat got jarred and I looked up. Color me shocked. I'd expected twenty-somethings, and this couple was in their early to mid-forties.

First thought: Ryan and I would be like that.

Next thought: Could I bleed out internally from a broken heart?

***

We landed on schedule, and by the time I got my luggage, it was ten at night Boston time. I was awake enough to drive – it was only seven in California – but I didn't know the roads here, and I wasn't going to show up at my cousin Theresa's town house close to midnight. Plus, I needed a shower something fierce, and I had to change my clothes.

I took out my phone and booked into the InterContinental for the night, and then arranged for Enterprise to pick me up at the hotel at nine am. I figured I'd get to Dutchford, Connecticut around 10:30. Usually, Theresa spent Saturday mornings at home puttering in her little garden.

When I got to my hotel room, I sat on the bed and checked my phone. Eight new texts. The first from Ziggy.

Where the fuck are you?

One from my mother.

Have a great time, sweetie. Call or text to let me know you're all right.

One from Lola.

Did you get where you're going yet? LMK you're okay.

The next from Bernadette.

When are you coming back?

The rest were from Ryan.

Let me know you're safe.

If you need anything, let me know.

I'll be right here waiting for you.

Now, I cried. Big, noisy, ugly crying. I mushed my face into the puffy white pillow and sobbed until I exhausted myself. This was exactly what I'd wanted to avoid. No, he didn't leave, and so far he hadn't judged, but the trust I had begun to place in him was a fragile thing and brand spankin' new. I didn't trust easily, and he knew it. Yet, he'd shattered that trust when he went behind my back to find out what happened at Cal. Even now, after I left, he didn't seem remorseful.

I stared at the black stains on the pillow. Mascara and eyeliner were probably the least offensive things bleached out of hotel sheets and pillowcases. Ew. I didn't want to think about that. I dragged myself to the bathroom. Classic racoon face. I stripped off my days'-old clothes and took a shower. Hard to believe I was doing the same thing less than twenty-four hours ago in Ryan's place.

With my eyes closed, I stood under the water and let its heat work out the airplane kinks. Not quite thirteen hours had passed from the time Ryan came to get me on Cottonwood until I fled his condo this morning. Almost every minute of those thirteen hours he had been focused on making me feel better. I didn't get it. How could the man who treated me like precious crystal betray me? From the get-go, when he'd approached me at Beans & Roast, he'd made it clear he was into me and wanted me. Last night, I understood the depth of his intentions, and for a few glorious hours I believed. Believed he wouldn't hurt me, lie to me, betray me, judge me. What I wouldn't give to feel that way all the time. I'd been nearly certain he was *that guy*. How could I've been so wrong?

He didn't apologize in his texts. He didn't ask where I was and when I was coming home. He wanted to know if I was safe and to tell me he was there for me, and that he was waiting until I came back. What did I do with that?

I turned off the shower, stepped out, and wrapped myself in a big towel, but not as big or soft as Ryan's. I toweled off my hair and went to the bedroom to unzip my suitcase and get out my toiletries bag and makeup bag. I always kept emergency mascara, eyeliner, and lipstick in my purse, but my makeup bag had everything I needed to transform myself. Which I'd have to do tomorrow before I saw Theresa. If I arrived on her doorstep all weepy and needy, I'd shoot myself. I didn't want her to feel compelled to "help" me the way shrinks do. I needed her warmth, love, understanding, smarts, and friendship.

I looked at Ryan's texts again and tried to decide if I should answer him. I was angry and hurt. He'd betrayed me in a way I never expected, especially from him. But I wasn't going to be mean and make him worry more than he already was. I knew he worried about me, especially after I'd freaked out and went running like a lunatic through the streets of Redwood Falls. I saw it on his face when I snuck glances over at him while he was driving me to his condo. His expression said genuinely upset, with a side of relieved.

Damn. I was over three thousand miles away from him, because of him, and I was worried about how he felt. Totally SAP. Well, from his texts, he was worried about me too, though I doubted he felt sad and pathetic. Maybe he was annoyed he got caught. More likely, he probably thought he didn't do anything wrong. Like he was entitled to know everything about me on his terms.

Well, fuck him.

I dumped all my clothes and shoes onto the bed and repacked my suitcase. I'd thrown everything in willy-nilly, and I needed to try to keep things de-wrinkled, not make it worse. As I was rolling my clothes, I thought about how about I'd spent more time pushing Ryan away than holding him close. Yet, he kept coming back for more. He was far from a pushover, and he wasn't the kind of man who let anyone walk all over him, but he kept at me no matter how much *get the fuck away* I threw at him. When he'd come to "question" me about Ziggy and her brothers, he had said straight up he didn't believe I wanted him out of my life.

Even now, as pissed off as I was, that was true. But after what he'd done, I didn't know how we'd ever be able to move forward. He hadn't only betrayed my trust, he meant to strip me of the walls, moats, and dungeons I'd built to keep the darkness hidden. Buried. He'd gotten a glimpse of what that beast could do to me. That he'd want to leave me defenseless was unfathomable, and scared me down to my toenails.

***

These people drove like lunatics. The Massachusetts Turnpike was a highway, and god knew I'd driven on enough of them living in California, but holy shit. This was the Indy 500 on crack. Cars zigzagged in and out of lanes for no other reason than to beat the car next to them in an imaginary race to whatever finish line the drivers had in their fucked-up brains. Typically, I drove about ten miles over the speed limit everywhere except in town. These imbeciles were flying past me like I was crawling along at thirty-five mph.

I'd rented an SUV crossover hybrid, and part of the deal was an E-ZPass since the turnpike's tollbooths were totally electronic. Tollbooths seemed to be an East Coast thing. I'd heard there were a few toll roads in SoCal, but I'd never driven on them. I didn't think there was one toll road north of LA. You'd think the tollbooths would slow people down, but they seemed to be like racehorses out of the gate when they cleared the tollbooths. Nuts.

I was thrilled when I saw the Dutchford exit.

Talk about picture-perfect cutesy New England. Beautiful big trees lined streets with houses spaced far from each other, each tucked behind wide lawns, or high walls covered in ivy. The little town was storybook, with shops that had charming signs hanging above their entryways, and restaurants and cafés had tables out on the sidewalks, wide colorful umbrellas shading the customers. I'd been here once, a couple of years ago, when Theresa had been shot by a lunatic ex-boyfriend of one her patients. I didn't remember much about the area since I spent all of my time in the hospital or the nearby hotel, and mostly that was to shower and sleep.

Theresa was my Uncle Tony and Aunt Connie's youngest daughter. A few years after Tony took his wife and kids to Connecticut, Theresa and her older sister, Laura, started to come to California to spend their summers with us. That was when we became best friends, and nothing had changed in twenty-one years. Two years older than me, Theresa was at Stanford when I went to Cal. We saw each other every couple of weeks. She'd stayed at Stanford for seven years altogether, working on her PhD, and was awarded her doctorate pretty quickly by those standards. Wicked smart, she was totally intuitive. She chose the right profession.

When she returned to Connecticut, we agreed to see each other at least twice a year. She came to California for a couple of weeks every January to escape the cold, and every summer we took a vacation together somewhere new. We talked on the phone all the time, and texted each other every day. If anyone in the world was my refuge, Theresa was it.

A couple of miles out of town, I pulled up in front of a row of redbrick town houses. Each house had a bright red door, black shutters, a teeny tiny lawn, and a wide front stoop. The only way you could differentiate one town house from the other were the plants and decorations on the stoops or little lawns. Without even looking at the house number, I knew which was Theresa's. The house with the most plants and flowers in abundant bloom. She had a twig-twined wreath on the door with seashells and star fish dangling from the twigs.

Parking wasn't allowed on the town house side of the street, but there were spots across the street, and I didn't have to walk far to get to her place.

With my backpack slung over my shoulder, I lugged the suitcase up the stoop and rang the doorbell. I waited a couple of minutes since Theresa was probably out back. When I heard nothing, I walked down to the end of the row of townhomes to see if there's a way to get to the back where I figured Theresa was repotting something on her patio. I turned down the block and saw there was an alleyway where the garages of each townhome faced, and there was another row of the same across the alleyway. The only problem, the alleyway was gated. Since Theresa's house was in the middle of the block, standing at the gate yelling wasn't going to do any good. I walked back to her house and rang the doorbell again. I waited a couple of minutes, then rang the bell and knocked on the door. That's when I heard Boo bark. I'd never met him, but I'd seen pictures, and he was thirty pounds of adorable. Black shaggy/curly hair, and a fuzzy face that was like a Schnauzer's except he had full floppy ears.

I banged on the door and called out, "Ter, you home?"

A few moments later I heard footfall approaching the door, then after another few seconds the door opened and an unbelievably handsome man, tall with serious blue eyes, was looking down at me like he knew who I was.

I was pretty sure he was Theresa's fiancé, but I'd never seen a picture 'cause he worked for the FBI and there was all sorts of security shit she couldn't tell me about, but it sounded intense. What she could've told me but didn't was this dude was a hunka-hunka burning love. "Who are you?"

"Ethan. Theresa's man."

It *was* him. My head jerked back, not from surprise as much as *wow, cuz, you landed you a hot one.* "No shit."

He fought a grin. "No shit."

He leaned forward and picked up my suitcase like it weighed five pounds, and I caught a whiff of him that told me I interrupted something. My brain didn't have time to censor my mouth. "You smell like sex."

As he moved back into the house, I caught his grin in full. Yeah, I interrupted something.

After he placed the suitcase in the hallway, I moved into the house behind him. Theresa, who had sex hair, walked toward the door and yelled, “Oh my god. Max. What are you doing here?”

For now, I gave her the short answer. “I’ve run away from home.”

Theresa leaned against Ethan’s side and said, “Holy shit” at the same time Boo jumped up to say hello.

“Down,” Ethan commanded in a super-deep voice. Boo plopped his butt on the floor, but his tail was going a mile a minute. I put him out of his misery, bent down, and gave him a good rub.

When I stood, Theresa came to me and wrapped her arms around my waist. I was significantly taller than her, and we’d stood like this many times with her head on my chest, my chin on her head. “What’s it going to be?” Theresa asked. “Breakfast, catching up, or heart-to-heart?”

I was facing her living room and saw moving boxes stacked in the corner. “Catching up and breakfast.” I turned my head to Ethan. “Don’t disappear. I want to get to know you.”

He smiled and the hallway lit up. Damn. They were going to have gorgeous kids. “I’ll put up the coffee.”

“None for me.”

Theresa disengaged. “Max is a tea drinker.” She looked up and said, “I have chamomile. We haven’t packed the kitchen yet. That’s last.”

Ethan walked down the hall toward the back of the town house. To my left was the living room, and to my right was a staircase. On the other side of the staircase was a narrow hallway. A closet door was at the top of the little hall, and large bifold doors were on the other side of the staircase. I guessed that was the laundry area.

I followed Theresa into the kitchen. Pretty glass-front white cabinets, white marble countertops with silver veining, throughout, including the island that separated the kitchen from the dining room. A large sliding glass door led out to Theresa’s famous back patio, and it was a sight to behold.

“Oooo. I’ve gotta see this.” I opened the slider and stepped onto a slate-tiled rectangle that was probably twelve feet deep and twenty feet wide. In the center was a rectangular table with a big sun umbrella through the middle. Four colorfully padded armchairs on white spiral coils surrounded the table. Along the fence on all sides were various plant holders, some in white wire in interesting shapes, like a bicycle with holders for pots, and others were antiqued with patina and rust. I guessed that every plant they had in her beloved garden center was represented in the dazzling array. A small trellis climbed up the wall alongside the slider, heavy with lilacs, which were planted into ground, the only place where the soil was exposed.

Theresa stood beside me and saw me admiring the lilacs. "I wasn't supposed to destroy the patio and plant directly in the ground, but I wanted lilacs and they're fussy about their roots. They need room to spread out. I had all the concrete pulled up, planted the bushes, then had the slate put in with the moss in between. This way their roots could breathe, and as they spread, the water would seep into the ground through the moss."

"It's gorgeous, Ter. A little paradise."

"Wait until you see the house. I have a conservatory, and an acre and a half."

"You're going to lose your mind, aren't you?"

She nodded, smiling. "I'm glad you're here."

"Me too. Can we eat out here?"

"Sure."

Ten minutes later, I'd set the table and was sitting with my tea, Theresa with her coffee, and we were waiting to dig into the toast on the table. Ethan came out carrying a large pan filled with scrambled eggs, and he spooned eggs onto each of our plates. He went into the kitchen to put the pan away, then joined us. I was putting copious amounts of blueberry jam on my toast, and Theresa was spreading cream cheese on a couple of slices of toast, which she put on Ethan's plate.

"Thanks, babe," he said, as he picked up a piece of toast and bit into it. His expression was full of gooey love.

They had it. That elusive thing most people search for their whole lives: real love filled with mutual admiration and respect. Theresa waxed poetic when she talked about him, and I didn't need to hear him say what was written so plainly on his face.

I dug into the eggs and found they were lightly sprinkled with cheddar cheese. I looked at Ethan. "Yum. You made these?"

He nodded, swallowed, then said, "Yeah. Theresa's teaching me how to cook. I'm getting good with breakfast. Nothing fancy. I leave that to her. But I'll be able to make pancakes and stuff like that for the kids."

I nearly choked on my eggs. I cut my gaze over to Theresa as I took a few sips of tea. "You're pregnant? On purpose?" She grinned and I jumped up, bent down, pulled her out of her chair, and hugged the shit out of her. "Ohmygod, ohmygod, ohmygod." I jumped up and down with her, then pushed her back and asked, "Who knows? How far along are you?" I looked at her body, which looked the same. Petite with a healthy ass and thighs. "How do you feel? Should you be doing all this boxing and lifting? Are you getting married soon?"

My gaze swung to Ethan, who was grinning so wide it had to hurt.

"Sit," Theresa said. I complied and waited while she sat, took Ethan's outstretched hand, and they laced their fingers. "I take it you haven't checked your email in a couple of days."

I shook my head. "Nope."

"I sent out e-wedding invitations. We're getting married in our backyard on Saturday, June thirtieth. Since July fourth falls in the middle of the week, we're calling it a pre-Fourth celebration. We invited the family, and close friends. About seventy-five people if absolutely everyone shows up. So far we've had fifty-six yes RSVPs and no one's said no. I'm counting you as number fifty-seven." I nodded. "We've got a big tent, a DJ, a dance floor, and a priest. The caterers are doing a huge buffet so people can graze all night. We're having an open bar, and we reserved forty rooms at the Marriot Courtyard in Milford. We contracted with a limo service to be on call to ferry people to the hotel. The caterers are coming back on Sunday. We're doing a family brunch at the house."

"Ho-lee shit."

"That must be a family thing," Ethan said.

Theresa looked at me and we cracked up. I told him, "Well, yeah. We all seem to say it the same way. I can't tell you why." I shrugged. "Genetics."

She nodded. "Anyway, to answer your questions, eleven weeks. Only you, Laurie, our moms and dads, and Trask knows."

"Trask?"

"My brother," Ethan answered.

"Ah. So, by June thirtieth, you'll be –"

"Right about thirteen weeks. We plan on telling everyone at the wedding."

"After the priest leaves," I said.

Ethan laughed. "I don't think this guy will give a shit. He's a hippie activist priest. He's staying to celebrate with us. He'll think it's great."

"A peace, love, and happiness dude."

"Exactly," he said.

"Cool." I turned to Theresa. "And the rest?"

"I feel fine. I pass out at night earlier than usual, and I sleep like a rock, but otherwise, I'm good. The doctor said I could box and wrap and pack. No heavy lifting. Ethan's arm is still healing, so every couple of days, one of the guys from the moving company comes over and stacks the boxes in the living room."

"When are you moving?"

"Next weekend," he said.

"Whoa. I'm in the way."

"Nonsense," Theresa said at the same time Ethan told me, "Bullshit."

"You gotta let me help, at least."

"Totally." Theresa smiled. "Ethan and I aren't working Thursday and Friday, so feel free to be motivated all you want while we're at work."

"I've got a moving log," Ethan said, wearing a serious expression. "Follow the log's numbering order, and on each box you put a number and a room designation. In the log you list the contents and to which room the stuff is going. This way we can direct the movers where to put everything, and we won't have to play dig through the box when we're looking for something."

I looked at Theresa. "He's not just a pretty face."

They both laughed.

"We'll pack the kitchen at the end of the week," she told me. "We've made a lot of headway already. There's not that much left."

"Tell me about the house."

Ethan spoke before Theresa could open her mouth. "The kitchen and bathrooms need to be updated. Every room needs to be repainted, and two rooms need to have the wallpaper stripped before we can paint. The floors need to be stripped, sanded, and revarnished, the driveway needs to be repaved, and those are the must-dos."

Theresa smiled. "It's perfect. It has four bedrooms, two and a half baths, a living room, dining room, study, laundry room, two-car garage, and a conservatory. The basement is finished, and we're making that into the family room."

"Wild guess. You're happy about the conservatory."

Ethan shook his head and Theresa laughed.

***

After we cleaned up, Ethan carried my suitcase upstairs to the guest bedroom, which, I was happy to see, was on the other end of the hallway from the master. It wasn't like they were in another wing of the house, but at least there was a linen closet and bathroom between us. I didn't want to cramp their style any more than I was already.

Ethan took Boo down the street for a walk and to play Frisbee, and I helped Theresa pack. She was putting all their hanging winter clothes in wardrobe boxes and I was packing sweaters and pants into regular boxes. She'd exhausted all their luggage days ago.

"Talk to me," she said casually. "This the same guy from the beginning of December?"

"Pffft," I replied. "I wasn't running away from him because I was into him. I had to disappear so he'd get the hint that I didn't want more than what we'd had. I was stressed because he was making me nuts."

"No wasn't enough?"

"I told him if I had to take out a restraining order, I would. By that time, Will knew he was going to be promoted. He had to wait until the guy he was replacing officially retired, but I told the asshole my best friend was a lieutenant in the police department. That coupled with a one-week trip to Albuquerque and Taos did the trick."

"And now?"

"It's what you think, and it's not. It's complicated, and I want a couple of days to sort it out in my head before I dump it on you."

"Fair enough. Pass me Ethan's flannel shirts. He put them on the high bar and I can't reach them.

Chapter Fourteen

Small Favors
Ryan

An entire weekend and not a word. I hadn't expected a phone call, but Max knew I worried, she could've let me know she was safe.

Her silence coupled with what Rico told me had me seriously considering getting on a plane. At this point I didn't care if we shouted the house down. We needed to get everything on the table, fight it out if she wouldn't talk with me reasonably, and move the fuck on with our lives. Together. Forever.

I'd never ached for anyone. What an abysmal feeling. Carrying on through the day, appearing to be competent and engaged, but knowing I was going through the motions. Of all the analogies I could conjure, I thought of Vincent D'Onofrio's character in *Men in Black* donning the skin of the dead human, and how ill-fitting it was. How his face sagged and how he lumbered, unable to mimic a real human gait. That's how I felt. Out of my body, yet in it. Out of my mind, but completely functional. A mass of riotous emotions, yet calm and in control when it came to work.

At home was a different story. Her scent lingered on my sheets, pillows, t-shirt, and sweats. Like a lovesick teenager, I lay in bed, my face pressed against her pillow, torturing myself with her essence. I yearned for her voice, her laughter, her wit, her irreverence, and her body next to mine in bed. There wasn't a single thing about her I didn't crave excepting her absence.

One of the many perks of living in this building was the gym and the pool. Neither world-class, but new machines, benches and weights, and the pool was clean, deep, almost always empty, and three lanes were lined off on the left side. The locker rooms connected to the gym and the pool, making the transition from one to the other seamless.

When I got back from San Francisco, I worked out for two hours and swam twenty laps after my workout. Saturday, I increased the laps to fifty, and by Sunday I was up to one hundred. The whole time I was swimming, I thought of each and every time Max ogled my body. A few times she didn't think I noticed, and those were the best. Her open appreciation was flattering and damn sexy. I made no such attempts at being surreptitious. When I regarded her, I did it right in front of her. I wanted her to know I enjoyed what I saw, and that I wanted it, all of it.

I hadn't lied when I told her we were raised to eat well and take care of our bodies. I grew up surfing, playing beach volleyball, running track, and playing baseball. My parents' idea of a family vacation was a trip to the mountains or a national park where we hiked all day and camped out at night. When I joined LAPD, my hours didn't allow for surfing and beach volleyball so I'd joined a twenty-four-hour gym. For years, my shifts were crazy, and I'd needed a physical outlet to balance the frustrations of the job. Now working out was part of my routine. I wasn't getting any younger, and staying strong and fit required more diligence than it had ten years ago.

As exhausted as I was at the end of the day, sleep eluded me. I wound up sitting in my easy chair watching *Jack Ryan*, and woke in the morning to find I'd fallen asleep in the middle of an episode.

The disjointed dichotomy of how I felt and what my job required was going to burn me out fast. Sunday night I set the alarm on my phone for the first time in my life. I'd never needed an alarm. If I had to be up at six, I set my body clock and got up at five to six. Now, I was too out of sync to rely on my mental fortitude, and I was glad for the alarm. I got out of the easy chair, took a shower, and while I was standing at the kitchen counter drinking coffee, I processed what Rico had told me.

As it turned out, his old partner had interviewed Max. She'd been at the frat party that night but had left a couple of hours before the rape. She'd been shocked by the news, and the officer, now detective – which was why it took a while for Rico to get back to me, his former partner was working a homicide and didn't have the time to talk until last Thursday – hadn't learned anything important from her.

What Rico hadn't remembered, but his partner had in vivid detail was the twin brother of the girl who had been raped was a member of the fraternity. He'd left the party for a while, but came back to escort his sister to her dorm. Apparently, he'd walked in on the rape in progress. He'd beaten the shit out of two of the guys, the one who was inside her, and the other who was trying to rape her mouth. The two who had already raped her and were watching took off when the brother went ballistic. Three ambulances were needed that night. The brother, who was a mess himself, rode to the hospital with his sister.

All four rapists were prosecuted to the fullest extent of the law. Unfortunately, that justice was unusual, but when I learned the twins' mother was a US Attorney and their father was a prominent corporate attorney, I knew there'd been a shit-ton of pressure on the Berkeley PD and the Alameda County DA's office to throw the book at those fuckwads. The two who were caught in the act pled out, and they testified against the other two. The judge gave all four of them the maximum sentence – eight years – with no possibility of parole, which was nowhere near enough. They were all out of prison and were all registered sex offenders. Two lived in San Diego, one lived in Menifee, and the other lived in Chico.

If the story of the rape hadn't been bad enough, two months after the girl was released from the hospital, she killed her twin then committed suicide in their parents' home.

Tragic, horrible, horrifying, and the kind of thing that would leave a scar on the psyche of a young, idealistic, impressionable college sophomore. What I couldn't understand was why Max was tormented with fear so primal she still had vicious nightmares ten years later. Will had called it "a rough patch," but what my woman was suffering was no rough patch. There was more to this story, and only Max had the key to unlocking the mystery as well as to the door that would let me in so I could help her slay the beast that was keeping her from being happy.

***

At ten am Camille knocked on my door. "Chief, you have a minute?"

"Sure. What's up?"

She came in, closed the door, and sat in one of the chairs in front of my desk. "Five bids have come in already, and I'm starting my due diligence. I'll close the bid at six, and as soon as I make my decision, I'll let you know."

"Anyone local?" I didn't want a former Redwood Falls cop investigating, but I trusted Camille would know that wouldn't be the best route.

"One from Sacramento, two from San Francisco, one from Sonoma, and one from Santa Rosa."

"Wide field. Good to know."

"Also, got word from the officers' union." I nodded for her to go on. "They're no longer handling the matter. Foster hired an outside attorney. Once he did that, the union's no longer obligated to represent him, and although the rep didn't say so, I have a feeling they're happy to distance themselves from this one."

"Same rep talked to you was the guy with Foster when he talked to Will?" My mind was such a jumble, I couldn't recall the guy's name.

"Yeah. Officer DeMarco. He's been on the force for about four years. Good cop." Right, DeMarco. I didn't know him, but by all reports, he was solid.

"They don't want to be painted with the same brush," I told her. With the shitstorm swirling over the incident, and the vultures circling to see how we handled what happened, no doubt the union took the out gladly and walked away from the mess.

"My take on it as well."

"Do we know if the lawyer is affiliated with any hate groups?"

She chuckled. "Foster hired Sam Glickman. He's been around forever. Sweet older man who has a heart of gold. He's big on lost causes." All evidence was pointing to Foster having opened his mouth before he'd engaged his brain and realized he had an audience. It'd cost him his career. Stupid dumb fuck.

Camille sat still as if she had something more to say.

"Anything else?" Please, god, I didn't want to talk about Max with anyone.

She took a breath. "I know the timing is bad, but my sister is in town for a few days and I wondered if I could take a couple of days off."

I was so relieved what she wanted had nothing to do with me and Max, I damn near sang out my answer. “At this point, two days isn’t going to change this case, Camille. Enjoy your time with your sister.”

Her shoulders relaxed. “Thanks, Chief. If you need me to come in, call. I’m not leaving town.”

I waved her off. “Go.”

She smiled, got up, and left my office.

By one-thirty my nerves were shot. I hadn’t had enough sleep, and I’d been drinking too much coffee. I needed to go home and have a swim, or a nap. Christ, I never took naps.

When I walked into my condo, I knew what I had to do to relieve the worry that was running riot through my brain. I took off my jacket, threw it on the couch, got my laptop from the sideboard drawer, sat at the dining room table and searched the name Calapiano in Connecticut. Thankfully, not a common name. It took twenty seconds to learn there were four Calapianos in Connecticut. Three minutes later, I’d tracked down Max’s aunt, uncle, and two cousins to their home and business addresses, and respective phone numbers. I didn’t see Max going to her aunt and uncle for refuge. Too much like being with her parents. One cousin was married with two small children, and it seemed unlikely their household would be calming. The other cousin was a psychotherapist. I’d bet my car that was who Max was staying with. I checked the time and hoped Dr. Calapiano was still in her office. I picked up my phone and dialed.

“Dr. Calapiano. Can I help you?”

I was surprised I got her and not a receptionist. “Hello. I’m Ryan Trent.”

“Ahh,” she said with a smile in her voice. “You’re Max’s man.”

I was so shocked by her statement, I asked, “She’s told you about me?”

“Actually, no. I’m what my fiancé calls hyper-intuitive. A side bonus in my profession.” Oh, I liked this woman. Definitely a relative of Max’s. Smart, quick, and not shy. “You’re calling from a Redwood Falls exchange. I know because a lot of my family lives there. Max is here, and I’m guessing she hasn’t let you know where she is and that she arrived safely so you tracked me down to find out if she’s all right. How am I doing?”

“Brilliantly. You sure you’re not an FBI profiler?”

She laughed. “When I go home tonight, I’ll have to share that one with Ethan, my fiancé. He works for the FBI.” Max was safe and staying with an FBI agent. Okay. I could dial down the frantic to a simmer. It didn’t help with the misery, but I’d take my wins where I could find them. “Can I ask, what do you do in Redwood Falls?”

“I’m the police chief.”

She started laughing loud and hard. “Sorry,” she stuttered, “sorry. That’s too rich.”

“Do I want to know why?”

“You know why,” she said without a trace of laughter in her voice.

I sighed. “I guess I do.” Of all people, Max chose a man who would press to get to the bottom of the darkness that lived inside her and would help her slay the beast.

“What I’m about to tell you could get me kicked out of the worldwide women’s club, the best friends club, and, potentially, my family. But I know what it is to find love, and I know with absolute certainty that it’s too precious to disregard. You sitting, Chief?”

“Yeah.”

“Max is in love with you.”

I closed my eyes and knew when I saw this woman for the first time, her man was not going to be thrilled with the kiss I intended to lay on her. The relief coursing through my system was so intense I felt weak from it. I wanted to cry.

“Ryan.”

“Yeah. It’s good to hear someone say what I believe is true. I love her too.”

“I know that or I wouldn’t’ve told you. Listen to me. You need to give her time. She’s here with me and Ethan, and trust me when I tell you she couldn’t be in safer hands. Within a couple of weeks, you’re going to receive mail from The Letter Club. Open it.”

I sensed she was up to something, but I didn’t know what, and I didn’t think it wise to ask. “Seems I’d be foolish to argue with a doctor.”

“You’d be foolish to argue with the one person who can help Max freely give you her heart. Now keep your shit together and let her be. I’m going to put your number in my cell, and I’ll text you in a few minutes so you have my number. If you get edgy, text me. Got it?”

I wondered if all the Calapiano women were bossy. "Got it. Can I call you Theresa?"

"I'd be insulted if you didn't."

"I don't know why you picked up your office phone, but I'm glad you did."

"My receptionist had to leave early. You lucked out."

I sure did. "Thank you. I think I might be able to sleep tonight." I had no idea why I was telling her that. She must be a *really* good shrink.

"Sweet dreams, Ryan."

She hung up.

Chapter Fifteen

The Set-Up
Theresa

Lying on Ethan's chest, I was catching my breath after particularly energetic sex. Between the pregnancy and Ethan's propensity to wear me out, I knew I had about ten minutes before I was in noddie-noddie land.

I raked my fingers through his chest hair. "Guess who called me today."

He smiled. "Long list of possibles. By the look of your lids, best give it over before you pass out."

This was one of the many fantastic things about being loved by Ethan. He *knew* me. He cared for me and took care of me. "Max's guy, Ryan Trent."

"Man's worried about his woman, I'm surprised he waited out the weekend."

"My guess, he was giving her room to respond to him on her terms. I don't doubt he called or texted her on Friday."

"Patient."

"Yeah. You're going to love what he does for a living."

He grabbed my ass with both hands and squeezed. "Spoon-fed that one. He's in law enforcement."

I grinned. "He's the chief of police in Redwood Falls."

"Man's gotta have patience to be a police chief. You settle his mind?"

"I did, and broke the girl code doing it."

"My little radical." His head came up and he kissed my mouth. "What'd you say?"

"I told him she's in love with him."

"That can't be a secret. She's a Times Square billboard advertising heartache."

My guy could be deadly serious, but he was funny and witty in equal measure. "He knows how she feels, but she hasn't told him yet."

"Ah."

"Yeah. He's really gone for her. Oh, oh, and when I guessed at a few things he asked if I was an FBI profiler."

Ethan chuckled. "You probably could be." He tapped his forefinger to my temple. "Spidey sense."

I ran my thumb over his eyebrows and down his nose. He was so gorgeous. "Miss Max has to get her shit together and make things right. She hasn't told me what's up, but whatever it is she has to get past it."

"Sound like you're getting ready to meddle."

I put my hand on his cheek. "I am. It's part of the reason she's here. She knows I'm going to push her in the direction she wants to go, but can't seem to get there on her own. I'm her cheerleading squad."

He chuckled. "You have a plan."

"I do. I'll let you know when it's in place."

He rolled us to our sides and pulled me against him chest to chest. "Go to sleep, Flower. You're on the wane." He wrapped his arms around me and kissed my forehead.

I sighed and dropped off immediately.

***

Ethan

With Theresa asleep and tucked safely under my arm, I stayed awake waiting for Max to come home. She'd called Laurie yesterday and they made arrangements to have lunch with Tony and Connie this afternoon. Afterward, Laurie's sister-in-law Andie and her man Lars were meeting them at Baz and Laurie's house to hang out with the kids until Baz came home. Then the adults were going out to dinner. Theresa told Max she should spend the night at Laurie's, but Max wanted to come back here. I knew she was a grown woman who'd traveled the world, often on her own, but she didn't know the roads, and she was driving at night. Learning her man was a top cop, I felt I was on watch on his behalf as well as ours.

When I heard the front door beep open, I extricated myself from Theresa's side, then pulled on jeans and a tee, shushed Boo, and went downstairs to set the security system and do my final walk-through.

Max was sitting at the dining room table dunking a tea bag into one of my FBI mugs.

"What is it with you guys? Ryan has an LAPD mug that's giant too."

I'd wondered where he worked before Redwood Falls. A lot of smaller cities drew on big-city talent for their police chiefs. I had to pretend I didn't know who Ryan was or else she'd ask how I found out. I sat to Max's right and asked, "Who's Ryan?"

She sighed. "That shouldn't be an existential question, but it sort of is."

"Okay, how about something easier? How'd your day go?"

That got her talking. "Last time I saw everyone was at the hospital a couple of years ago, and they'd looked like shit for obvious reasons." Theresa's scar was a daily reminder, but when someone brought up the shooting, my blood boiled and I wanted to kill the guy who'd hurt my Flower. "Uncle Tony and Aunt Connie look well, and were all hugs and smiles. They're totally up on the Ziggy sitch, except from her parents' point of view. Which means they know an eighth of the story. One thing I learned – I know Ter keeps you up to date on Ziggy – she dropped out of college after the beer bottle incident last week." That crazy broad was spiraling fast. "Uncle Stefano and Aunt Asta are insisting Ziggy needs to find a job if she's not going to school. Jury's out if they'll kick her to the curb if she doesn't comply. My money's on Ziggy."

I shook my head. "She's going from bad to worse."

"Ah, yeah." Max continued, "I see three ways Ziggy's life can go. One, she keeps on the way she is and she'll be in jail, or dead before she's thirty. Two, her hormones, oxytocin, vasopressin, or whatever the fuck is out of whack gets aligned either naturally or by medication, and she pulls her shit together and lives a productive life. Or three, someone comes along who gut-punches her emotionally and she falls for him, gets over herself, and lives a happy, productive life."

As she spoke about option three, her voice quavered and her gaze dropped to her lap. I waited a few long moments and thought, fuck it. If I was Ryan, I'd be going out of my mind being three thousand miles away from my woman, and I'd want me to give her a shove in the right direction. Theresa and I were a team. If she was Max's cheerleading squad, then so was I.

"Exercising my observational and listening skills here. Ryan is the guy who gut-punched you emotionally." She nodded and I saw a tear running down her cheek.

Fuck. Women crying sent me around the corner. I was a fixer by nature, but there was no one-size-fits-all way to get a woman to stop crying. I was going with tough love. Max seemed the type who would respond to that.

"Max, look at me." I deep-voiced her. She raised her head and her red-rimmed eyes were heartbreaking. "I don't know Ryan, but I'm going to tell you how I'd feel if my woman was on the other side of the country keeping herself from me." She didn't tell me to shut up, so I kept talking. "I'd be crazy with worry, out of my mind with loss, and I'd have to talk myself out of doing something rash or stupid fifty times a day so I wouldn't scare her and lose her."

She huffed out a short one-note laugh. "That sounds about right." She took the paper towel she was using as a napkin to wipe her eyes and dab her nose. "He's like you. All *I'm in charge*, and *I've got this*." She mimicked a man's voice and pushed her arms out to the side to make herself look bigger. I nearly laughed at her acting, and her accurate assessment, but I kept silent. "He's a police chief."

"Probably is a lot like me then."

She nodded and started twisting the paper towel. "Do you mind if I ask you something?"

"We're family, Max. You can ask me anything." That got me a little smile.

"If you knew there was something in Theresa's past she hadn't shared with you, would you look into it anyway?"

Good god. Theresa and I started writing to each other through The Letter Club, and used fake names. The whole point was to be anonymous. After a few letters, I'd sussed out there was a trauma in her past and asked her about it. She'd shut down and didn't write to me for weeks. The minute I'd discovered a way to learn who she was, I took it. That was when I read about the shooting. "Absolutely."

Her lips got tight and she smacked the table with her palm. "That's a betrayal of her trust. Why would you do that?"

Ah. Ryan went digging into Max's past. I knew something big had happened when she was in college, but Theresa was vague and I didn't press. But I wasn't Max's man.

"I'm FBI. If there's an answer to be had, I find it. If the answer has something to do with the woman I love, I'd find it fast. I'd need to know if it's something I can fix or help her fix. If it's bogging her down, I'd want to provide her with ways to get rid of it so we could move on with our future. No betrayal of trust, an act of love."

Her expression read astonished, which she confirmed. "That's…that's…a convoluted justification."

"Perhaps to the person who's hiding something. But to the man who loves her who has the tools to learn what's she hiding, it's the best way he knows to help her." I saw her getting ready to shit-shoot me. I held up my hand. "Hear me out. Everyone's got secrets. I'm fine with Theresa keeping hers. But if her secret is hindering our happiness, then it's not her secret anymore, it's our problem. If she tells me what the problem is, we can work it out that much faster. Her ability to share it would be an act of faith, love, and courage." Max's head snapped back like I slapped her across the face. Tough love was *tough*. "If she keeps the secret hidden, then I'm going to do everything I can to find out what it is, confront her, and force her to hash it out with me until we get to that place where it's something we worked through."

She didn't look entirely convinced, but I had her thinking.

"There are no words to express how much I love Theresa. I would fight to keep us together with everything I have, and I'd use everything and anything I could do to make that so. Our love is worth fighting for. I'd never let something from her past keep us from being happy."

She balled up the paper towel and put it on the table. "It's great to know she's got that from you."

"Sounds like you have that from Ryan."

She leaned forward and glared at me.

When I met Ryan, he was going to get an earful on how I fought part of this battle for his ass.

"How is that possible when we've known each other for..." she stopped for a moment, "five weeks. And half that time I've been avoiding him."

Damn. She was really making him work for it. Theresa was right. Ryan was gone for Max. "Is there a timetable for when people fall in love?"

That shut her up. I waited while she worked out her next parry.

In a surprisingly quiet voice – she'd been half shouting at me – she asked, "How do you know it's real if it happens so fast?"

"How do you ever know it's real? Either you feel it, or you don't."

"Fuck. This shit hurts."

"Don't know him, but from this conversation, sounds like he's worth fighting for. That makes the pain worth it."

She shook her head and said in a whisper so low I almost couldn't hear her, "When he finds out I'm not worth it, he'll go and all I'll have left is pain."

Jesus. She was in deep with him too. I'd never seen anyone fight being in love with such conviction. *What the fuck does she think she did?* Theresa told me Max felt guilty for something that happened to someone else and Max held herself responsible when she wasn't. Like I said, vague.

I reached forward and wrapped my hand around Max's. She looked up, her face a map of fear and anguish. "Theresa loves you fiercely. That's how I know you're worth it."

She squeezed my hand, let go. Got up, unhooked her bag from the back of her chair, and went upstairs.

Ryan Trent owed me a case of Hudson Baby Bourbon Whiskey.

***

Theresa

The next morning, in the shower, Ethan told me about his conversation with Max. He deserved a medal for being so understanding, so I gave him head. As he fisted my hair and grunted his release, I thought I'd never figure out who enjoyed this more.

While he walked Boo, I made coffee and filled his go-cup. Leaning against the counter, we ate homemade peach muffins, then he began his morning departure routine by going upstairs and taking care of business one last time. When he came back downstairs, he bent me over his arm, leaned down, and kissed me breathless. His new addition to the routine, he laid his hand over my belly for a moment. Back on script, he said, "Love you, Flower. Don't forget to set the alarm," then left via the door behind the stairs that went to the garage.

He was out of the house by six forty-five every morning. I liked the quiet time before I left for my office at eight-thirty. Sometimes I threw in a load of laundry, sometimes I cooked or baked something for dinner, but mostly, I sat outside on the patio with Boo and read the morning paper online.

Today, I took my laptop and stood at the kitchen counter going through The Letter Club website. I remembered reading something they'd sent me about new delivery options: overnight, two-day, or four-day. Of course, it cost extra and was added to the annual membership fee, but after hearing what Max said last night, we didn't have weeks to bandy back and forth with snail mail. I needed to put a fire under her ass, and put my plan into hyperdrive.

Without her permission, I signed up Max using the Mendon house address, and I opted for overnight mail. Then I texted Ryan and told him I needed his home mailing address. With the time difference, I didn't expect to hear from him for hours. Two minutes later he gave me the cop answer:

"What for?"

"Why aren't you sleeping?"

"Actually, I was. I got a work-related call a few minutes before you texted."

His job really was twenty-four-seven.

"Answer to Q – to sign you up for The Letter Club. It's a two-way street. When you get a letter from Max, you HAVE TO respond. You'll want to respond. They have overnight delivery. Expect a letter by Friday. There's a 24 hr delay. They verify you've (I've) given a real street address, etc. I'll tell Max I signed you up, and I'll figure out a way to tell her how I got your street address."

He texted his address and asked:

"How is she?"

"She had a good day yesterday. She saw my folks for lunch, hung out with my sister's kids, and went to dinner with my sister, her husband, his sister and her man."

"Where is she now?"

"Sleeping. She's still on Cali time. I'll catch up with her at lunch."

"Thank you for this."

"Go back to sleep. I need you in top form."

"Copy that."

I was a straightforward person, but I enjoyed a little mischief now and then. According to Ethan, I had a wide mischief streak. Maybe he was right 'cause I was enjoying the hell out of being clandestine.

After I signed up Ryan for TLC, I went upstairs to get ready for work. I took my laptop with me even though everything was password protected, and I had a laptop at work. I didn't want to take any chances Max would see something she shouldn't. I took Boo out for a quick walk, put him in his crate, stuffed my laptop, phone, and chargers into my messenger bag, and headed out, knowing I'd be back at lunchtime. I came home every day for lunch to take Boo for a walk and to hang out with him a little while. I told Max she could let him out of his crate when she got up, but I had a feeling I'd be home about the same time she'd be hitting consciousness.

Sure enough, when I walked in the house at twelve-fifteen, Max was standing on the back patio staring at who knew what in her oversize nightshirt. Boo was looking up as if he was verifying she was alive. He heard me before she did and came running into the kitchen, tail wagging and tongue out. Max turned when she saw him take off.

"Still comatose?" I asked.

She mumbled, "Is it lunchtime already?"

"Yep. Set the table for us outside, get some tea, and have a muffin. I made them yesterday."

"'Kay," she said absently.

I knew better than to bring up TLC now. I had to prime her for my onslaught. Regale her with tales of family and the bliss of being in love. I made a big salad, advanced prep for this evening, and put a little on a plate along with a slice of mushroom quiche leftover from yesterday. Completely on autopilot, Max came in, took down one of

Ethan's FBI mugs, filled it with water, and put the mug in the microwave. She got a plate and put a muffin on it, took the mug out after the ding, and dropped a teabag in it, then she shuffled outside and plopped into a chair. She'd been like this since she was a child. Max and mornings were not compatible. After she ate, she'd reanimate.

When she'd finished her muffin and was sipping the last of her tea I said, "I need you to do a couple of favors for me today."

"Sure. What?"

"Stop at the garden center and ask for Irv. They're holding a ton of burlap for me to wrap around the plants so they won't get destroyed in the move. I spoke to them this morning and paid for everything. They're expecting you, and they'll load the burlap and string into your car. No worries."

"Sounds easy. What else?"

"The moving company guy didn't bring over enough boxes and tape. All that's paid for too. They said they'd have the order ready for pickup any time after one. Ten big boxes, two dozen medium boxes, and two sleeves of tape. There are four rolls in each sleeve. They're not in town. You have to go to Putnam, which is about thirty minutes away. Don't get on the highway. The back roads are better, and the movers are off Route twenty-one just before you get to Putnam. I'll email directions to you. An incentive, there's a Dunkin' in Putnam."

Her eyes lit up. "Hot damn. I'll go there first."

"I figured." She grinned. "I expect to be home by five, the latest. We'll have time to do some more packing. I made salad already, and the lasagna is defrosting in the fridge. We'll pop it in the oven when I get home, and we'll use a baguette to make garlic bread. The lasagna will be ready by the time Ethan gets home a little after seven."

"That's late." I couldn't tell her Ryan would be out all hours of the night, but I knew that was in her future.

"That's traffic. If he leaves the office around five forty-five, he's home by seven-fifteen, seven-thirty. If he leaves the office at five, he's home by seven-thirty."

She leaned over and broke off a piece of my quiche. "I'm guessing he leaves at five forty-five."

“Yep. His commute will be seriously better when we’re in Mendon.”

“God, this is good. Is there more?”

“In the fridge.”

As she was getting up to go into the kitchen she said, “But you’ll have to commute, which you don’t have to now.”

“Twenty-five minutes on back roads. NBD,” I called out.

“What about Boo?” she asked as she came back with the glass pie dish with the two remaining slices of quiche.

“We’re fencing a half acre for him, and Ethan’s building him a doghouse big enough for two. We’re going to the shelter and getting him a friend.”

“Geez,” she said around a mouthful of quiche, “you’re taking on so much.”

“No. We’re starting our life in a house we’ll live in until we die. We’re going to raise our kids there and do all the things your parents and mine did for us growing up. I’m excited for each new thing, and I can’t wait to get into the house and start.”

She pointed her fork at my stomach. “That reminds me. Didn’t you tell me you guys were going to wait a couple of years to have kids?”

“I wanted to start right away, but Ethan said he wanted us to have alone time. I was okay with waiting, but it meant I couldn’t spread out the pregnancies as much as I wanted.”

Her eyes got wide. “How many kids are you going to have?”

I laughed. “Don’t look so horrified. You told me you want four kids. I’m only going for three.”

“Well,” she smirked, “I’m younger than you.” That right there told me all I needed to know. Max might be scared shitless, but she wanted what I wanted. We’d talked about it since we were preteens. All this moving and setting up house chatter was priming the pump for what I was going to lay on her when I came home from work.

“By two whole years.” I acted offended.

“Okay. Don’t whine.” Her fork was poised to stuff more quiche in her mouth. “What changed? Why aren’t you waiting?”

“A couple of weeks after Ethan returned to work, his colleague’s wife was told it was likely she wouldn’t ever have kids because she was going through early menopause. She’s thirty-seven. Ethan got freaked and reversed his thinking. He had a great childhood, and he's looking forward to having kids. He didn't want to take a chance on losing the opportunity." I put my hand on my belly. "Worked for me, and I gotta say, I enjoy all the trying."

"Slut."

"I'd wear the t-shirt proudly."

We laughed, she volunteered to clean up, I emailed directions to the garden center and to the moving company, and then I went back to work.

At a quarter to five, I opened the door to my town house, and walked into a rock concert. Max was blasting music while emptying the bookcase in the living room. I neutralized the alarm, then re-set it, then went to the dock in the living room – Max hadn't heard me – and lowered the volume.

She jumped and turned around at the same time. "Damn, Ter, you scared the shit out of me."

"Sorry, I didn't think I could shout over…"

"The Glorious Sons."

"Right. Them."

She laughed. "There's a box of Dunkin' on the kitchen counter. I felt the need to share in my craving."

"An equal opportunity addict. Nice." She curtsied. "Does Boo need to go out?"

"Nope. Full on Frisbee in the park for a half hour. He's good."

"Thanks." I bent down to give him a full body rub. "I'm going up to change. I'll be down in a few minutes."

"Oh, about ten minutes ago, I put the lasagna in the oven on three-fifty."

"You left the foil on?"

"Puh-leaze. Did we have the same *nonna*?"

"Right."

I went upstairs, pulled out my phone from the messenger bag, stowed it under the bed, and hit the bathroom. Then I changed into a slouchy tee and yoga pants. With phone in hand, I headed downstairs to put a fire under Max's ass.

Chapter Sixteen

Ambush
Max

It'd been about five years since I moved into my condo, but I remembered packing maxims. Don't fill a box with all books. Too heavy. Half books, half something soft, like pillows or towels. I was putting a pillow from the side chair on top of the books I'd packed when Theresa came downstairs.

"You put this in the log yet?" she asked.

"Yeah." I taped up the box and carried it to the stack in the corner.

"Don't do that. The moving guys will do that. Between now and Saturday morning, there's no point rearranging boxes." She grabbed my hand and pulled me onto the sofa. Damn. For a bitty thing, she was damn strong. "Talk to me. Please."

"Ethan told you about last night."

She nodded. "He did."

"Thank you for not telling him about –"

"Not my story to tell. As for how you feel about what happened, I could talk myself blue in the face and you wouldn't believe me." I dropped my head. All day long I'd been replaying my conversation with Ethan, trying to sort out how I felt about what he said. "Tell me," Theresa urged. "Why'd you run away from Ryan?"

"He went behind my back and had a cop in the Berkeley PD dig out the case. I don't know how Ryan found out something happened ten years ago, but once he had a timeframe, and I guess he knew where I went to school, that's no secret, he found a way to get answers I didn't want to give him."

"Ethan said he explained how from Ryan's point of view it wasn't a betrayal."

"Yeah. The thing he said that's sitting on my chest is how my secret is our problem." I hated that tears were rolling down my cheeks, but I couldn't stop them. "I didn't want to be an us. Every time I sent him away, he came back. Bossy, pushy, and fuckin' relentless."

Theresa got up and came back a moment later with a tissue box. I took it and blew my nose and wiped my cheeks.

"I have no worries you can handle bossy and pushy. You push back all the time. I bet he likes your ferocity."

In spite of myself I laughed. "He eats it up." She smiled. "Thursday, I lost it after his press conference. One of his cops fucked up." Her brows went up. I took my phone out of my back pocket and found a video of Ryan's press conference. "Here."

Theresa watched for a couple of minutes and handed the phone back to me. "If I didn't have Ethan, I'd chase Ryan until I caught him. He's fiiiine."

"You know how hard it is to yell at him when he looks like that?"

"I have some idea," she said, laughing. "Why'd you lose it after the press conference?"

"This is going to sound so stupid." I sighed. Knowing she'd sit there quietly and wait until I told her, I gave over and said, "All the staff and clients watched the press conference. When Bernadette turned off the TV, the women started saying shit about how commanding he was, and how handsome. One of them said she'd have ten of his children, and, no lie, I saw red. I thought, if anyone is going to have his children it's going to be me."

She grinned.

I got up and started pacing in front of the couch. "I didn't want to fall in love with him. When it hit me how deep I'd fallen, I ran out of the spa and wound up sitting at the top of Cottonwood Street for hours in the dark. A cop found me, and Ryan came and got me a few minutes later. He took care of me. He was sweet and gentle. He loves me. I did everything I could to chase him away."

"Why?"

"Because when he finds out what I did, he'll hate me and leave," I shouted.

Theresa snagged my arm and pulled me down onto the sofa. "Bullshit."

"He's a cop."

"And?"

"He'll know what happened to Lindsey was my fault."

"Goddammit, Max. It wasn't your fault." She tugged on my hand. "You didn't rape her. You didn't kill Artie, and you didn't commit suicide."

"But I got her drunk, then Artie and I left. She was alone. No one was there to protect her from those animals," I screamed.

"Did you hold her down and pour the drinks down her throat?"

I glared at her. "No, but I was drinking right along with her. We were smashed."

"Such an unusual thing to happen at a frat party." I didn't appreciate the sarcasm. "You told me you and Artie tried to get her to leave with you and she fought with you."

The tears threatened and I was back there in the hallway yanking on Lindsey's hand trying to drag her out the door with me. "She wouldn't listen. I begged her to go back to the dorm, but she pulled away and went back to the party."

"And Artie followed her and tried to get her to leave. Again."

"You know all this, Ter."

"So the fuck do you."

"Some friend. I left her there cuz I wanted to go back to my dorm room and fuck Artie."

"Another unusual occurrence for a nineteen-year-old college student."

"Okay," I shouted. "Let's pretend I absolved myself for passing out and not going back to the frat with Artie. Let's pretend I absolved myself for not being able to talk my boyfriend out of wanting to die because he didn't take care of his TWIN SISTER." Theresa held my gaze, fierce as ever, willing me to get to the nub of it. "I lied to the cops."

"How?"

"I didn't tell them Lindsey was my friend. I didn't tell them we got drunk together. I didn't tell them Artie and I tried to get her to leave and she wouldn't. I didn't tell them I was her brother's girlfriend. I didn't tell them we left the party together, and she was there alone."

"Would them knowing any of that have changed the outcome of their investigation?"

"That's a chickenshit way to look at it."

"For the love of god, how?"

I couldn't take this anymore. I'd replayed all of it over and over and over for ten years and I always came to the same conclusion. I felt sick, and I wanted this done. "Because if I'd told them, they would've known none of it would've happened if I'd dragged Lindsey out of that frat, even if I had to carry her."

"I've got a newsflash for your ass, Max. Those predators would've found another girl to rape that night. Were you supposed to save her too? Would it have made a difference if she wasn't your friend? Would it have been okay she was the victim because she wasn't your boyfriend's sister?"

"No," I screamed, "but at least Lindsey and Artie would be alive today."

"Artie, probably. Lindsey, no."

"What?"

"You told me a lot of Lindsey stories before that night. She wasn't stable. I can't say with certainty, but it sounds like she suffered from bipolar disorder, and I'm sure she was clinically depressed. Had she gotten help she might have made it. But along with your Lindsey stories were Artie's stories about their parents. They were absent from their children's lives, and they threw money at problems, not attention. If they hadn't seen what a disaster their daughter was before she went to college, they sure as hell didn't see it when she was in college. My guess, Lindsey would've committed suicide before she graduated. She was a mess, Max, and only professional help could've saved her."

"Is that supposed to make me feel better?"

"No, my sweet, sensitive, darling cousin. It's supposed to make you realize you can't control other people's choices."

I laid my head on Theresa's lap while she stroked my hair. She used to do this every year at the end of the summer the night before she had to go back home. Between summers, I always felt a little lost without her.

"How is it I've got seven inches and about sixty pounds on you, and you're the tough one?"

"Little dogs are always scrappier. We have to be." She kept stroking, her little hand a light and soothing weight on my head.

I knew all this emotional upheaval was part of the march to Theresa's goal post. "Okay, Ter. Bottom line me."

"I signed you and Ryan up for The Letter Club. They have overnight mail now, and you two have to talk. Unless you don't want to talk to him ever again."

"Jesus. You don't cut a girl a break."

"Option one. You go back home and let him know he's out of your life, and eventually he moves on and finds someone else and they get married and have kids." That felt as good as being stabbed in the heart with a serrated-edge knife. "Option two. You stay here for a while, get a license to cut hair and hang out with the East Coast fam. Maybe you look into getting your PhD. We have two Ivy League schools within driving distance. Ryan moves on with his life, finds someone else, they get married and have kids." And she keeps on stabbing. "Option three. You trust his love and you lay it all out on the table. If he bolts, fuck him. He didn't deserve you. If he's the man I think he is, he'll understand and be supportive. He marries you, you have your four kids, and visit the East Coast fam frequently."

I sat up. "You're brutal."

"And you're not a coward. You found him, Max. The one. You know how many people find the one? Maybe twenty percent, and I'm probably being generous. Most people settle. Some have happy, healthy marriages, but their love is a warm glow, not a blazing fire."

She took my hand, squeezed, and continued, "When I was sitting with fifty cops waiting for Ethan to come out of surgery, I decided I'd never hold anything back from him. If I'm pissed, he'll hear about it. If we disagree, we'll fight it out until we get through it. If I'm horny, I'll jump him. I was so scared I was going to lose him ten minutes after I found him, I swore to myself that we were going to live our lives out loud and to the fullest." She touched her chest. Something she did unconsciously since the shooting when her emotions were close to the surface. "I almost died. I'm alive, in love, pregnant, moving into a new house, rescuing another dog, and getting married. Life's short and precarious. Don't survive it, jump in with both feet and truly live it."

Boo got up from his bed and stood in front of Theresa and stared at her. "He has to go out, doesn't he?"

"Yep." She put her hand on my cheek. "You want to call him?"

I shook my head. "I'll do The Letter Club thing. This way if he bails, I won't have to hear him say it, and I won't make a fool of myself on the phone."

"Take Boo out, and I'll set the table. When you come back in, while we're making the garlic bread, I'll tell you how TLC works. Tonight you'll write him a letter, and tomorrow I'll take it to the office and put it in the overnight mail. Deal?"

I opened my arms and she came in for the hug. "Deal," I whispered into her ear. We separated, and I snapped my fingers. "C'mon, Boo. You and I are going for a walk."

***

Theresa

Ethan loved everything I cooked. After he'd recovered enough to go out, he'd come to three of my cooking club dinners. After every one, he'd said, "They don't cook as well as you." Taste buds blinded by love, but I'd take it.

After dinner – there were two servings of lasagna left – and a dessert of assorted donuts – did we eat enough carbs tonight? – we cleaned up and left Max sitting in front of her laptop at the dining room table.

Now, we were leaning against the headboard, legs tangled on top of the covers, catching up on last season's episodes of *Endeavour*. We shared a love for British detective procedurals. When episode two ended, Ethan shut off the TV. "How'd it go today?"

"Rough, but we got there. The big plan is I signed her and Ryan up for TLC. They have to communicate, and writing letters is intimate but remote. I thought she'd need that. He texted me his home address. The man's all in. Whatever it takes to get Max back to him. She doesn't want to talk to him until she's sure he won't bail, which is what I figured, so she said she'd write to him. That's what she was doing on her laptop. Writing his letter. TLC has an overnight mail option now. After they do their twenty-four-hour verification, Ryan should have her letter by Friday."

"Huh. I wouldn't've wanted that in the beginning. I liked the anticipation of getting your letters, and I needed the time to process I was falling in love with a woman I didn't know, and had never met. For a while, I worried you didn't feel the same way."

I stretched up and kissed his cheek. "I get that." I smiled. My man had a soft heart. "Their situation is different."

"Undoubtedly. She okay?"

I put my hand out and flipped it palm up, palm down a couple of times. "A little shaky, but better than she had been. It's a leap into the unknown for her. Your talk last night made a real impression and helped her come to terms with Ryan's motivations. Have I thanked you for that?"

He grinned. "I seem to recall something transpiring in the shower this morning, but I might need to be reminded."

I took my time reminding him, and he took his time reminding me how I got pregnant.

The next morning, as Ethan was watching a video of Ryan's press conference on his iPad, I picked up an envelope addressed to TLC that had been leaning against the white ceramic cannister that held the multicolored spatulas.

Chapter Seventeen

Deep
Ryan

The mail was delivered around eleven am, and overnight envelopes and packages were left with the guard at the front desk. I didn't know if the overnight mail came in with the regular mail, or was delivered at a different time. I'd never thought about mail delivery before in my life. Today I was consumed with it.

Even though work had been busy, Tuesday through Friday was time slogging through quicksand. After Theresa told me Max was in love me, I was able to get past the maudlin, and I was sleeping in my bed about five hours a night, but no, I hadn't changed the sheets. The call at four Tuesday morning had me out of bed and heading to the hospital. One of my officers was sideswiped by a semitruck. The driver, a long-hauler, had fallen asleep at the wheel. My officer suffered a few fractured ribs, a concussion, and a broken wrist. The truck driver had a broken arm and a concussion. Given the state of the vehicles, they got off easy.

Camille came back to work on Wednesday, closed the bids, and spent Wednesday and Thursday doing her due diligence. Thursday, before she left to go home, she gave me her selection, the firm from Sacramento, which was owned by a retired FBI agent who'd worked out of the Roseville office. I wondered if Ethan knew the guy. The firm had six investigators, three former FBI agents, two retired cops from Sacramento PD, and one retired cop from the Davis PD. In the bid, the firm stated the woman from Davis was available for an immediate investigation. I signed the necessary paperwork and put it on Camille's desk. I figured shit would be good and stirred up by Monday.

As a courtesy, and mostly to keep him off my ass, I called the mayor and told him we expected the investigation to begin on Monday. I didn't share any details, which caused a few stutters in the conversation, but overall he seemed mollified.

I'd had my Friday morning staff meeting with Camille, my two commanders, and four lieutenants. Of the many things I liked about being the chief of a smaller workforce, knowing my command staff personally was high on the list. While the meetings were informal by LAPD standards, the quality of the work had improved under my guidance and had gone from good to superior. We were tightening up the slack, smoothing out the rough edges, and communication had improved tenfold.

Camille hung back after the rest of the team left. "Within an hour of sending the email telling the firm they got the bid, I received a call from the investigator, Eden O'Farrell. She'll be here in a couple of hours. Do you want to meet her?"

I planned to head home to check the mail. Two hours would put O'Farrell here at one. "Why don't you bring her by when she's on her way out. A quick hello."

"Got it, Chief." She left the conference room, and I followed, heading to my office to get my jacket and keys.

All the regular mail had been delivered, but the overnight hadn't. The guard told me way more than I needed to know about the different delivery times, but it seemed the bulk of the overnight envelopes arrived between three and four. I went upstairs and made myself a bowl of pasta, and added pesto sauce. The daily extended workouts had me hungrier than usual, and I found myself carb-ing up at lunch. I couldn't help the stray thought, but I prayed by next week I'd be enjoying a different kind of workout. I had to forcibly push the image of Max underneath me out of my head. I'd jacked off so many times since she'd left, I was on my way to carpel tunnel syndrome.

Back at the office, I was reading end of week reports when Camille knocked on my door. "Got a minute, Chief?"

I waved her in, and behind her was a middle-aged good-looking woman of average height and weight wearing a dark blue pant suit over a light blue blouse. She wore minimal jewelry, and her blonde hair was pulled back into a bun. She had clear blue eyes, and an attractive face relatively free of makeup. A cop's cop if I ever saw one. She stuck out her hand and said, "Eden O'Farrell. Pleasure to meet you, Chief." We shook quickly. She put that same hand in her jacket pocket and took out a business card, which she proffered and I accepted.

I knew she'd retired from the Davis PD as a lieutenant, had a good reputation, and was well regarded by the cops who'd worked under her. I did my due diligence too. "Miss all this?" I tilted my head toward the offices down the hall from mine.

"Occasionally. But I find this work fascinating and varied."

"You have any questions, or need anything, let Assistant Chief Radcliffe know. Nice to meet you."

"You too, Chief." O'Farrell and Camille left.

I hoped our investigator did her job meticulously. We needed a capable, insightful person whose investigation would be beyond reproach.

I left the office at four and headed home.

***

Ryan,

I suppose one of the reasons I put up with Ziggy is because I see a little of myself in her. Not the violence or self-destructive behavior, but the joie de vivre and insouciance, both of which I lost on a night I'm sure you now know about. Well, the salient facts. This is the whole story:

I met Lindsey Wentworth in a sociology class at the beginning of my sophomore year. She was hilarious. Off-the-wall humor and a wild outlook on life. We lived in the same dorm and became fast friends. A couple of weeks after we started hanging out, her twin brother, Arturo – everyone called him Artie – stopped by her room and we all went out for dinner. After that, Artie and I started seeing each other. The three of us were together a lot, but not all the time. I had other friends, and so did Artie, who lived in "that" frat house. At first I thought Lindsey was a loner, but over time I realized she did strange things and she didn't think they were odd. Like sitting outside late at night in her shorts and a t-shirt cross-legged on the grass with her laptop working on a paper. Artie and I had been out clubbing, came back to the dorm, and saw her typing away furiously. I freaked because she was alone in the dark so late at night, and she wasn't dressed for the cold weather, but Artie seemed to take it in stride and knew how to coax her back into the dorm. Theresa thinks Lindsey was bipolar and suffered from clinical depression. I'm no shrink, but something was wrong with Lindsey, that's for sure.

After the night we found Lindsey in the dark, Artie started telling me stories about how their parents hardly saw them. When they were little, they had a nanny who cooked their meals, took them to school, helped with their homework – all the things parents should do. The family had holidays together, and went on one family vacation a year to places like Gstaad. The parents would hang out with Lindsey and Artie for a couple of hours then the nanny would take over. They had dinner separate from the parents, and the nanny put them to bed and slept in a room adjacent to theirs. Their parents had their own suite on another floor. When Lindsey and Artie went to high school – all their schools were elite private schools –the nanny kept an eye on them, chauffeured them to school until they got their own cars, and the housekeeper made all their meals. I often wonder if those parents look back on their disaffection and neglect and hate themselves for it.

On the night of the frat party, Lindsey and I had been drinking way more than usual. We'd started in the dorm and continued at the party. We danced, laughed, and were having a good time until Lindsey got out of control. Artie and I wanted to go back to my room, and we agreed we had to get Lindsey to come back to the dorm so she could crash and sleep it off. We had the hugest fight in the frat house front hallway. I was tugging on Lindsey's arm, my hand in hers, literally dragging her toward the door. She was shouting all sorts of terrible things at me, but I knew she was drunk. I did everything I could to get her to come with me. The whole time, Artie was standing behind me using his coaxing voice to try to get her to leave with us.

She broke out of my hold and ran back into the party and got swallowed up in the crowd. Artie went after and I stayed in the hallway. He was gone for a while. I was still pretty sloshed and don't remember how much time went by, but it'd been enough for me to sit on the steps while I waited for him. When he came back, he didn't have Lindsey, but he had a red hand mark on his cheek. She'd slapped him hard and refused to come back to the dorm. I don't know if the alcohol made whatever was wrong with her worse, but

Artie always had been able to get her to do what he asked her to do. Not that night.

We left. She was alone. No one to look out for her, no one to protect her. If I live to be two hundred, I'll never forgive myself.

Artie and I went back to my dorm room. Later, I learned, he left when I passed out. He wanted to check on Lindsey. When he got back to the frat house, he looked for her and found her. I'm sure you know the rest of what happened that night.

The next morning, really early, a cop banged on my door and woke me. He told me what happened. Then he asked me a bunch of questions about the party, and if any guys were hitting on Lindsey and that kind of thing. I told him she'd been drinking, and didn't want to leave, but otherwise everything was fine when I left, and that I didn't return to the party, that I'd come back to the dorm and fell asleep. I didn't tell him Lindsey was my friend, her brother was my boyfriend, and that she'd fought us when we tried to get her to leave. I didn't tell him Artie and I had been together in my room while Lindsey was alone at the party.

You're a cop. I knew if I told you all this, you'd be disgusted with me, and you should be. I'm disgusted with myself. Nothing I shared with the cop was a lie, and nothing I should have told him would've made a difference in what happened with the case. But I abandoned Lindsey literally and figuratively, and I cut Artie out of the picture entirely. I'm ashamed of myself. That morning I learned I'm not a good person.

Artie came by the next day and we cried together. He kept saying it was his fault. He was responsible for his sister and he failed her. When he told the cops he'd left for a little while, he never said where he went, and, apparently, they never asked. As the days went on, he told me he wanted to die. He couldn't face himself for abandoning her. Lindsey never came back to Cal, and Artie dropped out about a week after the last time I saw him. We talked on the phone a few times. In each conversation, he was worse than the one before. He told me he couldn't see a way to make things better. I never called anyone to share how despondent he was, not even Theresa – well, not until after.

I know in my heart, Artie told Lindsey to kill him. By then, I'm sure he felt it was the penance he deserved at her hand. She killed herself for obvious reasons, not the least of which was she couldn't go on without Artie.

If it wasn't for Theresa, I don't know how I would have made it. She helped me find a therapist, and I saw the therapist the whole time I was at Cal, except for the summers when I went home. The shrink was kind, and she really helped me keep it together. The week before I graduated was the last time I saw her. She said I had the "tools" to cope, move on, and heal. I guess my tools are rusty.

My parents don't know what happened. Only Theresa and Lola know – and I figure Will since Lola tells him everything. And now you.

I graduated with a degree in anthropology, and had been accepted into Cal's PhD program, but I couldn't do it. I needed to be home near family, but I didn't want to work in the vineyard or the winery. I decided to go to beauty school and got my license. I worked in a couple of places before I moved over to Shangri-la Spa five years ago.

I understand now why you went digging into my past. You have Ethan to thank for that. More importantly, I'll understand if you don't want to see me or talk to me. I won't be angry with you, and you don't have to worry about me anymore.

Thank you for being so good to me last Thursday night, I'll never forget it.

Be happy.

Max

In my whole life, I never cried as hard and for so long as I did when I finished reading that letter. My sweet, precious Max. My heart physically hurt for hours.

***

By the time I pulled myself together, had a cup of coffee, and answered a few work-related texts, it was nearly six. I wondered if nine pm was too late to call Theresa. The worst that could happen was I'd get voice mail.

Three rings, then a deep-voiced man answered the phone. "Trent?"

Ethan. "Hey, man. Hope it's not too late."

"Nah. We're in bed watching TV."

"Well, shit."

He chuckled. "No, really. We're moving into our new house tomorrow and we're resting up for the big day."

"Congrats. I hope the move goes well. Always a pain in the ass."

"Ain't that the truth. You wanna talk to Ter."

"Yeah."

I heard the phone transfer and then Theresa's throaty voice. Seemed the Calapiano women had that in common. "Ryan. What's up?"

"Before I start, how is she?"

"Tired. We conscripted her to help us pack for our big move tomorrow. We have a new house."

"I heard. Great news. Really, she okay otherwise?"

"Yep. Really. I've kept her busy."

"Good. Good. Listen, she told me everything. I can't respond to all that in a letter. I want her to see me when I tell her what I have to say."

The smile in Theresa's voice was unmistakable. "I understand. Write enough to hold her until Wednesday. You're welcome to stay at the house, but I'm guessing you'll want privacy, so I'll book you into the hotel where we reserved a block of rooms for the wedding. That work for you?"

"Wedding?"

"Ethan told you about the move but not the wedding." She must've held the phone away from her face. I heard a muffled "Niiice," and Ethan chuckling. Her voice was clear when she said, "We're getting married in the backyard of our new house next weekend. I expect to see you at the wedding."

"I'll be there." I rubbed my face. "Okay. I'll write something, and get everything in order on this end. I'll come to the house on Wednesday after I check in. Text me the addresses."

"Will do. And, Ryan."

"Yeah?"

"Thank you for being the man I thought you were."

I shook my head. "See ya Wednesday, Ter."

Two minutes later I had the addresses I needed. I got out my laptop and made plane reservations. Then I stared at the blank white screen and tried to put together the right words in my head.

Chapter Eighteen

Muscle
Max

Moving sucked. We'd packed up the kitchen on Thursday, along with the linen closet and the remaining household items in the garage. There was nothing to eat. The fridge and freezer were empty and their doors were open. We ordered in salads, a large pizza, and a couple of calzones. Ethan was a big guy, and he ate like one. He looked to be six-two. Ryan was taller, and they had about the same build, but Ethan was broader, wider in the chest. Ryan was sculpted and defined. A surfer's body.

Annnd here I was thinking about Ryan's body. Again. I had no idea why since he was going to get that letter tomorrow and after he read it, he'd be saying *adios* to any future we might've had. It was for the best. I was aunt material. Lola was a couple of weeks away from popping, and I yearned to be conscripted into babysitting. Theresa wouldn't be coming to California in January. Her baby was due January fifth. I figured I'd come back east after Christmas and would be here for the birth and hang around for a week or so to help out. Not that Laurie and Aunt Connie wouldn't be at the house every day, but I figured, it takes a village.

Within months, I'd have two kids who I'd love and I'd get to spoil. That'd fill the baby gaps.

No, I wasn't going to dwell on the thought of Ryan and my kids. I limited my mental and emotional self-flagellation to specific past events. No need to expand my repertoire.

After we ate, we all walked to the park and Theresa and I watched Ethan play Frisbee with Boo. "He's a good guy," I told her, as if it were a surprise. I mean, geesh, she was pregnant and marrying him. "He's going to be a great dad."

"I know." She sighed. "We've Skyped with his folks every Sunday for the past six months. They're the nicest people. Ethan's like his dad. Steady and even-keeled. Mr. Berenikoff has all the patience in the world. He needs it. Mrs. Berenikoff is a force of nature."

"I'd hoped you'd get an easy new last name. No such luck."

She laughed. "Everyone in the little town where they live calls them Mr. and Mrs. B."

"Saves time. Where's he from again?"

"Oregon, mid-state, but he lived in Portland for about twelve years when he worked for their PD."

Before I could ask another Ethan question, my phone rang. "Mom," I told Theresa. "Hiya, Mom." I put her on FaceTime. "I'm here in Connecticut with Theresa." I turned the phone to Theresa.

"Oh, fantastic. Hi, honey." Mom waved. "You look great. How are you? Excited about the wedding?"

"Hi, Aunt Merrie. You look great too. I'm sure Max prays she got all your beauty genes."

Mom gave a movie star smile. "I'm going to have to buy you a bigger present."

We laughed. "Yep. I'm excited," Theresa told Mom. "But for the next couple of days, we're focused on moving. Max has been a huge help. A cleaning service will be over at the new house tomorrow. We'll be out of the town house on Saturday, the cleaning service is coming to the town house on Sunday, and the new owners are moving in on Monday."

"So much going on. I can't wait to see the new house."

"It's awesome," Theresa said. "It has a real conservatory."

"Oh, how lovely. Listen, honey, I don't want to keep you girls, but I wanted to let Max know that Dad and I will be there Friday afternoon with enough time to get ready for the rehearsal dinner. Our plane lands in Boston around five on Thursday, and we're spending the night. We thought to have dinner out, then walk around a little, take in the city. Then we'll do the same for breakfast. We'll leave Boston around noon on Friday and head over your way."

"Okay. Call me after you check in so we know you got in okay."

"Will do, sweetie. Can't wait to see you, Ter. I'm so happy for you."

"Hang on, Aunt Merrie." Theresa ran to get Ethan.

While he clicked Boo's leash to his halter, and they walked back to me, Mom told me Dad bought a new suit for the wedding, which was code for she made him buy a new suit and he didn't want to, but he did it anyway to shut her up.

I handed the phone to Theresa. "Aunt Merrie, this is Ethan. Ethan, this is Max's mom, my Aunt Merrie."

"Oh my," Mom gushed. "Look at those eyes."

We all laughed.

"Nice to meet you, ma'am."

"No ma'am. Aunt Merrie. I was just telling the girls our plans. Dominic and I will see you a week from tomorrow."

"Can't wait, Aunt Merrie."

Mom's smile surpassed movie star. She was smitten. Within the next hour, my sister Donna, our Aunt Asta, our Aunt Gwyn, and Lola would know all about Ethan's good looks, and how polite he was. "Bye. See you soon."

I put the phone in my back pocket. "I have two words to prepare you for our family."

"Hit me," Ethan said.

"We're Italian."

***

Friday was spent wrapping the plants. There were more of those suckers on that little patio than expected. Like they were an optical illusion, I'd get a row done, and another popped up out of nowhere. Theresa wanted to dig up the lilacs and use quick-set concrete to seal the hole, but Ethan put the ixnay on that.

"Who gives a fuck. The house is sold. If the new owners don't like 'em, they'll deal with it. You can plant all the lilacs you want at our house." He raised his brows. "We good?"

She grinned. "We're good."

Theresa was going to be well looked after the rest of her life. Ethan was a *really* good guy.

After we wrapped the plants, including the ones on the front stoop, Ethan went into the attic to do a last check while Theresa and

I went through the rest of the house looking for anything we might've missed. Only our personal electronics, a few towels, our toiletries, and the bedding were left. We saved a big box for the soft stuff, and I had my big piece of luggage where we'd stuff in the toiletries.

Ethan came downstairs and said, "The attic's all clear. I'm going to look in the garage one last time. After that, we'll get some lunch, and go over to the house to make sure the cleaning service got everything we wanted done, done, before they leave at five."

"Good, 'cause I'm starving." Theresa rubbed her belly.

"Asian?" Ethan asked.

"Vietnamese," she answered.

He nodded and went to the garage.

"You're turning him into a foodie," I said.

"It isn't a long trip. He loves to eat, and he likes trying new flavors. Apparently, his mom is a good cook, but it's mostly traditional food. You know, meatloaf and stuff like that. His exposure to other cultures' cuisine didn't start until he lived in Portland."

"Now that you'll be closer to Boston, you guys will have lots more choices."

She rubbed her hands together. "I can hardly wait."

When each of us made a last visit to the *baño*, I checked my phone again. Not that I thought Ryan would call or text, and I would've heard that anyway, but I wanted to check the time. Only ten in the morning in California. Too early for overnight mail to've arrived. Damn. I wanted to know the end was the end so I could adjust my thinking accordingly. I was going to be stuck between selecting Theresa's options one or two. I loved being with her, but she and Ethan needed newly married alone time. Plus, they had a house to get in shape and a kid on the way. Option two was out. My life was back in Redwood Falls. I'd have to suck-it-up-buttercup and find ways to avoid Ryan.

I had the advantage there. I worked on the other side of town from city hall, I had no reason to go to the police department, and I was going to be neck-deep in Auntie Max duty with Lola's kid. They hadn't wanted to know the sex. It didn't make a difference to me, and I knew they'd be thrilled either way.

If I had a hankering for Mandarin Paradise, I'd get takeout. If I wanted great Italian food, and I didn't want to cook it, I could go to my parents' house for dinner. Meredith Calapiano, nee Sorrentino, was a *maestra* in the kitchen. Her people were from Napoli, and their food dated back to Greco-Roman times. Her *pasta e fagioli* was a work of art, and her *spaghetti alle vongole* put me in the best kind of food coma. Don't get me started on her desserts. If I wanted to get foodventurous, I'd go to Santa Rosa. I could always stay at my Aunt Gwyn and Uncle Ren's or Aunt Asta and Uncle Stefano's. Well, maybe not Aunt Asta's if Ziggy lived there.

"Max?" Theresa yelled. "You fall in?"

I was so busy laying out my return home avoidance plan, I forgot I was standing at the sink and was supposed to wash my hands. "Coming," I shouted.

***

Ho-lee shit. Their house was unbelievably fantastic. Boo thought so too. He bounced on the seat next to me, then threw his head out the window and started whining. We were riding in Ethan's man-size SUV. Boo had plenty of room to express his delight. Ethan was right about the house. There were a lot of cosmetic things that needed to be done, and the kitchen and bathrooms needed updating. But Theresa was more right.

As we drove up, I saw a wide front porch with thick white columns. A place where their family could sit in comfort and shade and watch the world go by. The rooms were large and airy, and the layout had flow. Good *feng shui*. I'd buy the house for the conservatory alone. Multipaned windows with an angled glass ceiling, this place looked like something out of an old English manor. There were mature trees far enough from the house that Ethan wouldn't worry they'd cave in the roof if they fell, but they were close enough to shade a large part of property. When Theresa had told me Ethan was going to build her a greenhouse, that she was going to fence in a half acre for Boo and his new friend, and that she was going to put in a large circle of pavers and create an outdoor dining room and kitchen, I thought that was a lot to ask of a backyard. Not this place. Everything she envisioned would look amazing.

Of course, most of it would take years, except the fencing and the doghouse, but still, to have all that room to create a livable outdoor space was divine.

She came outside with Boo, whose tongue was hanging out of his mouth, his doggie face broadcasting glee. She stood next to me and asked, "What do you think?"

"It's totally you and absolutely perfect." She came in for a hug and we swayed. "Show me where everything's going to be for the wedding."

We walked off where the tent was going, which would be past the seating for the ceremony – the chairs would be brought to the tables inside the tent afterward – and on which side of the tent the buffet would be laid, and where the dance floor would be. The wedding was going to be spectacular.

Theresa had gotten her dress a few days before I arrived – I was sorry I hadn't been there with her when she picked it out, but Laurie and Aunt Connie were with her – and the shop was holding it until after the move was done. We were supposed to go into Boston to pick it up on Wednesday.

Ethan came out back and said, "They did a good job."

"Marguerite said they were the best."

Ethan's brows dropped at Theresa's statement. "Marguerite gets a kickback from all the businesses she refers to her clients."

Theresa laid her hand on his chest and it looked so small against his big body, but I swear, the moment she touched him, his brows came up and his face relaxed. "You know," she cooed, "not everyone is a criminal."

"Point taken," he answered as he wrapped his arms around her.

I walked away and gave them their moment. Actually, I walked away because it hurt to watch them. They were what love looked like. I wondered, if when Ryan and I were dancing we'd been filmed, would I say we were what love looked like. No matter what happened after he read my letter, those two hours will remain embedded in my heart. I'd always be able to conjure those feelings. In my mind's eye, I'd always be able to see *us*.

I was leaning on a porch column when Ethan and Theresa came around to the front of the house. For a moment they didn't see me, and I watched them have a whole conversation with their eyes as they walked with their hands linked.

They'd found that elusive intangible thing that bound people together. More than love, their connection that was soul deep. In equal measure, I was thrilled for Theresa as I was envious.

***

Saturday was organized chaos. I woke knowing Ryan had received my letter, and I got that feeling in my stomach. You know, the sinking, dropping-into-a-hole sensation when something bad happened. I was past nauseous. I was hollow.

But my cuz was moving to her new house so I roused myself at the ungodly hour of seven in the morning. The movers were coming at eight and I had to be ready. I went to the bathroom, took care of business, dressed, stripped the bed, and went downstairs to put the bedding and the towels on top of Ethan and Theresa's in the only open box left in the town house. Ethan had numbered and labeled the box. I took the roll of tape and sealed it up. I'd put my toiletries bag in my luggage, and left it upstairs for Theresa to do the same. Since she was standing in the kitchen drinking from a white paper cup with a picture of a steaming mug, I figured her stuff was in the luggage.

"G'morning," I mumbled.

She laughed. "I'm impressed. Up, motoring, and talking. Do you remember what seven in the morning looks like?"

"Funny, brat. I remember it well since I've stumbled home at seven in the morning more times than I can count."

"Ahh. Your misspent youth."

"Well spent. I had a blast." I picked up a cup with the letter M on it. "This mine?"

"Yep. I got you a chai latte."

I took a sip. Ambrosia. "You're forgiven for the snark."

She pushed a white paper bag toward me. "There's blueberry scones in this one." She pushed another white paper bag toward me with a leaf drawn on it. "There's maple frosted craisin scones in this one."

Of course, I went for the maple frosted scones. I'd eat maple frosted anything. I heard Ethan coming down the stairs. He carried my suitcase to the front door, came into the kitchen and took my backpack off his shoulder, and put it on the counter.

"Thanks," I said after I washed down some scone with my latte. "I sealed the box. You have the log?"

"Yeah. I'd entered the box already. We're good to go."

I looked out at the patio empty of everything except the table, chairs, and umbrella stand. We'd packed the chair cushions, had wrapped the umbrella, and moved the plants into the garage. The movers were going to load them last.

The plan was when the movers arrived, they'd put my suitcase and the big box with the bedding and towels in my rental along with a thirty-pack of toilet paper, two bottles of Windex, a twelve-pack of paper towels, and a flat of one-quart water bottles. All sitting by the front door – Ethan had done too much, and Theresa had yelled at him. Then, the movers would carry the eight medium boxes with kitchen stuff that were currently sitting on the kitchen counters to Theresa's car. Flatware, plates, mugs, glasses, coffee, the coffeemaker, scissors, knives, spatulas, wooden spoons, a couple of pots, and a couple of pans. Theresa had bought a huge roll of super-thin tan nubby rubber drawer lining and had left that in the car for the past few days. After we were all loaded up, she'd drive her car to the house, and I'd tag behind her. Ethan was staying behind to "supervise" the movers, and would follow the loaded truck to the house.

"Remember," he said, looking at me intently, "Theresa doesn't carry anything except her little shoulder bag."

I flicked two fingers from my forehead. "I'm all over it, sir."

"Smartass is also a genetic trait you Calapiano women share," he told Theresa.

She grinned. "We own that with pride."

We heard the moving truck roll up. Theresa and I used the bathrooms one more time.

***

Eighty-thirty that night we were sitting at the dining room table in the spacious dining room in Ethan and Theresa's new house, the detritus of round foil containers, paper bags, takeaway bowls, and water bottles scattered over the table.

"Well." Theresa patted her stomach. "We found a great Mexican restaurant right off the bat."

“I give it my California seal of approval.” I pointed to the leftover salsa and chips. “The real deal.”

“Real deal, I need to hit the bed,” Ethan said. “I want to get an early start on squaring away the living room and family room.”

Tomorrow, two of Ethan’s friends were bringing his stuff from storage. According to him, it wasn’t much, but he had a good sofa they’d used in the family room, a coffee table and a couple of end tables to go with it, and another bedroom’s worth of furniture. Though the highboy was going in the master bedroom. Theresa and I were finishing the kitchen and unpacking the wardrobe boxes. They’d left their clothes in their dresser, but we had to make sure the drawers were in the correct slots. If we had the energy, we’d tackle the linen closets. Yes, plural. Oh, the joys of having closet space. A person could live in the walk-in closet in the master bedroom.

The WiFi was on, and tomorrow Ethan and his buds were hanging the TVs in the master, the family room, and the guest room, which was where Ethan’s bachelor furniture was going. The furniture from the small town house bedroom I’d stayed in – the bed was a double – was going into the baby’s room. There was plenty of space for a crib and changing table if they decided to keep the bed. In the intervening six months, they’d have two rooms for guests.

When Theresa got up to clear the table, I waved her away, and she hugged me good night and went to bed with her man for the first time in her new house. The great news about the floor plan upstairs: the master bedroom was to the right on the staircase, to the left was an open space she told me they were going to use as a playroom, then there was a large linen closet, a bedroom, a Jack and Jill bathroom connecting another bedroom, and at the end of the hall, the guest bedroom. Hooray. I was on the other side of the house from them. They thought I was going to sleep in the baby’s room tonight, but hell no, I was bunking on the sofa in the living room. They deserved to have their privacy. I felt like an interloper. Tonight should’ve been theirs alone. At least I could give them the upstairs to themselves.

While I was cleaning up, my mind went where it’d been going ninety percent of the time for the past five weeks – to Ryan. Given that I hadn’t received a text telling me to fuck off, I figured he would be gentle with his good-bye. Or maybe he wouldn’t bother and silence would be my answer.

Random thought: Would he give up that sweet condo to live in a house like this?

My brain. I often wondered where the stray thoughts and non sequiturs came from.

I refused to dwell on something I couldn't change, like Ryan's mind. Okay, one last thing – I took my shot and laid myself bare. As Theresa said, if knowing the truth and how I felt ran him off, then fuck him. He didn't deserve me. Well, I wasn't quite all in on that line of thinking, but I'd embrace it. Then I made myself a promise: until I got on the plane next Sunday night I was going to be upbeat, positive, and one hundred percent supportive of and for my cousin. This was her week, and I was going to help make it as special as I could.

I took out my laptop to watch a movie and found out the sofa was unbelievably comfortable.

***

"Max." I felt a hand on my shoulder. "Max. Wake up."

I rolled over and looked up into freakin' amazing blue eyes. It took me a moment to get my bearings. Ethan. The man leaning over the back of the couch was Ethan. "Hey," I mumbled.

"You didn't have to do that."

Oh god, he wanted me to have a conversation with him. I slapped my hand over my mouth as I yawned huge. "Sorry. Do what?"

"Sleep down here."

Theresa said he was really intuitive. I wondered if that was an FBI requirement. "Yeah, I did." I pushed myself up on my elbows and scooched back to lean on the armrest. "Last night was your first night in your new house. It was supposed to be alone time. I crashed your party. The least I could do was give you some privacy."

"Sweet, but unnecessary." He stood and pointed toward the kitchen. "I'm making coffee. You want tea?"

"I'm going to head upstairs to take a shower and clean out the cobwebs. What time is it?"

"Almost seven."

I shuddered. "I'll never understand morning people."

He chuckled. "When I was a cop, for years I worked the second or third shift. It took some getting used to going back to days."

I got up and walked toward the staircase. "You couldn't pay me enough to be at work before ten."

He gave me a knowing smirk but didn't say anything. Sleeping dogs and all that.

Ninety minutes later I was clean, in jeans and my "Highway to Hell" t-shirt. I'd spiked my hair, swiped on a little makeup, was wearing my Vans slip-ons, and felt semiconscious. Boo greeted me at the bottom of the stairs, which were in front of French doors that sectioned off a little vestibule through which was the front door.

"Hey, buddy." I bent down and gave him a body rub.

"I'll take one of those."

I looked up and saw a wicked handsome man wearing a sly smirk. I stood and told him, "Keep dreaming, *federale*," as I passed him on my way to the kitchen. I heard booming laughter following me.

Theresa was leaning against Ethan, who was leaning against the island. Across from them was the most all-American guy I'd ever seen outside a Ralph Lauren advertisement. He smiled and his bright white teeth didn't seem real. "I see you met Fernando," he said.

The offender in question stood beside me as if he was invited. "Unfortunately," I replied. "And you are…"

"Wondering where you've been all my life."

I rolled my eyes and looked at Ethan, who was grinning. "Please tell me all of them aren't walking talking stereotypes."

Theresa cracked up. "This is Adam. He's actually much more civilized than Fernando."

"Oh geez. That's not a ringing endorsement, is it?"

"Be nice, *mujer*." Fernando was way too close to me. "I brought breakfast."

"*We* brought breakfast," Adam clarified.

I stepped farther into the kitchen and saw two Dunkin' boxes on the counter next to the coffee pot. "Ohmygod. I'm in love."

"It's the smile," Adam said. "Gets 'em every time."

"It's the donuts," Theresa corrected him. "You two," she shook her head, "don't stand a chance."

"Challenge accepted, Teresita."

I ripped off a couple of sheets of paper towel, wrapped up a cinnamon donut and a maple frosted donut, grabbed a bottle of water from the fridge, and said, "Got work to do. Thanks for breakfast," then went upstairs and started opening the wardrobe boxes.

Adam and Fernando didn't fuck around. They got to work too and hauled all of Ethan's bachelor bedroom furniture upstairs. They brought the highboy into the master and put it where Theresa directed, then they went down the hall. I heard drills whirring, and about fifteen minutes later, clomping down the stairs. Theresa and I checked out the guest room and we were impressed. The guys had put the bed together. The wooden headboard matched the dresser, which they moved near the wall opposite the bed that they'd set between the two windows. We figured they hadn't put the dresser flush against the wall because they had to put up the flat-screen.

By lunchtime, all the TVs were in place, the family room looked like a family room, and all the guys were sprawled on the L-shaped sofa watching the Red Sox pre-game show. Theresa and I took Boo and went to the Subway in Country Hills Plaza and got six sandwiches, three salads, and assorted bags of chips. Then we stopped in the liquor store and got a couple of six-packs of beer. After we got home, we stood at the kitchen island, split a sandwich, and each had a salad. When we went into the family room to hang out for a few minutes, all the food was gone. It was like we hadn't shopped.

Theresa and I were upstairs finishing getting the linen closet together when Ethan shouted up the guys were leaving. We went downstairs where Theresa hugged Adam and Fernando and thanked them.

"See you on Saturday." Adam winked.

"Save a dance for me, *mujer*," Fernando told me.

Then they were gone.

Two ticks after the front door closed, Ethan grabbed Theresa's hand and said, "Come lie down. You need a nap."

I went upstairs, finished putting the last few things in the linen closet, and took everything I needed to make up the bed to the guest bedroom. Somewhere there was a comforter that fit the bed, but for now the comforter that was on the bed in the town house was fine. If not big enough for the bed, it covered me. I didn't expect to fall asleep, but I knocked out the minute my head hit the pillow.

When I woke, the sun was setting. After I used the *baño*, I went downstairs and let Boo out of his crate. There was a note on the island telling me Ethan and Theresa went into Milford to go grocery shopping. Boo's bowls were next to the sink, so I figured he hadn't eaten yet. I fed him, then put on his halter and took him out back and we walked around until he did his business.

Ethan and Theresa came back a half hour later, and I helped them unpack the groceries. We made a spinach, artichoke hearts, and peppers frittata, and had a mini antipasto plate of cheese, prosciutto, and fruit.

Even though Theresa and I had napped, we all went to bed early.

Moving was exhausting.

***

Monday morning I dragged my sluggo body out of bed at eight, which was close enough to my regular wakey-wakey time that I couldn't bitch and moan. Ethan was taking the day off work – he was working full days the rest of the week, if you can believe that – to "supervise" the security system installation people. I understood this stuff was within his professional purview, and I knew how he was about security. I'd had a fifteen-minute tutorial on the town house system. I didn't think him getting shot bothered him at all. It was the danger of his job spreading to Theresa that had him hypervigilant. Then there was that lunatic who'd shot her instead of her patient, who was the intended target. Even though Ethan didn't know Theresa at the time, she told me he hurt for her every single day like he'd lived it. That fuckin' scar surely didn't help.

After a shower and all the other bathroom stuff, I headed downstairs in drawstring sweats and a long-sleeve tee. Today was unwrapping and arranging plants on the porch and back deck day. Translation: getting dirty and sweaty day.

Theresa, dressed for work, was in the kitchen eating pancakes. She was going in for a half day. "Hey." I walked over and gave her a quick hug. "Ethan make those?"

She nodded with her mouth full.

"Any batter left?" She nodded again. "Starting to feel like you're eating for two?" More nodding.

After a sip of coffee, she said, "I left the diagram of where I think I want what. I'm sure with your eye you'll correct any mistakes or improve on my plant OCD-ness."

I walked over to the stove turned on the flame under the nonstick pan, sprayed some olive oil pan coat, and ladled in three dollops of batter. "What time will you be home?" I asked over my shoulder.

"'Round four."

The movers put all the plant stands and plants at the side of the house. Poor things were probably screaming to get out of the burlap. Ethan had the movers leave the hand truck just inside the garage door. He was the most organized person I'd ever met. Since the security guys were working up front – we could hear them on the porch – my morning would be spent making the back deck gorgie. Ethan expected a location switch after lunch.

"Geez, these are yummy," I commented after my first mouthful of pancake. "You're a good teacher."

She smirked. "He's a great student."

"I think we're heading into TMI territory."

She laughed as she rinsed off her plate, cup, and fork, and put them in the dishwasher. "I'm outta here. I have a ten o'clock." She slung her backpack over her shoulder – fancy in tufted peach leather with tiny gold balls marking the diamond pattern – and grinned. "I love my house." She waved and went out front, surely to find Ethan to do more than wave good-bye.

As I was coming around the side of the house to get more plants – I was enjoying doing this way more than I'd expected – a mail truck pulled up in front of the end of the driveway. I figured, I'd get the mail, put it in the kitchen, and grab a bottle of water while I was there. The mailman came out of the truck and I swear, he looked like he was cast for the role. Mid-fifties, a little paunch, his gray/blue shorts hung to his knees, his hair, what was left of it, was more salt than pepper, and he had an Einstein 'do. He wore black-rimmed cheaters at the end of his nose as he shuffled the mail, then he ducked into the truck for a moment and came back with a large overnight delivery envelope.

My heart skipped a few beats.

"Hi." He put the cheaters in his top pocket then stuck out his hand. "I'm Lester Moody. You the new lady of the house?"

Before I could answer, Ethan appeared at my side. He stuck out his hand and said, "Ethan Berenikoff. I live here with my wife. This is our cousin."

"Well, how-do. Welcome to the neighborhood." Lester handed the mail to Ethan and my focus was riveted on that overnight mail envelope.

"Thanks. You our regular guy?"

"Ayuh. Had this route for near-on fourteen years."

Ethan smiled. "Sorry. We have workmen in the house. Have to get back in."

Lester nodded. "Moving is a lot of work. You folks take care." He got in his truck and puttered down the lane.

Ethan took my hand, walked me around the side of the house, and released me when he sat on the top step to the deck. He handed me the big envelope, and I leaned against the wooden bannister and yanked the tab that opened the overnight mail.

Agápi mou,

I was seventeen on New Year's Eve 2000. My friend Lalo had a huge party on the beach behind his folks' house. Alcohol and weed were being passed around all night. There were fireworks over the ocean at midnight, and after, we set off our own illegal fireworks. If we'd stopped by 1:00, no one would've cared. But we were obnoxious teenagers, and around 2:30 the cops came by to tell us to knock it off. They saw the discarded bottles, they smelled the weed, and they saw how old we were. I missed getting arrested by the skin of my teeth. Lalo's dad came onto the beach and talked the cops around. After they left, we got an earful from a pissed-off father, and we spent the next hour cleaning up, putting out the fire, and dragging the chairs and shit back to the house.

When I was twenty, I had a clunker. An old GTO that needed more work than the money and time I had to fix it up. One Friday night, a few friends piled in the car and I drove us to Santa Monica. We walked up and down the Third Street Promenade trying to look cool while taking in all the pretty girls. Then we ate at Falafel King and called it a night. We'd had a good time until we went back to the car and five gang members started giving us shit about the state of the GTO.

You know the saying young, dumb, and full of come? That was us. Instead of getting in the car and driving away, we threw down with the bangers and two of us got stabbed. I was one of them. Luckily, the wound was near my belly button and the knife was a small switchblade. It didn't penetrate deep. Hurt like a mother, but no internal organs were involved. My friend Shawn wasn't so fortunate. He was stabbed in the shoulder, and the injury did some damage. To save face, we lied to the cops and told them we got jumped.

Of course, none of what I shared comes close to what you lived through. The point I'm trying to make is at nineteen years old, if you had lied, you would've joined the extremely large club of college students who have done the same. But you didn't lie. What you didn't do was share. You weren't obligated to share. If the officer had asked you if you were friends with Lindsey, I know you would've told him the truth. He didn't ask because it wasn't germane to what he needed to learn. Let it go.

As for how you feel, there are no words that would be adequate to express how sorry I am that any of it happened. If you'd told me in person, I would've gathered you in my arms and held you until you knew you were safe and that your memories couldn't hurt you unless you let them. Please don't let them.

I'm looking forward to seeing your smile and hearing your laughter.

Ryan

I sunk onto a step and reread the letter. Then I looked up at Ethan and said, "He's not mad at me."

"For the record, I don't know what happened. Theresa never told me, and she never will. She shared some shit went down when you were in college. That's it. Ryan…I didn't expect him to be angry. I'm sure he's upset you're not there with him. Since we agree he's like me, I'll tell you how I'd feel. I would've wanted to show you it's okay to tell me anything. I would've talked myself hoarse to make you understand that. He's in your corner, Max. He'll fight your side. Forever, if you let him."

I blinked rapidly a few times. I wasn't going to fall apart again. I had no reason to. The other night, when I was in self-torture mode, I looked up *agápi mou*. It meant *my love*. Since that horrible-turned-charmed Thursday night, he'd been telling me he loved me. Until now, I didn't believe him.

I leaned up and put my hand on Ethan's knee. "I've been thrilled for Theresa that you guys found each other. I didn't expect the side bonus of gaining a good friend in the bargain."

He laid his hand over mine. "Same." He smiled, stood, and went into the house.

I took my phone out of my back pocket and called Theresa.

Chapter Nineteen

Best Laid Plans
Ryan

I checked the tracking. Max got my letter yesterday. I hadn't heard from her, but I knew her well enough by now to expect she'd take a minute to formulate her response. Tomorrow, she could tell me in person.

Yesterday, our investigator did her job. Admirably, from what Camille told me. All day Monday, officers who'd worked with Eric Foster, who'd trained Eric Foster, who'd taught Eric Foster in the academy, were interviewed in a small conference room adjacent to Camille's office.

Eden had come in at seven am to catch the officers coming off the third shift, and she stayed until eight at night. She'd talked to eleven people. Then she'd briefed Camille. No one had ever heard Foster make one disparaging remark about anyone for any reason. He'd never exhibited any abhorrent behavior, and was a fine student and a good cop. Camille had the same reaction I did. No one, especially in our line of work, would have nothing to say about someone they had contact with or arrested. Eric Foster was exceedingly cautious because he was in the closet. The racist's closet. My guess, he was part of some group whose leadership had become savvy and cautioned the members to keep their mouths shut. If they looked and behaved like model citizens, they'd be able to get away with spewing – and probably acting on – their deranged ideology. Foster's outburst came from extreme job pressure. Aside from being a fucking racist, he wasn't cut out for this type of work, and his lid blew when he couldn't handle a tense situation.

Today, Eden had come in a little before eight and had three interviews scheduled before her interview with Eric Foster and his attorney. She's blocked out from eleven to six, and would pick it up tomorrow if need be.

I'd be long gone by the time Foster came in. I'd come in at six and was bugging out at nine-thirty, the latest. My flight left SFO around one and I wanted to make sure I got to the airport on time. I'd hoped I'd have enough time to stop at a jewelry store in San Francisco before my flight. I needed to be here this morning for a meeting with the mayor. He had one hour to be his usual demanding and taxing self. He knew I had to leave to catch a plane, which meant I'd get a double earful since I wouldn't be at his beck and call for days. No petulant child was more difficult than that man.

By nine-ten I was heading out of town. Every mile I got closer to SFO I felt lighter knowing that tonight Max would be where she belonged. In my bed, by my side. I'd told Theresa I wouldn't be at the house until eleven. She texted back she and Ethan didn't care.

I'd mapped out where the jewelry store I wanted was and the closest location was only a half hour away from the hotel. Thursday – no way I was putting on clothes tomorrow – I'd find an excuse to go to the Natwick Mall, and Max would get once and for all I wasn't fucking around. She and I were going to be together forever, and she'd be wearing the evidence of that promise by Thursday afternoon.

When my phone rang, I looked at the car's display and saw it was Camille. She wouldn't be calling unless it was important. I took the call.

"What's up?"

"Chief, I'm so sorry, really, but you have to come back. Now."

Fuck. "Gimme a minute. I have to pull off the road." I was twenty minutes away from SFO. The next exit was coming up, and when I was in a bank parking lot, I asked, "What happened?"

"Eden was interviewing Foster and she was pressing him hard. He lost it. He grabbed her arm and near pulled her across the table. Sam Glickman fell off his chair from the force of the table slamming into him. Eden was able to extricate herself from Foster's hold, but he came at her and was able to land a jawbreaker before two officers pulled him off her. Foster was arrested and is being booked into our jail. Sam and Eden are on the way to the hospital. The whole thing was recorded. You have to hear it to believe it. Foster screaming 'I got a Jew lawyer and you're still out for blood you fuckin' bitch' and other vile things along that vein. He used the N word about fifteen times, and he didn't stop shouting the whole way down to booking. When I say he lost it, I mean he cracked. Keeping all that shit bottled up for who knows how long, it all boiled over today."

Fuckfuckfuck. Fuck. "Are you all right?" I put the bars on my roof, turned on the lights, pulled out of the parking lot, hung a u-ey and got back on the 101 heading north.

"Yes, Chief. A little rattled, to be honest, but I wasn't hurt. One of the officers who pulled Foster off Eden took one in the face. The EMTs said he didn't need more than ice and Aleve, but he's got a split lip and his cheek started to swell. I sent him home."

"Who is it?"

"Officer Ngo."

One of my hires. "He's married, right?"

"Right. Has a couple of kids. A day or two resting at home with his family and he'll be good as new."

What a clusterfuck. "I'm on my way back. Have you talked to Miranda Cummins yet?"

"I have. She's coordinating with Bradon Fellows. This is one of those times I wished we had city manager, not a 'strong mayor.'"

I didn't say *You and me both*, but I sure as hell believed it. Hiram was going to lose his mind, such as it was. "I'll call Hiram and tell him I'm on my way back. You keep everything business as usual, and tell the command staff I'll want to meet with them sometime around two. I've got to get Hiram in line first."

"Copy that, Chief."

I hung up and called Theresa.

***

The mayor was intolerable, and I'd had enough of him to last two lifetimes. With so much on the line, I knew I had to take him in hand or get the fuck out.

"Sir. Would you take a ride with me?" That threw him.

"Uh…well…ah, I guess."

We went to my official chief's car, a typical black Crown Vic. I drove it only when I had to. I hated the damn thing. When Hiram was buckled in, I drove us through some of the older neighborhoods where traditional Craftsmen homes and mini gingerbread Victorians were abundant.

"What do you see, sir?"

"Houses, Trent," he blustered. "What are you getting at?"

"I see families, sir. Neighborhoods filled with families who rely on us to protect them."

"Well, yes. Of course."

I pulled over at the end of the street in front of an old but well-maintained cottage. "You hired me not only for my expertise and experience, but because I believe in families and maintaining an environment for them to thrive. Isn't that what you believe, sir?"

"You know I do." He wasn't smart enough to know what I was doing, but he understood he was being manipulated and he didn't like it.

"In the past ten months, have I given you any reason to doubt my commitment to this community?"

"Not until you took off today in the middle of a crisis."

"Sir, there was no crisis when I left. As I explained when I told you I was leaving, I have to tend to a family matter, which, since you believe in families, I know you'd want me to be able to handle."

He huffed. I had him there and he knew it.

"Nonetheless, twenty minutes from the airport, I turned around and came back to Redwood Falls." Now he couldn't say anything without sounding like the ass he was. "Sir, I'm asking you point blank. If you're unhappy with my job performance and wish for me to leave my post, let me know. I'll take care of my family matter, come back, pack my desk, and go."

I had him over a barrel. If he fired me, the community would go up in arms. I'd made damn sure I'd cultivated all the appropriate community leaders, many of whom shared that no one had ever bothered meeting with them, no less ask their opinions on policing. The last police chief wasn't a bad cop, but he'd been a throwback to the 1970s, and he had been in that chair for too long. Hiram was also out of touch with modern society. The city he'd grown up in was gone. I represented everything he hated about change. But he'd hired me because I was and still am the best person to bring modern policing and community relations to Redwood Falls, and to build the infrastructure for a healthy future.

"All right, Trent. You're a slick one, I'll give you that. And the community and your cops like you. I'd be signing my retirement papers if I let you go. But I'm not pleased with the whole Foster business."

Score. "I'm not pleased with the whole Foster business either, sir. However, from every indication, everyone did their due diligence when he was hired, which was over a year before I got here. Sometimes, no matter how deep you dig, you don't know what a man is thinking and what he believes. Foster went out of his way to appear to be a good guy to hide his twisted mind. Frankly, we should consider ourselves lucky we got off this easy."

"I beg your pardon."

"Sir, the video that went viral was mild compared to what could've happened. The incident today was in a contained environment, and the whole thing was recorded. There'll be no disputing the facts. He'll be arraigned tomorrow, and I'm sure his new attorney will ask for a psych eval, which will reveal he's not fit for duty. I have no doubt he'll be remanded to a facility that deals with people who have severe mental illness. We'll be able to fire him after we get confirmation he's not fit for duty. Our lawyers will walk you through the steps, but at the end of the day, we'll be off the hook for his behavior not only today, but for what happened a couple of weeks ago. Sad for him, a great result for us."

"Huh. Maybe you do know what you're doing."

I chuckled and started the car.

"I hear you're seeing the oldest Calapiano girl."

Max would kill him for calling her a girl. "I am." Small cities. The gossip mill was the best working machinery in Redwood Falls.

"Gonna marry her?"

"If she'll have me."

He humphed. "Well, that'll tie you to the community for good."

"My intention, sir."

***

After the command staff meeting, I went to the hospital. Eden had to have her jaw wired. She'd typed on her iPad, "I've been meaning to lose ten pounds." If she ever wanted back into a cop shop, I'd hire her in a heartbeat.

Sam had a concussion and a bruised rib. He wanted to go home, but his wife told him to do what the doctors said, which was stay overnight in the hospital so they could monitor him. I enjoyed them, and meant to keep up with Sam. He was a hidden treasure in the Falls. He knew everyone and, from what Camille said, was widely respected.

Down the road a couple of years, after everyone got used to my being so "slick," I planned to institute a citizens' police council to provide recommendations where we needed to focus our attention, and if there were issues with our officers, we wanted to hear about it and solve the problems. Sam would make a great CPC leader.

What I'd told Hiram would happen went down in court the next morning. Foster was sent to a facility for psych eval. I knew the way the rest would play out.

The day went by in a blur. Mostly, I spent my time being seen by my staff and I even made a trip to city hall to say a quick hello to Hiram. He preened, and I said to myself, *my work here is done.* In essence, I was letting everyone know they had nothing to worry about. In the afternoon I visited Officer Phuong Ngo at home. His kids were adorable and couldn't get over the color of my eyes. The little one, who was three, kept yelling, "Fake. Fake." Ngo's face looked a little worse for the wear, but he assured me he'd be back to work on Friday.

I dragged myself into my condo at six pm with a smile on my face. A couple of hours ago Max texted:

"I'll be home late Sunday night. See you then."

No, you'd see me tomorrow evening. I'd changed my ticket to an early morning flight, and would be in Boston a little after four pm. Since, by the time I got there, I'd've lost nearly two days with her, on the way to Mendon, I was stopping at the Natwick Mall.

I went to bed at eight. I had to leave the Falls by two in the morning.

***

I'd read that ancient coffee came from the forests of Ethiopia. Well done, Ethiopia. On behalf of all groggy people everywhere, we salute you. I'd downed a cup on the way to SFO, and it held me until I got on the plane. I fell asleep when we were taxiing, and woke when the captain said, "We're beginning our descent into Boston." I had a garment bag and a carry-on rolling suitcase. I went straight to the car rental shuttle and within fifteen minutes I was in an upgraded-to-luxury sedan and was heading to Natwick Mall in traffic that rivaled LA's.

By the time I got to Ethan and Theresa's house it was seven pm. Thank god for long June days. It helped being able to see where I was going. I'd never been to Massachusetts, but I knew I'd be back here a lot since part of my soon-to-be family lived in New England. If Max could hear my thoughts, she'd say *arrogant and presumptive.* I'd tell her there were no other options.

I sat for a moment admiring the big, beautiful house while I caught my breath. I wasn't nervous, but I was nearly shaking with want and need. I thought of what Rico had said about enjoying the war he waged to win his wife. Some of our war had been fun, but what Max had suffered was no joke. I was going to encourage her to go back into therapy. Those ghosts hadn't been laid to rest, and they needed to be. A less sensitive person might not have felt what had happened so deeply, but my woman had a heart of gold. Her reaction was pure Max.

As if conjured by the thought, she came around the side of the house carrying a plant. She didn't see me. She was paying attention to not falling up the steps to the porch. God, she looked like heaven walking. Tight jeans that loved her ass, a t-shirt that hugged her ample tits, and her hair was spiked up. Her face was buried in the plant, but I caught a glimpse of big hoop earrings.

I got out of the car and closed the door as quietly as I could, and then walked up the lawn to the porch steps and watched her ass as she placed the plant in one corner then shifted it to the other. I must've moved and she jumped up to see who it was.

"Ohmygod, ohmygod, ohmygod." She slapped her hand on a big white column. "What are you doing here?"

I saw her knees begin to buckle and I rushed forward and caught her in my arms. "I'm here for you, *agápi mou.*"

She threw her arms around my neck and mumbled into my chest, "I know what that means."

I put my hand under her chin and lifted her head. I could swim for hours in the depths of her dark brown eyes. I smiled. "You are my love, Max. My one and only. Please say you'll be mine."

She gave me her lopsided smile. The one where she didn't fully commit to the smile, but she had a knowing expression on her beautiful face. "I've been yours since Beans and Roast. Though it took a while for my head to catch up to my heart."

"All synced up now?"

"Yeah." Now I got the full smile.

"Good." I hadn't planned to do this the moment I saw her, but I felt like I'd been waiting years for her to be mine. I put my hand into the front pocket of my jeans and pulled out her ring. That box was way too clunky. "Mine forever and always." I had to give the ring a little push to lodge at the base of her finger, which was fitting given our bumpy ride.

"Geez." She turned her hand in a few different positions as she admired the ring. "Did you sell the car to buy this?"

I chuckled. "No. Do you like it?"

She sighed and gave me a bored look. "It'll do." I leaned in to kiss her, but she put her finger over my lips. "Are you mine forever and always?"

Max lifted her finger when my lips moved. "*Glikia mou,* you stole my breath with your laughter, and I fell in love with your smile. At the risk of being gooey, I'm really here to get my heart back. You took it with you when you left."

She ducked her chin. "Seems I don't mind that kind of gooey."

"I'll keep that in mind." Then she lifted her head and got up on her tiptoes to put her lips against mine. "You can ravish me now."

I wrapped my arms around her tight, bent her back, and took her mouth the way Max needed to be kissed. Thoroughly, deeply, intensely, and for a really, really long time. When I straightened us, she said breathily, "I've been meaning to tell you this for a while." I raised my brows. "You're an exceptional kisser."

"That's the PG on-the-porch version."

"When do I get the X-rated version?"

"After I say hello to your cousins, get your bags, and we check into our hotel room."

"That seems like a terribly long time to wait."

I nipped her bottom lip. "Behave."

***

Theresa and Ethan looked pretty much the way I'd pictured them. I was no mystery. My mug was all over the internet. While Theresa and Max oohed and ahhed over her ring, Ethan took me on a quick tour of the house, pointing out the "years' worth of home improvements" he had to look forward to. Great house, and I told him so. I also thanked him. He mentioned a case of whiskey that sounded like it was going to set me back a few hundred dollars. I didn't mind one fuckin' bit.

When we got to Max's room, I stuffed the clothes lying on a chair into her suitcase, got her toiletries, and somehow managed to fit all that shit into the bag that was sitting on the bathroom's vanity counter. I zipped it all up, took her messenger bag and threw it over my shoulder, and brought her stuff downstairs. I put the bags by the front door and went into the kitchen.

When I draped my arm around Max's shoulder, she reached up and wrapped her fingers around my hand. For what seemed like decades, I'd wished for this ease of affection, this display of emotion, the freedom to assert our devotion. I'd missed what I'd never had, but relished having it now.

"Stay for dinner," Theresa insisted. "You must be starving."

"Flower." Ethan said a hundred words in that one.

"Right." She smiled at us. "Get gone. We'll see you tomorrow night at the rehearsal dinner."

Max giggled, a sound I'd never heard from her. Its gaiety an indication of the woman I'd always known Max to be was now going to spread her wings and fly straight into our bliss.

On the car ride to the hotel, Max told me stories about the move, about how Ethan's arm was healing because he'd been shot last December and he was pissed off he couldn't help more, though from the sound of it, he did a lot. The big news: Theresa was about three months pregnant. When they went to pick up her dress, the seamstress told her to try it on, and good thing. While she didn't look pregnant, her waist had thickened and they had to wait while the seams were let out from the ribs to the hips.

This Max, the chatty, happy, bubbly woman sitting across from me, was the woman I saw laughing with her whole body. She'd freed herself from the chains of doubt and believed in me, in our love. The feeling was exhilarating, and I couldn't wait to show her how thrilled I was.

We checked into a renovated hotel used mostly by businesspeople. Our room was a small suite done in grays and taupe with a narrow living room with a small kidney-shaped sofa, a curved side chair, a desk, and a small cabinet that had a microwave on a shelf and a small fridge behind the cabinet doors. There was a TV on top, angled toward the couch. The bedroom had a king-size bed, side tables, a flat-screen on the wall above the dresser, and a tiled bathroom. Basic, but slightly upscale. Frankly, as long as it was clean and the bed was comfortable, that was all we needed. We were staying naked until we had to go to the rehearsal dinner.

I double locked the door, hung my garment bag in the closet, and pulled our suitcases into the bedroom. Max went into the bathroom and I sat on the bed to take off my boots. My socks had barely come off when she walked out of the bathroom completely naked.

I gripped the bed as my heart skittered in my chest. Her body was a thing of beauty, and every man's wet dream. Ripe, full tits, soft curves, and juicy hips and thighs. My gaze travelled back up to hers and she was smiling, enjoying my reaction.

"Everything you hoped for?" she asked in that throaty voice that was so damn sexy.

"So much more."

She walked to me and I rested my hands on her hips. Her skin was soft and supple, and feeling her without restrictions seemed too good to be true. She pushed my shoulders and I lay back, more than happy to let her take the lead. I was feasting with my eyes and hands, and felt quite certain she had every intention of engaging the rest of my body.

She stood between my legs and bent over, her tits hanging over my torso as she unbuttoned my shirt, and then pushed the sides open. "Have I told you," she rasped, "how much I love your chest?"

"You've supplied some clues."

"Uh-huh." She put a knee on the bed on one side of my hips then repeated the motion with the other knee. She leaned down and pressed her lusciousness against my body and moved slowly, rubbing herself against me. My dick began to weep in my jeans. "Mmmm," she moaned. "I knew it would feel divine to rub my breasts against your chest. I've wanted to do this for what seems like years."

Damn, to hear her echo my sentiments meant she'd been right there with me, but hiding behind her walls. Those suckers were rubble now, and I was getting the full effect of everything Max had to offer.

She lifted up and pressed her lips to the notch at the bottom of my throat. "This is so sexy. You wear your shirts open, and the view is an invitation." She ran her tongue over my pecs and flicked it over my nipples then latched on to one, and I felt that in my balls. I brought my hands up and started caressing her back. She continued her exploration, running her tongue down the hair between my pecs until she got to my belly button. She lifted up and ran her finger over the small pucker next to it. "Knife wound?"

"It is."

"You guys were so stupid." She bent down to kiss the scar, then undid my belt and unbuttoned my jeans. She laid her hand over my straining cock. "I don't want to hurt you. You take off your pants." She swung one leg over and was kneeling beside me when I got rid of my jeans and my briefs. "Wow." She licked her lips. "My own personal sucker." She bent over, her tits pressing on my thigh, and ran her tongue over the head of my cock. It jumped up to meet her lips and she laughed. "Steady, boy. I'll get there." She wrapped her fingers around the base and stroked slowly as she took me in her mouth.

My eyes rolled back in my head, and I willed myself to keep it together. I tucked my hands under my neck and forced my lids open. I had to watch this. I'd wanted her since the day I met her, and I wasn't going to miss a moment of her giving me head. Her profile was an erotic picture. A hollowed cheek, her mouth wrapped around me sliding up and down, and her hand working me. Between the visual and the sensation, I was seconds away from blowing. I cupped her face. "The first time, I want to come inside you."

She sucked up and my dick popped out of her mouth. "You ever go ungloved?" I shook my head. "Me neither. We're going to starting now. I want to feel every inch of you."

Ungloved inside of Max. I wasn't going to last long. Before my brain completely shut down I asked, "We going for a kid already?"

She smiled. "Not quite yet. I'm on the pill."

Using my elbows, I pulled myself into the middle of the mattress and Max straddled me again. This time her trimmed dark triangle rested just below my balls.

"Slow, *bello*. I want to feel you before we combust."

I grinned. *Zero to fuck me.* Max's term for how fast we ignited. I was fine with slow. I was interested to see how long it would last. She moved forward and lowered herself onto my dick, her hot wet pussy gripping me in a fist of warmth. I balled my hands in the covers, knowing the moment I grabbed her hips, slow would become a passing thought.

"Damn, *glikia mou,* you feel too good."

"Hmmm?" Her eyes were closed and her head was thrown back as she used her hands, gripping my thighs to help raise and lower herself on me. "How can this be too good?"

"Your pussy's so delicious I'm not going to last."

She opened her eyes and leaned forward, her tits brushing my chest. I raised up on my elbows and drew her light brown nipple into my mouth as I started to pump into her. Damn, she tasted like sunshine on a warm day: hot, bright, and earthy. I sucked deep and nipped at the nub, which made her moan and move faster. She was rubbing her clit against my body as she fucked me harder and harder. I moved to her other nipple and swirled my tongue around its edge over and over until she begged, "More please, more."

I flipped us over and got on my knees, yanking her up by her hips, and within moments of sinking inside her, I was pistoning, my hips working overtime as I used my thumb and forefinger on her clit, pinching and releasing over and over. I watched myself move in and out of her body, overcome by the sight, the sensations, and the knowledge that finally, god, finally we were truly together.

She started screaming, "Ryan, Ryan, Ryan," and I felt the walls of her pussy spasming as she let out a low rumbly moan. I gripped her hips harder and slammed into her once, twice, and the third time my back bowed as I came so hard I actually shook from it, my groan resounding in the room as my release jetted out of me.

I put my hands under her back and pulled her up to me until her cheek was against mine, and I could feel the warm gush of her breath against me. "I love you, I love you, I love you," she murmured in my ear. "I'll always love you." I wrapped my arms around her tight and pressed my face into her neck. I couldn't speak. The emotions of getting everything I ever wanted swamped me and all I could do was hold on to the woman who owned me.

***

We fell asleep for a little while, then Max got up to use the bathroom, and when she came back to bed, I did the same. I got under the covers and flicked them back and straddled her before she could ask what I was up to.

"I've been waiting forever to do this." I kissed my way down the center of her body, threw her legs over my shoulders, and put my mouth over her pussy.

Nothing ever tasted sweeter. Like honey with a side of orange, her juices dripped down my throat as I lapped at her lower lips. When I ran my tongue in a circle around her clit, she grabbed onto my hair and pressed my face into her. I sucked on her clit, then flicked it with my tongue, and I kept alternating between the two until her legs crossed over my back and her heels dug into me.

As she was coming, she yelled, "Too much, too much." But I didn't stop. I buried my tongue inside her and ran my fingers up and down the crease of her ass until my thumb rested on her tight hole, and I pressed. The walls of her pussy pulled at my tongue and I pressed harder, my thumb pushing inside her. She was bucking against my face and yanking my hair as her climax took over and she was moaning and panting. I pulled my thumb from her body and licked the inside of her thighs to get up every last drop of her essence.

When I lowered her ass to the bed, her legs fell from my shoulders and she appeared boneless beneath me. My inner Cro-Magnon man wanted to beat his chest then bang around the cave for a while.

"Hungry?" I asked.

"Huh?" she barely replied.

"Food. Nourishment. Fuel. I'm nowhere near finished with you."

She lifted her head and looked at me like I was crazy. "Aren't you exhausted?"

I grinned. "I slept on the plane."

Her head dropped to the bed. "Yeah. I guess I could eat something."

The hotel had room service, but their dining room was closed. They had a list of nearby restaurants that delivered. Unfortunately, most of them were closed too. The suburbs. We ordered pizza and mozzarella sticks. I pulled on my pants when the order was delivered, gave the guy a tip, closed and double locked the door, and got naked again.

We sat on the bed and ate.

"This isn't bad, but I can't wait until you taste my pizza."

"*Glikia mou,* I'll eat anything you feed me."

She liked that. Her eyes sparkled. "You cook any Greek dishes?"

"Easy stuff. Falafel, hummus, *dolmas*."

"Yum. You ever make *spanakopita*?"

"No. You?"

"Nope, but I could try. I love that stuff."

I put the leftovers – there wasn't much, I was hungry – in the little fridge. Then I got into bed, wrapped myself around my woman, and we fell asleep.

In the middle of the night, I reached around and caressed her luscious tits and she responded almost immediately by pushing her ass into my groin. I slid into her wet pussy and told her, "You are my dream come true." Slowly, we moved together, building the fire, but banking it, working each other up then backing off until the sensations were heightened in intensity. When I took her nipples between my fingers and stared rolling, she gasped and moaned, pushing harder against me, her juices coating my thighs.

I moved one hand down her body and lightly brushed my fingers over her clit as I pinched and rolled her nipple. Slow became urgent, and I rammed into her, my fingers pinching her nipple and clit. We came together, her pussy milking it out of me, my hips bucking wildly as she bit down on my arm and sucked my skin.

"I think," she managed to get out between heaving breaths, "we're going to have to be in our seventies before we can do slow through the whole thing."

I laughed into her neck, my semi-hard dick kicking inside her pussy.

We fell asleep like that. Connected.

Chapter Twenty

We're Italian
Max

Every woman wanted to be sore the way I was sore. Ryan kept me naked until four o'clock Friday afternoon, then we had no choice but to get ready for the rehearsal dinner. My man was inventive. After we'd done our morning bathroom business, we had a shower. I wasn't tiny like Theresa, and I wasn't skinny like a model. Hell I wasn't thin at all, so the idea of wrapping my legs around Ryan's body while he held me up against the shower wall seemed improbable. He didn't even try to go there. Instead, he bent me at the waist, told me to put my arms straight out and lean into the wall opposite the showerhead. He rested one hand on my back as he played with my body.

He had such talented fingers, and within seconds he had me dripping and wiggling my ass, signaling he better get that gorgeous cock inside me. He blocked the shower stream and I was able to keep purchase on the wall as he held my hips and sunk into me. He held me still, and it drove me crazy not to move, but I waited, knowing he had something planned.

"Don't move until I tell you to move." He squeezed my hips to emphasize his domination. "Understand?"

"Uh-huh," I breathed out.

He leaned on my back, reached around, and ran one finger of each hand around the edge of my nipples. Slowly, gently, torturing me until he pinched both nipples not hard enough to hurt, but enough pressure that I felt that zing in my clit. Damn, it felt so good I thrust back into him. In a flash, his hands left my breasts, one lodged on my hip and the other cracked a smack across my butt.

Ho-lee shit. If someone had asked me two days ago what I'd do if a man smacked my ass, I would've said I'd turn around and punch him in the face. With Ryan, his smack made my insides quiver, and I knew it was part of the play. Him controlling my release. I also knew with a certainty that was tattooed on my brain: he *would* eat a bullet before hurting me.

"I said, don't move." He kicked my legs farther apart, leaned on my back again, and took up where he left off. By now, my nipples were so sensitized, any touch made my legs shake. When I was sure I was going to collapse, he moved his hand to my clit, and at the same time he pinched it, he started thrusting inside me. I was gone. Screaming and slapping the wall, his arm around my waist the only thing holding me up.

When his groan filled the bathroom and bounced off the tile, he sagged over me, holding me tight while kissing my shoulder. "You all right?" he asked, his voice thick and husky.

I turned my head and saw his jewel eyes full of sex and love. "You keep this up, I won't be able to walk for a week." His smile reached his eyes. "But if you stop, I'll never talk to you again." He laughed and I felt him move inside me.

We had breakfast in the room, and enough sex to say we engaged in a valiant effort to make up for lost time. I was preening in the full-length mirror next to the closet. Ryan came up behind me, wrapped his arms around my waist, and rested his chin on my shoulder. Our faces looked so relaxed no one at the rehearsal dinner would miss it, including my folks.

"We have well fucked written all over us."

He grinned. "That a problem?"

I shook my head. "No. But fair warning, we're Italian. If someone observes something, they talk about it, regardless of the appropriateness of the topic."

"I've been inoculated." He squeezed my waist. "The Greek side of my family is the same."

"And yet, your father still married your mother."

"He never talks about such things, but I'd lay good money on him following my mother with his tongue hanging out." I smiled at him in the mirror. "I know what you're thinking. It must be hereditary."

I turned in his arms and got red lipstick all over his face and mouth.

***

The rehearsal dinner was the only event of the wedding weekend Theresa and Ethan didn't have at their house. Too much tumult the night before the wedding. In a nod to Ethan's home state, although Theresa said it was all about the food, the dinner was held at The Oregon Club, about twenty-five minutes away in Ashland, the restaurant aptly named since there was an Ashland in Oregon where they hosted the world-famous Oregon Shakespeare Festival.

There were thirty-two of us. We took over the interior of the restaurant, though patio dining was open to the public. We walked in and my mother took one look at us, said, "Oh my," and that got everyone going. My left hand wasn't my own for a while. Within minutes of our arrival, Ryan had a word with my dad, and they went outside. I was a little concerned. My dad had a spikey temper and could lose control of his brain-to-tongue censor in a flash. But when they came back about fifteen minutes later, my father looked like he'd won the lottery.

Ryan came over to me and put his arm around my waist. I leaned in and asked, "What was that about?"

"Told him my intentions."

"Well, duh. We're engaged."

"It's a guy thing." I looked up and narrowed my eyes. He smiled. "Don't worry. He's happy."

My gaze traveled the room and I found my father in the corner near the tiny bar drinking a glass of wine, of course. He was in a man huddle with my all my uncles, and it looked like he was bragging, and they appeared to be eating it up.

Thank god. There'd be no family drama because of me.

"Okay."

***

I could write a book about how glorious, beautiful, and perfect Ethan and Theresa's wedding was. Including the bride, groom, and the priest – who was exactly as Ethan had billed – there were eighty people, all of whom were glowing with happiness for the newlyweds. Theresa and I were standing on the deck taking in the gathering.

"Gotta say, having cops and FBI agents," I nodded to the guys standing together with beer bottles in their hands, Ethan and Ryan among them, "at a wedding that's being guarded by four of Don Di Caro's bodyguards," Theresa and I scanned the perimeter, "has surreal written all over it."

Theresa laughed then said, "Ethan told me law enforcement is used to complicated relationships."

"Well this sure as hell defines that statement."

"He understands the Don and my family's connection."

"Ter, your dad works on the legit side of the Don's business. You're the one who's special to Alessandro Di Caro. After you stepped in front of a bullet for his daughter, he'd do anything for you, and you know it."

She shrugged. "I'm glad they're all here."

"I can't believe Sofia has a baby."

"Right?"

"Lola's next. I spoke to her today and she's ready to pop."

"I'll miss having you here, but I'm glad you'll be home for her."

I felt the tears threatening, but today was a joyous day, and I wasn't going to do anything weepy. Okay, I cried a little during the ceremony, but only Ryan saw that. "I'll miss you too, Ter. But I'll be back after Christmas as an official vigil member."

"Can't wait." She held out her arms and we hugged for a really long time.

Without Theresa…and Ethan, I wouldn't have Ryan.

***

On the plane going home, Ryan told me, "We're buying a house."

"Why?" I asked. Aside from being a random thing to say when I was half asleep, it didn't make sense. Although we hadn't discussed it, I figured I'd sell my condo and move in with him. His place was four times the size of mine, was new and fancy, and it was where I'd had the most romantic night of my life. Although, if Ryan kept up with the gooey, I had a feeling I'd have occasion to say that a lot over the course of our lifetime together. “You have a great condo. I love the terrace.”

“Houses have garages,” he said with the authority of a prominent architect.

“Your building has a garage.” I had an intimate acquaintance with that garage.

“True, but I can’t lay you out on the hood of my car and bury my face in your pussy in the condo’s garage.”

I smirked. “I see your point.”

Epilogue

Gooey
Ryan

We went home and Max moved her clothes into my place and put the rest of her stuff in storage. Well located, and well-priced, her condo sold in under three weeks. She banked the money for a down payment on our house. Nine weeks after escrow closed, we said "I do" under a gazebo behind her family's winery. Unlike Ethan and Theresa's intimate backyard affair, we had an obscene number of people at our wedding. I'd heard three hundred and ninety, but since all I had to do was show up in a suit and tie, promise to do things I knew I was going to do anyway, slip another ring on Max's finger, kiss my bride, and dance with her all night, I didn't care what her family put together. I met cousins from Italy, Toronto, and Australia. She met cousins from Greece, New York, and Florida. We had stacks of plates put aside for the inevitable throwing and breaking, and there was plenty of *Opa* shouted throughout the night. Many of Max's cousins happily adopted the custom and were enthusiastic participants.

Outside of marrying Max, my favorite wedding moment was when Max met Oscar. I'd primed the pump, and Oscar came dressed in an expensive tailored black suit and a white silk shirt that made his yellow-brown eyes even brighter against his café-au-lait skin. He walked up to her on the dance floor and asked me in his deep, rich, cultured voice, "May I cut in?" then turned, took her left hand, and turned it over palm up. He bent his long body at the waist and pressed his lips against her wrist. She swooned and didn't seem to put her feet back on the floor until he stopped dancing with her ten minutes later.

As part of their wedding present, he and Randall generously gave us their house in Mendocino for five days, to where we escaped while the wedding was still in full swing. We planned to have an extended honeymoon next spring in Scandinavia, where no one from any side of our families lived.

Max had agreed she needed to go back into therapy. She didn't want to continue wearing the shroud she'd wrapped herself in ten years ago. Without Theresa's help, Max found someone she liked, and started seeing the therapist once a week after work. Sometimes she came home visibly shaken, and those nights the only thing I could do to make her feel better was to wrap her in my arms and hold her close. To her credit, she kept going back even though I knew working through that horror show was tough stuff.

Now we were house hunting. We'd seen seven homes already with no success. There were three fundamental things we disagreed on. I wanted a newer build: she wanted an older home. I wanted a manageable yard, no more than a quarter acre: she wanted an acre or more. I wanted a ranch-style house, and, you guessed it, she wanted a two-story home. Our realtor looked like she wanted to slit her wrists after our second viewing.

I was sitting in my office going through the PD's upcoming annual budget proposal when Will knocked on the door. "Got a minute, Chief?"

I waved him in and he sat in one of the chairs in front of my desk. "How's Aiden?" Will took out his phone and handed it to me. The kid was cute, but he'd started teething and some pictures were drool heavy. "He's going to be a bruiser."

Will nodded and took back his phone. "Lola's already telling me she doesn't want him to play football." He shook his head. "Too much aggression, too many head injuries, too many broken bones. She nearly threw her shoe at me when I asked if she wanted me to sign him up now for a knitting circle."

I couldn't help it, I cracked up.

"Laugh it up, Chief. I can't wait 'til it's you. Remember, I *know* Max."

I sobered immediately. "Don't," I said, using my command tone.

Will chuckled. "Actually, I'm here to help you with your housing crisis."

"I didn't know I had a housing crisis." Actually, I did, but I wasn't ready to admit it yet.

"According to Lola, you and Max are at an impasse. I think I found you a solution."

"I'm listening."

He pulled a folded piece of paper from his top pocket and handed it to me. I unfolded it and saw it was a for-sale flyer.

"I know the house. It's about a mile from the winery." From the photo it looked old. Not good. Green painted wood siding and a shake roof. But it was a single story. A bonus. "It was built in nineteen fifty-four. I know, I know, not new enough. But the roof is synthetic shake tile and it has a fifty-year warranty, and the entire house was remodeled two years ago. It's turnkey."

There was no price on the flyer, and that said out of our wallet's range. "What's the catch?"

"The old folks, the Barnetts, owned the house and when they died, they left it to their grandson, Robbie, who was four years ahead of us in school. Anyway, he's the one who fixed up the house. Last week he found out his company's transferring him to Denver. His sister lives in Auburn and is settled there. She doesn't want the house, so he's selling it."

"How much property?"

"Well, here's the thing." Fuck. This was about to get complicated. "The house sits on sixty-five acres." I must've looked as horrified as I felt. "Wait, hold up. You can make this work." I nodded for him to go on even though I knew this wasn't going to work at all. "For reasons only Dominic Calapiano knows, the Barnetts didn't want to sell the land to him to expand the vineyard. Robbie knows the price tag for the house with all that land in wine country is too high for anyone except a vintner to purchase."

I saw where this was going. "You want me to have my father-in-law buy the house for the acreage and sell the house back to me with a normal amount of land."

Will winced and scratched his head. "Well, technically, Robbie can't sell the property to Dominic. The terms of his inheritance prohibit it."

Fuck me. "You're telling me to ask my father-in-law for…"

“Twenty million dollars,” Will stuttered. I felt my brows touch my hairline. “But,” he rushed to say, “that includes the house, which would go for about five hundred thousand with a half-acre of land.”

I put my face in my hands. Now I knew why Will was really here. “Max knows about this already,” I told my palms.

“Um, yeah. Lola knows Robbie’s ex-girlfriend who told Lola who told Max.” Goddamn small cities.

“Has Max seen the house?”

Will took a deep breath. “She and Lola drove by the house this morning before Max went to work. She hasn’t seen the inside, but Lola said Max said she could live in that single-story since it’s up on a hill and has a great view.”

I felt like I was back in junior high school. *Lola said Max said I could call her.*

“I take it she knows the whole Robbie-can’t-sell-to-Dominic story.”

“Ah, yup.”

“I can’t believe I’m asking you this. Has she talked to her father yet?”

Will brightened. “That’s the good news. She doesn’t want to approach him until she talks to you since… Chief, don’t fire me, but this is what Lola told me Max said.” I could hardly wait. “She didn’t want to offend your male sensibilities.”

I pulled my gun out of its holster and put it on the desk. “Please,” I said with all due seriousness, “shoot me now.”

Will tried not to laugh, but it sputtered out of him in bursts.

I re-holstered my gun and stood. “It seems I have somewhere to be.”

Will stood and said, “Good luck, Chief,” then he half ran out of my office.

***

On Tuesdays, Max worked late, which meant I took advantage of her hours and worked late only that night so I didn’t have to the rest of the week, emergencies excepted. Tonight I’d gotten home before her and I was leaning against the kitchen counter sipping Lagavulin when she walked in.

"Hey." She came right to me, put her bag on the counter, wrapped her arms around my neck, and laid a wet one on me. I looked down to see she was in her chunky-heeled boots. No need for tiptoes with those heels. "You taste like whiskey." I lifted the glass. She tilted her head. "What's up?"

I took another sip and asked, "Guess how I spent my afternoon?"

"Police related?" I shook my head. She smiled. "Jewelry related?" I smiled back and shook my head. "I've exhausted my possibilities."

I put the glass on the counter and said, "I went twenty million dollars in debt."

She took a step back. "What?"

"Actually, we went twenty million dollars in debt. California is a community property state and we don't have pre-nup."

She narrowed her eyes. "How many of those have you had?"

"Nowhere near enough."

"Should I be worried?"

I never wanted her to worry so I stopped being obtuse and slightly freaked out and told her what I knew would make her happy. "You know that house you and Lola went by today?"

"No," she rasped out, her expression a mix of alarm and joy.

"Oh yeah."

"Ohmygod, ohmygod, ohmygod. My father went for it."

"Your father couldn't call his banker fast enough."

She threw her arms around me and peppered my neck with kisses. Then she unbuttoned my shirt – this was something she loved to do and did it often – and rested her head on my chest. "Can we lie in the bed and look at *Daybreak* while you're telling me this?"

I took her hand and when we got to the bedroom, she took off her boots and socks – I was already barefoot – and we grabbed the shams, propped them on the footboard, lay down, and looked at my mother's art.

"Here's the deal. It's a fourteen-day escrow."

She snugged up against me and put her head on my shoulder. "Wow, quick."

"Cash talks. Twenty million dollars screams. Loud."

"I'll say."

"Your father agreed to maintain a one-acre barrier between the vineyard and our house and yard. We're getting a half-acre of land."

"Geez. We'll have my family's vineyard as our only neighbor. How cool is that?"

I smiled and kissed her forehead. "Pretty damn cool." I put my arm around her shoulders and ran my fingers over her soft skin. "The day after escrow closes with Robbie, your father is buying sixty-four and a half acres of land from me for nineteen and a half million dollars."

"In other words, on paper, yeah, but you're giving him back his money."

"The bank's money, but yes."

She moved so she could see my face. "Have you been inside the house?"

"I have, and you'll see it tomorrow at lunch. Robbie's meeting us there."

"Do you love it?"

Actually, I was surprised at how much I liked the house. The reno fit the setting, and all that new meant we wouldn't have to do a damn thing – except paint if Max didn't like the interior colors – for many years. I was particularly happy about the roof, the two-year-old water heater, furnace, new duct work, AC system, and back deck. "I do. It's roomier than it looks."

"The flyer said four bedrooms, three bathrooms."

"True. Good-size rooms. Lots of open space and natural light."

"I can't wait." She laid her head on my pec, then popped right back up and fixed her gaze on mine. "Thank you for the wonderful life you've given me, will give me and our kids, and for never giving up on me."

And that right there made being twenty million dollars in debt absolutely, one hundred and ten percent worth it.

"With everything I am, I love you, Max, and I always will."

PLAYLIST

Ain't No Mountain High Enough – Marvin Gaye & Tammi Terrell
Anyone Who Had a Heart – Luther Vandross
Best Part – H.E.R.
Hard Place – H.E.R.
Here You Come Again – Dolly Parton
In Case You Didn't Know – Brett Young
Just Give Me A Reason – P!nk & Nate Ruess
Let Me Love You – Mario – Teddy Swims version
Never Too Much – Luther Vandross
Nobody's Love – Maroon 5
Nothing Like You – Dan + Shay
Ocean Eyes – Billie Eilish
Sugar – Maroon 5
What Ifs – Kane Brown

TURN THE PAGE FOR A SNEAK PEEK AT:
NOTHING ELSE BUT YOU
The Letter Club – Book 1

Nothing Else But You

#65's first letter

Hi,

I saw your posts/ads/whatever on social media and thought this is such a cool idea. It reminds me of pen pals from back in the day. The idea that we're anonymous seems like a good way to get to know new people without all the judgment. I can't stand all the BS on social media. Everyone has an opinion, and I guess it's their right to express it, but some people should just keep their yaps shut. And some of the snaps... Where's your dignity. This, though. Words on a page and nothing else seems free-er and more honest. I'd lay down a hundy for a little honesty.

Anyway, a little about me: I'm nineteen and a sophomore in an Ivy League college. We're currently on winter break. According to your rules, that's all I'm allowed to say because, well, we have to be anonymous. I have no idea what I'm going to major in. My dad wants me to follow in the family business, but I'm not into it. Big conflict there. My mom says she wants me to be happy, but she doesn't go against my dad so lots of I love you phone calls and texts from her and not much else. I have two younger sisters, both in high school, and they don't get what the big is. When I'm home and my dad puts on the pressure, they roll their eyes, take out their phones, and tell me I'm ruining dinner. I don't go home much.

I like old things. Which is sort of obvi given the letter-writing gig. I don't see myself as a history prof or anything like that. I'm not scholarly. And I don't see myself owning an antiques shop. Not my vibe. I'm thinking salvation diving. You know, where one of those boats with the amazing technology goes out and hunts for buried treasure thousands of feet below the sea.

There are so many sunken ships from hundreds of years ago with all kinds of things lying at the bottom of the ocean. Bonus: most of the shipwrecks are off coasts of places I'd love to visit like Bermuda, Greece, Key West. I know how to dive, but for fun. And I've been on boats, but I don't know how to work on one, so maybe not. I'll look into whether one of them offers summer internships. It'll be a good way to find out if I'm cut out for that sort of thing.

Meanwhile, I'm taking a few different kinds of classes to see if anything clicks. Mostly, though, I spend my time practicing. I'm on one of my school's sports team. I don't know if I'm allowed to say which sport, but I get banged up a lot. Pretty brutal physically, but it requires mental acuity mostly. You know, strategy and all that.

Now, your turn.

G

Ten days later
1st response to letter #65 from letter #493

Hi,
Waving!!!
OMG!!! We're soul mates!!! I just know it!!! I'm at an Ivy League school too!!! I don't know my major either, but I'm a legacy, so it's all good. I don't have to decide anything really. I mean I'd love to go into fashion design, but only if I could have my own house, you know. Working for anyone else just won't happen. I'm thinking of the intern thing too just so I can see what's required. I mean how many people I'll have to hire and stuff like that.

Can't wait to hear back from you!!!

C

Eleven days later
2nd response to letter #65 from letter #845

G,
You're a lucky bastard and you have nothing to complain about. Life sucks for most of us mere mortals who have to work for a living. Right now I'm on second shift at a food processing plant and let me tell you it sucks. Life is a grind and I'm not even 20 yet and I know it doesn't get any better than this. I'm saving up to have my tubes tied so I never get stuck with any brats. It's bad enough I have to support myself. Kids. No way.

L

Eight days later
3rd response to letter #65 from letter #993

So inspired to meet you, G. I see this means of communication as an inter-spatial plane where souls can meet and meld. Imagine, through mere words we can find what makes us "us" without bone and sinew, muscle and blood. Through the energy of the mind we can reach the deep core of our being and extend that energy to other creatures.

Have you ever sat with your cat and had a conversation? I've had so many deep, meaningful interactions with Miss Adelaine. She's helped me establish many interspecies connections that I've forged over the years. One in particular is noteworthy. About six months ago, I was walking through the forest behind my house, and a chipmunk, barely larger than my hand, called out to me from a tree branch. He introduced himself as Seymour, then spent a goodly amount of time admonishing me for my bad recycling habits. We proceeded to have the most wonderful conversation about ecologically sound products, and a better way to live and recycle. He changed my life in so many ways, and Miss Adelaine agrees: we are moving forward to become a fully sustainable household.

Of course, we've been using solar energy for years, but water collection and drainage has improved to the point where all my showers are supported by rainwater. Certainly, in drier stretches, I avail myself of the lake, but I do NOT use any cleansing products when I take my ablutions there.

I can feel our souls touching already and I can't wait to learn more about your innermost thoughts and desires.

X

Three weeks later
4th response to letter #65 from letter #1287

Hey, G. Yeah, I feel you about not knowing the life plan thing. One day everything seemed totally in sync and the next, I'm packing up my car and moving across the country. I've been in my new place for a few months now, and while it's diff for sure, starting over has allowed me a certain freedom. I gave up social media entirely – too much noise – and found focusing on real one-on-one people time an eye opener. Like facial cues. I've never noticed how much people give away with little tics, twitches, and blinks. Talk about a lie detector, so often the words do not match up with what the face is saying. But, at heart, I'm a writer. So, when I saw the ad in the local newspaper about The Letter Club, I figured, sure, why not. I know you can't see me to tell whether I'm blowing smoke, but I guess you'll be able to read the honesty in my words, or you'll enjoy what you think is a good tale. Either way, it gives me an outlet.

Right now, I'm taking classes at the community college focusing on language, literature, and writing. I can't handle more than two classes a semester since I work full-time in a hardware store. Don't laugh. It's not as far a cry away from my writer dream as you'd think. Sure, a socket wrench isn't necessarily a thing of beauty, unless you need one desperately to fix a leaking pipe in a tight place. Then, the damn thing is your whole world. Plus, I like the customers. Most of them have been coming here forever, or their parents came here. There's something to be said for continuity, which small-town life provides. Sure, it's incestual in a groupthink kind of way, and it's gossipy, but this place leans left so it appeals to my social cause side.

Working here gives me fodder for my writing, and it connects me with people in a more meaningful way, which, my writing prof says, is what makes good character development...learning people, their stories and their motivations. And, of course, the job pays the bills, which is critical since I like my car, a good roof over my head, running water, electricity, and to eat.

So that's a brief introduction to me.

Be well, and don't get banged up too badly. I like sports, but only if no one gets hurt.

M

One week after receiving M's letter
G's first reply letter

Yo, Ace. See what I did there? Ace and helpful hardware person. Not lame. Clever. Inventive. Shows a connection to retro pop culture.

Moving on.

I'm impressed you know what you want to do with your life. It seems every other person at school is going through the motions. Showing up at class, studying, hitting a bong, chillin' with a binge-watch, but completely clueless as to what's going to happen after they graduate. Yeah, some have it all figured out. The true Ivy Leaguers. They're so self-directed they mow down people in the halls. But mostly, I see the spectrum of vague confusion to absolute panic.

I'm two steps up the ladder from vague confusion. Being the oldest kid in my fam, and the default heir, until the middle of my junior year in high school, I thought I knew exactly what my life was going to look like. I'd laid out everything in my head, and it was crystal clear. In retrospect, it was narrow, but at the time, knowing how everything was going to play out gave me a sense of security I didn't even know I had.

Then, a week after we came back from winter break, a freshman went into the cafeteria during lunch and started shooting. The good news, he was scrawny and the rifle's recoil knocked him on his ass. The bad news, he hit two people before he went down. One, a teacher, died.

Fucked-up shit. Did my head in. Insult to injury, my parents went into total flip-out mode and made me go to a prep school to finish out my last year and a half of high school. I was two hours from home. I couldn't hang with my friends. I didn't know anyone at the new school, and I had to see a shrink twice a week to talk about the shooting. The shrink was cool, and she helped, but I needed to be with my friends.

Sorry to get so heavy, but shit like that has a way of re-shaping your life. I was never in danger. I was out on the field in practice. But it happened. And nothing has been the same since.

Your turn.

G

Ten days later

Mirabelle locked herself in the storage closet behind the breakroom to cry about G's letter. She knew better than to read anything remotely personal at work, but all her mail went to a P.O. box, and the only time she had to collect it was during her lunch break. Thankfully, the post office was a two-block walk from Gusk's Hardware Store. Typically, she stuffed her bills and random fliers in her car, and still had plenty of time to return to Gusk's, eat her sandwich, and schmooze with one of her coworkers before she had to go back out on the floor. But when she saw The Letter Club's return address in its now familiar light green on the top left corner of a thick white envelope, she couldn't wait. She'd hoped it was G writing back, and not one of the many weird first letters she'd gotten through TLC.

She'd been chewing when she got to the paragraph about the school shooting and nearly choked on her food. Mrs. Berenikoff got up out of her chair, came around the table, and started whacking Mirabelle on the back, which was saying something since Mrs. B could take a sumo wrestler, no problem. After Mirabelle assured Mrs. B the food had gone down the wrong pipe – as if there was more than one esophagus – Mirabelle excused herself and pretended to go to the bathroom, when, in fact, she hid in the storage closet, tucked her fist against her mouth, and wept for ten minutes straight.

Yeah, too much too soon, but damn. Now she knew – sort of – a person who had that happen in his school. Fucked-up shit, indeed.

The minute her shift ended, she stuffed her blue apron – she'd have to tell G it wasn't red – in her locker, grabbed her backpack, and beat feet out to her car. Her world literature class didn't start until seven, and she was fine with sacrificing dinner to get to the campus library to do some research.

She found an empty computer in the back corner of the lab, signed on, and began researching school shootings from four years ago. Fuuuuck, there were so many it made her gut wrench, her heart hurt, and her head spin. She considered herself a pacifist, but she wondered how Congress would react if a shooter showed up when they were all in sesh. Bet waaay stricter gun control laws would be put in place a day later.

Narrowing her search, she looked for *one teacher dead from a shooting in January*. Four results popped up, which led to G's school shooting.

GUNMAN SUBDUED BY CLASSMATES

In a show of bravery, ten high school students rushed classmate Jordan Welsh after he opened fire in the cafeteria during lunch at Sagawick Valley High School in Dutchford, Connecticut.

She skimmed the article, saw a photo of the shooter, and found a video clip of the boys who had saved the day. None of them were G. He had been at practice. But now she knew where he'd gone to school. One state over and forty miles away from where she'd spent nineteen years of her life until nine months ago. What were the odds? She tried to remember the shooting. It had been close enough for the local news to carry it, but nothing. No surprise given what had been going on in her life.

Next step in investigating a guy she didn't know and would never meet, find the yearbook for his sophomore year since he'd left Sagawick before most schools took their yearbook photos.

But not tonight. She had fifteen minutes to get to class, which was on the other side of campus.

Tomorrow. She'd sit down in front of the computer tomorrow.

ABOUT THE AUTHOR

Elle Wright has been writing stories since she was a child, which led her to a career in journalism. She enjoys reporting life as much as making up a world she can control. She lives on the east coast of the United States where most of her large, noisy family resides. When she isn't in front of her computer, she loves to travel, garden, hang out with her dogs, and take in the brisk sea air that she's told is supposed to help calm her. She's been testing that theory for a while now.

CONNECT WITH ELLE:

Twitter: @ElleWright18
Instagram: @Elle_Wright_Writes
FB: facebook.com/elle.wright.1460

www.BOROUGHSPUBLISHINGGROUP.com

If you enjoyed this book, please write a review. Our authors appreciate the feedback, and it helps future readers find books they love. We welcome your comments and invite you to send them to info@boroughspublishinggroup.com. Follow us on Facebook, Twitter and Instagram, and be sure to sign up for our newsletter for surprises and new releases from your favorite authors.

Are you an aspiring writer? Check out www.boroughspublishinggroup.com/submit and see if we can help you make your dreams come true.

www.ingramcontent.com/pod-product-compliance
Lightning Source LLC
LaVergne TN
LVHW010058110826
845155LV00028B/396

* 9 7 8 1 9 5 3 8 1 0 0 3 8 *